STURGEON
FEVER

Sturgeon Fever
The Tug is The Drug
Copyright © 2023 by Robert Owen

This is a work of fiction. Names, characters, places and incidents are either products of the author's imagination or are used fictitiously. Any resemblance to actual events, locales or persons, living or dead, is entirely coincidental.

Additional copies may be ordered from the publisher for educational, business, promotional or premium use.
For information, contact ALIVE Book Publishing at:
alivebookpublishing.com.

Book and cover design by Alex P. Johnson

ISBN 13
978-1-63132-214-3

Library of Congress Control Number: 2023917246
Library of Congress Cataloging-in-Publication Data
is available upon request.

First Edition

Published in the United States of America by ALIVE Book Publishing
an imprint of Advanced Publishing LLC
3200 A Danville Blvd., Suite 204, Alamo, California 94507
alivebookpublishing.com

PRINTED IN THE UNITED STATES OF AMERICA

10 9 8 7 6 5 4 3 2 1

STURGEON FEVER

THE TUG IS THE DRUG

Robert Owen

ABOOKS

Alive Book Publishing

INTRODUCTION

SAN FRANCISCO BAY AREA
CONCORD, CALIFORNIA

1969, INDIAN SUMMER

It was almost 6:00 p.m. with three hours of daylight left, the temperature was still 104 degrees. I was wearing Sears Toughskins jeans cut off above the knees, black Converse Chuck Taylor high-tops and no shirt. Third grade was right around the corner. My bicycle was upside down in the driveway, the back wheel spinning so I could true up the spokes. She was a 1967 blue Schwinn Stingray with a python seat, a springer front end and a kickback two speed hub. It didn't come with that equipment; I had customized it by trading parts with other kids back in Arizona. She was a radical two-wheeler for her day.

Our family had just moved from Phoenix, Arizona to Concord, California in July. We had lived in the new house only one month. My father was backing up in the driveway with his company-issued white '69 Chevrolet El Camino pickup when I noticed a brand new fishing rod, tackle box and gear.

Dad was wearing creased khaki pants, black slip-on boots, and a white V-neck T-shirt. He was sporting Ray-Ban Pilots with gold frames and mirrored lenses, his salt and pepper hair greased back and the customary Pall Mall non-filter hanging from the right side of his mouth. The Old Man said, "Put together a couple of sandwiches and a six-pack of Pepsi-Colas. We're going fishin'."

The cab of the El Camino had black rubber floors, a white Motorola two-way radio under the dash with green and red-faceted bulbs. You could smell Old Spice and Pall Malls. There was no air-conditioning, but the windows were down with the wing windows open. He was checking himself in the rear-view mirror, running his fingertip comb through his greased hair and cleaning his Ray-Bans with his white handkerchief. Dad blew into the end of the pack of smokes and then shook one out. I will never forget the smell of the lighter fluid as he opened the Zippo one-handed, flipping the top open with a flick of his thumb, lighting up, and clicking the lighter shut in one smooth motion.

"The stripers are making their fall migratory run. It's the beginning of the season," the Old Man explained as we pulled out. "It's slack tide. The current will start to go out within the hour." Dad wound the 250-cubic-inch straight in-line six-cylinder pretty tight as he shifted through the gears. He wished under his breath that the pickup truck had a V-8 with a four-on-the-floor or even an automatic transmission instead of the straight six-cylinder with the three-on-the-tree, but it was a Southern Pacific Pipeline company-issued vehicle, and that was stock factory equipment.

We headed west on Highway 4 then took I-680 north. Dad was talking about the heat wave; he didn't think the temperature would go below 100 degrees all night. We drove over the Benicia Bridge leaving Martinez, the Shell oil refinery to the left, Tosco to the right and Exxon across the channel on the Benicia side. This was the first time I saw the most impressive thing I had ever seen: the National Reserve Mothball Fleet. The Liberty Ships were lined up north by south, bow by stern, as they waited for a call of duty that might never come. They just lay in anchor like a floating graveyard full of heroes. All of these had served in naval combat as far back as World War II. Each row moored six to ten ships, over two hundred of these were anchored, almost all the way past Suisun Bay. As we drove across the bridge, I could see the heat shimmering on the surface, creating the illusion of a mirage. The surface of the water blazed with an exact mirror image, an inverted reflection of everything on the surface: the ships, the towers, and the stacks of the re-fineries standing like giant castles down the banks of the channel from Benicia clear to Suisun Bay.

The Old Man said, "This heat wave with no wind at slack tide, this is called 'dead calm.'"

There wasn't a single ripple for a hundred miles from San Francisco to Stockton and as far as Sacramento. We drove through Benicia to Dillon Point then came to a locked gate where Dad mumbled something about pipeline jurisdiction, producing a key ring with an assortment of brass keys. He worked for Southern Pacific Pipeline where he was the Northern California Superintendent. The way he looked at it, if he had a key, it was the company's jurisdiction, so he had the right to go anywhere, anytime he wanted. Going through the keys one by one, Dad smiled as he hit pay dirt on his third or fourth try. He drove through the gate then I shut and locked it behind us. The tires broke traction on the gravel road as the feather-light tail end of the El Camino fishtailed, snaking through the S-turns.

The fishermen were lined up and down the bank, casting lures or fishing with cut bait. Dad rigged his twelve-foot green Daiwa spinning rod with the black D.A.M. Quick reel. Even though it was brand new, he checked the 20-pound monofilament P-Line by trying to break it with his hands. "I don't know how old this is or how long it's been on the shelf," the Old Man admitted. The line passed the test when he tied a fisherman's knot: seven twists then back through the eye.

I asked, "Why only 20-pound-test? Why not 50 in case you catch a monster?"

He said, "Twenty is plenty." Using the arc of the rod and proper drag adjustment, a good angler could bring in Moby Dick on 20-pound test if he played the fish right."

First he tied on a fast snap-barrel swivel, where he clipped on the pet-spoon lure, chrome with red feathers and a yellow pork-rind trailer. He pulled off his boots while sitting on the tailgate. Dad put on green chest-high waders then walked slowly down into the water where there was a man about every twenty feet, mostly Chinese Americans.

I watched him try to cast without much luck in the beginning. The first one went behind snagging weeds, the second maybe 10 feet in front of him. The men snickered at his lack of experience, but Dad stopped that with one glance at the loudest guy. At six-two and 285 pounds, he towered over all the men there. One thing for sure, he was the wrong guy to make mad; Dad could hand out an ass whoopin' *real quick*. As he got the hang of the rod and reel, he was soon casting as far as anyone on the bank.

FISH ON

There were guys reeling in keepers: 20-30-inch, 5-10-pound striped bass. As the bite started getting hot with the tide going out, Dad gained confidence with each cast, when his long arms jerked from his shoulders, the rod hair pinned

180 degrees, the tip in the water with the reel spitting line.

My dad got *real* serious *real* fast. He and every man there thought he had hooked a record bass, at least a 50-pound wall hanger. The crowd gathered around as the battle wore on. Dad walked to his left against the current then downriver to the right as the fish fought for its life. After a full two and a half hours of the Old Man fighting the fish marlin style, cranking back the rod then then reeling down, Dad thought the fish was ready to come in, but it got a second wind and ran with the current downriver, spooling him until there were only a few thin wraps of line left on the reel. It ran upriver against the outgoing tide. After running right then left, it headed straight out to deep water. It seemed to have stopped moving altogether, so Dad leaned back, the rod bent in a vicious arc. He stood so far from the bank that the water was almost pouring in over the front of the chest-high waders.

Dad thought the fish had snagged up or got itself wrapped around something. As he started to walk backwards toward the bank, the other fishermen commented that somehow he must have caught a big stingray, which was why he could not land the fish.

The Old Man said, "I'll either bring it in or break it off."

Out of nowhere, a tall, well-aged fisherman walked slowly toward my father. He was Indian, about six feet tall, wearing faded Wranglers, well-worn Rough Out cowboy boots, a faded green army coat, with an old straw cowboy hat. The band around the hat was made from a row of sturgeon spikes. He offered his help, fishing a master padlock out of his coat pocket.

"Let me show you an old Indian trick," the man said, clipping the lock on my dad's line and instructing him to crank the rod. The Indian man said, "When the fish feels the lock on his lips, he will run again."

This method was effective where the fish came off the bottom. Dad took about ten steps backwards then reeled in as he walked forward. He repeated this, continuously bringing the fish closer to shore. The crowd was thinning out as it was just about dark when the fish, which definitely wasn't a striped bass, was dragged tail-first from the water onto the green moss-covered rocks. By now, the tide was all the way out.

I ran down to my father's side and asked, "What kind of fish, Dad?"

He said, "I don't know, but I think it has to be some kind of shark, maybe a young great white."

Only two other anglers were left, and they were pointing at the massive fish screaming, "STER-JON! STER-JON! Good to eat. Good to eat."

Somehow Dad had managed to snag the sturgeon by the tail, with the barb of the hook penetrating above the rear dorsal fin. That's why it was able to fight so long and hard; it was impossible to turn its head. I tried to get closer, but Dad stopped me with the butt of the rod. He reached into his pocket and pulled out a small black Case folding penknife. He opened the larger of the two blades with his thumb. Using only one hand, he was about to cut the line when another angler asked if they could have the fish.

The Old Man said, "If you want it, go down and get it."

The two men went down to the sturgeon but were not prepared. The fish was now rested and the fight was on. One of the men tried to pull the line, the other tried to drag it by its gills. As soon as the man's hands touched the fish, which was probably all of six feet, the monster took its final stand.

With a kick of its tail, the entire fish became electrified, and the massive sturj' thrashed like a crocodile, rolling over and over, cutting the line with the razor-sharp scutes running down its back.

When it was over, the fish was long gone. All the men had to show for their effort were some cuts and bruises.

The old Indian walked over and picked up his lock. "Works every time," he said then he just walked away with a grin on his face.

Dad said, "Wish I had a picture, because there's no way anybody at work would believe the story about the one that got away."

I could not have known it at the time, but that day would have a major effect on the rest of my life. I didn't know it of course, back then, but I caught a bad case of sturgeon fever. True story.

CHAPTER 1

NO STRANGER TO DANGER, 1994

It was Friday night. The weather was just starting to get to the point where you could wear a T-shirt without having to worry about a jacket. After some light maintenance, I left the *General* moored at the marina. I was in a foul mood, knowing there were only one or two ways for a sure-fire cure, wishing I was on my motorcycle but it was back at the house, turning over the ignition in the 1970 El Camino, listening to it catch while just barely bumping the key.

When I salvaged the pickup from McHugh's Auto Wreckers way back when, she was on her way to the car crusher. It was missing both doors, and most of the front end, she had no drive train whatsoever. As far back as I could remember I always wanted an El Camino, since my dad told me that the El-Co was a "Cowboy Cadillac," half car, half pickup. You could haul a small load with the comfort of a car.

I had been tinkering with this one for almost twenty years. I painted her myself in my dad's garage, a candy apple-cranberry red lacquer job with a touch of blue pearl. With a white undercoat primer/sealer and ten coats of hand-rubbed clear the paint looked wet, so deep you could stick a finger in it, with the white undercoat making it light reflective, the paint poppin' like a red ruby ring. It was outfitted with fully-reversed 15 x 10 inch, in-set stock Chevrolet Corvette rally wheels with BFGoodrich Radial T/A tires, 50-series. There was not one single mechanical part stock from the factory, from the super-charged 454-cubic-inch big-block, equipped with nitrous oxide, the 700R4 automatic transmission, the Jaguar independent rear end, or the air-bag suspension. The exhaust consisted of Hooker Headers with the quietest turbo-style mufflers available, with over 600 horsepower at 6,000 RPM, trying to keep it incognito as much as possible. A street legal hot rod was referred to as a "sleeper." After warming her up, I pulled out of the marina then headed into Martini town.

It was just about 11:00 p.m. I knew what I was doing was dead wrong. If I were asleep right now, that would make only four hours of sleep. Having the *General* chartered, we would get underway at 0600 hours sharp. No matter what time I would go to bed, I'd wake up around 3:00 a.m., worrying about last-minute details, bait, etc. Driving past the four downtown local bars: La Beau's, Ferry Street Landing, then College Lane where a few people lingered out in front along with a couple of bikes, and Shorty's, a bar well-known for bikers and union steamfitters from the surrounding oil refineries—knowing this from personal experience, for I am a proud card-holding member in good standing with the Steamfitters Local Union 342.

I parked the El Camino out of sight so if Johnny Law came driving by, he wouldn't see my pickup—one ticket away from losing my license, a deuce, a 502 violation for driving under the influence, would sink me completely. I walked through the back door, scanned and took inventory of everything going on inside: no immediate enemies or current part-time girlfriends. I recognized a few of the men and probably all the women, having had priors with more than one in the room. There were two, maybe three bikes parked outside where I counted six or seven guys wearing chaps over their jeans. I call them "sidewalk commanders." Laughing to myself I visualized them all dancing with each other to the song "Born to Be Wild"—a bunch of wannabes. I took a seat at the end of the bar where I could see both the front and back doors, as well as the women's bathroom. My chair of choice allowed me to see people as they came in: the perfect place to get a close inspection of the babes because when they are in a bar drinking, they always have to use the ladies' room—the perfect seat.

There I was just sitting there, minding my own business, nursing my first beer when she came walking by. We had visual lock, extreme eye contact. I liked what I saw, knowing she was feeling the same, remembering the rules as I smiled then broke away my gaze, not wanting to act too interested, maybe just a little hard to get. She was young, guessing her to be close to twenty-one. Me being more than ten years her senior, she definitely wasn't "Miss Right," but she was positively "Miss Right Now." As she went into the ladies' room, I tried to pretend not to pay attention. I heard a few loud bikes pull up in front, so I looked in the direction of all the commotion when I smelled a familiar scent, Ciara perfume. To my right, the girl I was thinking about had very quietly taken the bar stool at my side. As I took a hard, close look into her big brown eyes the first thing I saw set alarms ringing in my head. She was obviously under the influence of more than one street drug, the irises surrounding her dilated pupils alive with activity. They looked like miniature electrical pulses as she was trying to focus. I usually don't get blown off course so easily, but I think the small brain had already taken over my thought process. She was definitely in her physical prime but not yet completely grown-up or entirely a mature, adult woman. Her skin still held the elasticity of youth where she had not borne a child. One hundred percent trouble if I ever saw it.

She was sporting a black tube top, tight mini-skirt, and four-inch stiletto heels. Her hair was dyed a gold blonde with brownish roots trying to surface. She looked like a million dollars in the neon glow of the bar room lights. We stared into each other's eyes kind of like a stare-down to see who would talk or look away first. She started to break out in a devilish grin. Stupid me, sitting there flattering myself thinking I was dazzling this young lady when I heard heavy footsteps coming from behind. I knew I'd been had. The only reason this blonde was so interested in me was to make the guy standing behind me jealous. Not having spoken a word to her or even asked her name, I still knew I was in trouble. She had heard his bike pull up then sat next to me in a hurry to set the stage.

THINGS DON'T GO RIGHT—START A FIGHT

I thought about attempting to walk away or talk my way out of the mess when I felt a heavy hand on my right shoulder spin me around on my bar stool. Still seated with my best smile across my face, I looked directly at a stomach like that of a big-time wrestler stretching a black Harley-Davidson T-shirt. The stomach was connected to the six-foot four-inch, 300-pound-plus jealous biker. I left the marina looking for one of two things, finding both of them at the same time.

As soon as my boots hit the floor, in one continuous motion from him spinning me clockwise on my bar stool, I lashed out with a right-hand back swing low in his stomach. I used the side of my fist like a hammer when he dropped both hands in a natural reaction. I was already rolling my right forearm up, driving the back of my knuckles into his nose, crushing cartilage. The blood sprayed from both nostrils down his black beard and chest. He let out a roar like a wounded bear then bull-rushed me all the way to the back wall. I could tell by the way the big man drove me with my feet not even touching the ground that he probably had played a little high school football. He moved with incredible speed and agility for a man his size and weight.

When my back hit the wood paneling, I heard a blood-curdling, bone-cracking sound. I prayed it wasn't my spine. He took a few steps back to ram me into the wall again with my arms pinned at my side in a bear hug. Not being able to breathe, my eyes were ready to pop out of their sockets, so I bent at the waist, leaning back as far as possible, arching my spine then whipping my upper body, attempting a head butt that did not work out as planned. Our foreheads met evenly, letting out a loud crack like a professional baseball player knocking one out of the park with a wooden bat. I couldn't believe I almost knocked *myself* out. It had no effect whatsoever on the big man, it didn't even phase him.

I had no other choice but to attempt the head butt again. The lights were beginning to go out as my vision blurred, I experienced a feeling similar to déjà vu. Everything moved in slow motion, where I could no longer hear, just a loud ringing in my ears. When I leaned back this time, bending my neck back until the back of my head was almost touching between my shoulder blades, I threw my head forward with such force that my chin touched my chest as I connected with the bridge of his already broken nose. The big man attempted to squeeze the remaining life out of me, holding my back as well as my head pinned to the wall. His giant melon head felt like a bowling ball grinding against my skull. I gasped for breath through my open mouth. His eyebrow ended up between my upper and lower teeth, so I twisted my head looking into his shocked face then bit down with all my might, tasting salty sweat, torn skin tissue, and warm coppery blood.

Feeling his grip loosen a fraction of an inch, I was able to free my arms. As he drove for the wall again, his tree trunk neck was all gilled up, the veins sticking out like one-inch ropes under the skin like a sevengill shark. Forming cups with both my hands then clapping his ears, I tried to burst his ear drums, but he seemed to get stronger, more violent. I had no choice. Fearing for my life as the lights were going out fast from the lack of oxygen to my brain and the bear hug restricting the blood flow to my internal organs, I drove both thumbs into his eyes, extending both arms to full lock. He jerked his head back and dropped me real quick. Even though he was temporarily blinded, he somehow managed to charge again. This time I let him come then side stepped as he came in, wrapping my right arm around his thick, bull neck and grabbing my right wrist with my left hand where his face was behind me. I let him charge full speed into the wall where his head connected with a solid bang hard enough to shiver the timbers of the bar. Without hesitation, still having a hold with the reverse head lock, I lifted my legs up, pile-driving his big head into the ground. This was effective as it thumped his melon pretty good, but not enough to knock him completely out. He just stayed there on all fours, shaking his bloody head like a big confused bear.

I rolled out and away, where everything was happening fast. I got to my feet, and the entire crowd exploded in a classic bar-room brawl. I looked for his friends, ducking stray punches as I made my way out the same way I came in, the back door.

Hot-footing it to the El-Co, I unlocked the driver's door and got behind the wheel, turning the key, firing up the big block then shifting into low gear all in one continuous move, then started to drive away when the blonde came walking up.

She stood in front of the truck and yelled out, "Hey, aren't you forgetting something?"

To the winner go the spoils. Looking at the attractive young lady standing in front of my truck made me wonder if she was interested in me or if she was just still trying to make the bear inside the bar mad. If she wanted to go with me, then she was completely twisted. I knew in my heart she was nothing but trouble, but I always had a soft spot for girls that were head cases. The more messed up in the head, the better in the bed. She walked up to the driver's side window of the truck. I rolled down the window, taking a good look around for the boyfriend. Then she planted a kiss, full on my mouth. Even with the smell of the cheap perfume and the hard liquor on her breath, I have to admit it was an impressive kiss. Holding my left foot on the brake with the truck in gear, I told her to go around to the other side and get in. When she walked around the back of the truck, I floored the foot feeder.

The big block reacted with the fuel-injected, supercharged power plant breaking the tires loose on the feather light rear end of the El Camino. White smoke rolled from the rear wheel wells as I brought the front end around, sweeping through the corner with my steering wheel turned all the way to the right. The entire intersection was filled with smoke from me burning the tires. I let off the gas and pulled up to a red light. Out of nowhere, a Z-28 IROC Camaro with a good-looking brunette at the wheel pulled up beside me, windows down. She looked at me, and I looked back.

She asked, "Is there anything to do in this town?"

I replied, "Follow me to the marina. We could go have a drink on my boat."

She said, "Lead the way."

Off we went. On the way there I'd looked for one of two things. I looked at my wristwatch and it was only 11:20. I had been in a good brawl and had a good-looking lady following me to the water all in less than half an hour; that had to be some kind of world record. God bless America. Her name was Andrea. It turns out we had a lot in common. She was a car buff who liked to drink, and she was at home on the water. We had a little party on the *Sturgeon General*. When she left at 0300, I handed her a business card with my pager number. She left with a big smile on her face. I stayed up and went to work.

CHAPTER 2

THE GENERAL

The *Sturgeon General* was a 1973 Owens—one of, if not the oldest manufacturer of ships or boats of every style, dating back to 1925. At 36-feet with a 12-foot beam, she was powered by twin in-line six-cylinder diesel Caterpillars, 180-horse for each of the twin screws. At the end of each driveshaft, I had installed dual counter rotating stainless steel dual props, a very expensive modification, but it paid for itself with massive fuel efficiency. A charter sport fishing boat of this style was called a six-pack because it was designed to entertain four fishermen, a deckhand, and of course, the captain and owner-operator, which in this case was me, Mike Stone.

You couldn't have asked for better weather conditions, with just a hint of a southeast prevailing breeze. I had been on duty since about 3:00 a.m. After warming up the Cat's, I double then triple checked everything from the bilge pumps, life jackets, the horn, blowers, and anything else that had to do with safety. My first concern being captain was the well-being of everyone onboard as well as being closely inspected on a regular basis by the coast guard. Moored in the slip next to the *General*, I kept a 1961 23-foot Chris-Craft. She was an old woody in pristine condition with lots of freshly lacquered teak and mahogany. The entire boat was naturally stained wood except for the bottom, anti-fouling paint, of course. She was a beautiful boat and ran strong.

I had taken a blue-printed and balanced 409-cubic-inch with two staggered four-barrel carburetors out of a 1962 S.S. Chevrolet Impala, then shoe-horned it into the tight motor house. There was no outdrive, just a shaft directly off the flywheel connected to a universal joint with a solid brass alloy drive line out the stern. This is referred to as a Velvet or V-Drive. She was good for almost fifty knots. Her name, stenciled in 6-inch gold leaf cursive scroll lettering across the stern, was the "*Aquaholic*," because she was addicted to the water. She was an older boat being a '61, but she was designed with a deep modified hull to pound through the waves.

Both of my boats were outfitted with state-of-the-art electronics, global positioning systems, ship to shore radios, and top-of-the-line depth sounder fish-finders. Whenever I had a charter going out, I would take her out early to scout some well-known hot spots to see if I could scope any sturgeon. This saved me a lot of fuel plus wear and tear on the *General*. A normal charter was six to eight hours, depending on the tides, the weather and how hot the sturgeon were biting. If I could put the *General* on top of the fish, the better the chance of the bite, the better odds that one of these yahoos would set the hook—one or two of these guys goes home with a sturj' the better for business. Don't get me wrong, I love to fish, but I didn't come out here to make friends. After all, business is business.

I motored out of the marina about 0400 sharp, with just a fraction of a fingernail moon. The tide was coming in, so the surface of the water was fairly flat. On an incoming tide, the current runs the same direction as the prevailing southeast winds, just a light wind chop, no popcorn or sign of whitecaps. I left the marina, motoring past the breakwater marked with the red and green navigational markers, tapping the horn twice in case another boat was on its way in. Navigating left, downriver, I let my eyes focus on the darkness by squinting to dilate my pupils while counting to ten. I fire-walled the fuel feeder where she was instantly on plane, traveling across the flat, steel-colored water. I barely had enough time to adjust the trim tabs for greater fuel efficiency. The cold wind was in my face, filling my lungs with fresh, clean air. I got more of the hull out of the water, creating less drag on the bottom. I let her unwind for a minute with the 409 begging for more. She's so fine, my 409. The open exhaust through the transom echoed off the low hills surrounding the channel, like music to my ears.

I throttled down fast to five knots while spinning the helm hard to port to avoid my back wake washing over the stern, now at one of my favorite sturgeon holes, the Ozol Pier.

This dock is a receiving terminal for tanker ships transporting raw fuel from China. The gasoline is a base product that needs to be further refined with additives mixed in to bring it up to acceptable market grade. The pier comes away from the tank farm holding facility on the hill. The well-lit pier runs perpendicular from the facility, then T's out bullheaded, running parallel with the bank. Doesn't matter if you're on an incoming or outgoing tide the pier had produced fish for many years, for the bottom is clam bed. If you can find a clam bed you can usually find sturgeon activity.

Not seeing anything on the fish finder, nothing promising at either end of the dock, I cruised past the ancient remains of a dock called White's Landing, where up until about 1978 you could still rent a 12- or 14-foot aluminum boat. When I was only twelve years old, my father would drop me off by myself on Saturday morning then pick me up Sunday afternoon. We had a Montgomery Ward's 9 hp Sea King outboard. We would haul the outboard in the supplied wheelbarrow, ice chest in tow. He would leave me with an ice chest, fishing rod, and bait where I would fish straight through to Sunday afternoon. Dad would be waiting in his El Camino to pick me up. They don't make kids like they used to.

I reversed course, headed upriver, and ran with the current as I motored toward the Benicia Bridge to the most famous sturgeon territory on the planet: the United States Naval Reserve, the Mothball Fleet.

CHAPTER 3

THE GLOMAR EXPLORER

I was holding my tachometer to 4,000 rpm, enjoying the boat ride, cruising at about 40 miles per hour or 35 knots—the peace and tranquility of the water. The throaty, open exhaust coming out the dual three-inch straight pipes penetrated the stern above the water line. I looked over my left shoulder at the white foam wake, which was breaking at an endless "V" behind the *Aquaholic's* single screw. I said a short, quick prayer to God, thanking him for my blessings, which to me were moments like this. I also asked forgiveness for my many sins.

Motoring past the north side of the bridge with the *Glomar Explorer* coming up on my portside—the *Glomar*, designed by multi-billionaire Howard Hughes, was built in less than six months in 1973 by Sun Shipbuilding & Dry Dock Co. It was built for an intricate CIA undertaking: code name Jennifer. The mission of the *Glomar* was to raise a Soviet nuclear submarine, the K-129 that had sunk in the Pacific. The Soviet Golf-class ballistic missile sub sank on April 11, 1968 approximately 750 miles northwest of Hawaii. Naval Intelligence at Pearl Harbor had tracked the sub, learning of its fate through underwater listening devices. After months of futile searching by soviet vessels, it became apparent that only the United States knew the location of the sunken submarine. Under the cover of a deep sea mining mission, with the Soviets bird-dogging the entire operation, the U.S. Navy Seals were able to raise and salvage a good portion of the sub, including three nuclear missiles, two nuclear torpedoes, the ship's code machine, and various crypto code books. The *Glomar Explorer* cost $200 million to build, where it was in service from 1973 to 1975. She is 620 feet long and 116 feet wide. Legend has it the inside of the ship is hollow where it hoisted the lost Russian submarine up into its belly under the nose of the Soviets in complete stealth. The *Glomar Explorer* was now mothballed here in Suisun Bay where it could be seen from the Benicia Bridge on U.S. Highway 680.

The heavy wooden hull powered through the light waves, the 409 purring like a kitten, coming up the main shipping deep water channel when something caught my eye on the screen of the fish-finder. This was a common area for sturgeon, so slowing down to idle I kept my eyes glued to the screens of both fish finders. In both boats, I had installed a Bottom Line Sidefinder Tournament Leader 3300 with side view so I could scan below the boat as well as horizontally out both sides. The second one, a backup being a relatively low-cost Hummingbird which showed me only two things: the bottom in solid black and any fish or object in black horizontal bars, 1/8-inch equaling one foot. This was a practically bulletproof method of locating then estimating the size of the sturgeon.

What I saw made me shake my head. I looked twice because the black bar was continuous across the 3-inch screen. I turned the power switch off then back on to reset the readout. Sure enough, it was still there. Thinking the possibilities over in my head, I concluded that this boxcar, which was reading at a depth of 46 feet with the bottom at 48, was one of three things: three or four very large sturj' swimming end to end, a school of striped bass swimming in a tight group, or a school of shad. In all my years of fishing, I had never seen anything close to this. Remembering a story my father had told me many years ago where the Southern Pacific Pipeline Company had high-pressure petroleum pipelines connecting the refineries. These pipes lay on the bottom of the channel. Divers took photographs of the lines as part of maintenance/inspection; there was one picture with an extra line. After magnification, they saw it wasn't a pipe but a massive sturgeon lying parallel with the lines. The legends of the workers who built the Benicia Bridge swore they saw sturgeon of over twenty feet. They refused to dive. I remember hearing stories about an occasional lost whale swimming this far upriver, coming under the Golden Gate through the San Francisco Bay.

I had actually seen with my own eyes a humpback whale that was way off course, drawing a lot of attention; he was nicknamed Humphrey. They named a restaurant in Antioch after that whale, which is upriver about ten miles. I looked at my black Seiko Diver Watch and read 5:15 a.m. I was running short on time. The black boxcar was gone, and I needed to get back to the *General*, so I wound the 409 pretty tight. I was back in my slip in record time, making a mental note about the mystery boxcar.

I had booked six fishermen who were standing on the dock when I pulled into my slip. They were bright-eyed and bushy-tailed, raring to go. I collected $100 in cash from each, totaling $600. Booking an expedition on the *Sturgeon General* was about $25 more than other charters in the area, such as the *Happy Hooker* or the *Fin Attic*. I had a good reputation for bringing home a high percentage of sturgeon. Whenever I have a fresh group of anglers, I always hold a quick safety meeting once everyone is onboard, briefly explaining about the tide going in and back out, twice a day—that if somehow someone was to go overboard or if there was some type of accident where they ended up in the water, then they would have to swim with the current, not against it, toward the nearest shore or other boats.

We got underway, motoring along at maybe 12 knots, keeping the tachometer under 2,000 rpm, and listening to the Cat's purr. We headed back upriver toward the fleet. I kept a close eye on the fish finder as we went past the *Glomar Explorer* but failed to pick up any sign, so we slowly crept into Suisun Bay to scope for sturgeon when the bottom started to rise up, veering out of the deep-water shipping channel. With the water becoming shallow, I didn't want to scare any fish away with the prop wash from the *General's* twin screws, so I dropped anchor above the green buoy, channel marker number four. With the tide coming in at maybe 6 knots, the current was overpowering the breeze, so the bow held steady, pointing downriver toward the Benicia Bridge, the stern faced directly at the sandbar, which runs parallel to the fleet, separating the rows of ships from the main shipping channel. The trick was to cast toward the sandbar into the shallows where the sturgeon lay with their backs just below the surface, enjoying the heat from the sun, getting a break from having to fight the strong current in the deeper water.

I passed out four Shakespeare Ugly Stiks, medium light action, outfitted with Shimano Charter Special conventional bait casting reels. The Ugly Stik is an imitation of the Fenwick Pacificstik, the best sturgeon rod ever made. I always tried to hang out on the deck to keep an eye on the rod tips because a sturj' hits so gently, and generally the fish will stay down current from whatever it's going to eat. Sucking with its large toothless mouth with its leathery lips, it has a cruncher in the back of its mouth which pulverizes its food before swallowing. The sturgeon is a bottom feeder. People say the bigger the fish, the softer it will bite. The younger, immature sturj' is known as a shaker because when you pull one in the fish will shake so hard that it will actually bounce two or three feet off the deck. The young and dumb shaker will hit much more aggressively, more like a striped bass, which is more of a predator species.

After getting the anglers set with their rods positioned, four out the back over the stern, one out each side, port and starboard, we sat without any sign of a bite. We would sit for only thirty minutes if there was no action—six rods in the water are equivalent to one man fishing for three hours. I weighed anchor with my automatic hoist then headed back out to the edge of the channel where I began seeing some good signs. Quite often the sturgeon will forage for grass shrimp or other types of bait fish where the food will accumulate on shelves or low spots and divots. We got set up, and immediately the rod tips were getting pumped. The fishermen were far from experienced sturgeon anglers—even though they knew how to fish, setting the hook on a sturj' was a completely different story. I gave the guys a chance before I offered advice or pointers where needed. The best method is to leave the rod alone. A couple of pumps with the rod tip, same as with a small catfish, the trick is to quietly pick up the rod, thumb on the spool, other hand on the forward handle section of the rod while gently lifting the rod in a forward motion. Give up a little slack, thus letting your bait drift down into the sturgeon's mouth. When he pulls the third time, an experienced angler will yank back on the rod, trying to break the rod in half, bring the rod forward again reeling up slack, then set the hook again, burying the #7 hook into the tough, leather lips of the mighty sturj'. This technique was taught to me by a business agent and friend of mine from the Steamfitters Union Hall. Most fishermen are not aware of this method, and as soon as they get a hit, they usually pull the "Quick Draw Mc-Graw," jerking the rod back as soon as they get a bite, and go home skunked (empty handed).

CHAPTER 4

THE STURGEON GODS

The first couple of bites were missed, so I offered my help. After some simple direction, the guy who was paying the most attention came back solid. The Ugly Stik bent down toward the water. The Shimano Charter Special reel gave up line as the fish ran with the current about fifty or sixty yards, then in a classic sturgeon maneuver, headed straight for the surface, coming completely out of the water much like a marlin, spinning through the air, throwing its head side to side like a pit bull shaking a poodle. Trying to dislodge the #7 hook from its lip, rolling midair, the sturgeon wrapped the line around its body in an attempt to cut it with the large bony scutes, better known as spikes, which are located in front of the dorsal fin, running lengthwise up the back to just behind its head, that serve as a form of armor, where a stainless steel or heavy 50-pound monofilament leader is required to prevent the line from being cut.

I instructed him to yank back on the rod, to make the fish unwind. With the fish still clear of the water, it was tail-walking across the surface of the water like a dolphin. I noticed he was close to 60 inches. The sturj' must be between 46 to 72 inches. This rule is due to the course of reproduction where the undersized young and dumb sturj' is more aggressive, being easily caught. The oversized fish is able to produce a much larger quantity of eggs.

The sturgeon's back was almost black from many years of sunning in shallow water. The stomach, as always, was snow white. This proved to be an experienced fish, probably having been caught more than once before. The fish now swam directly at the back of the boat, attempting to create slack, and then tried to spit the hook. His next move was an attempt to wrap the line around the props. This is prevented by stomping your feet on the floorboard of the boat to scare the fish away. It made a run under the boat then tried to wrap itself around the anchor line in an attempt to break free, so I grabbed the rod then came down the side of the boat with my feet on the walk-around. After unwinding the line from the anchor rope, I handed the rod back to the angler and the sturj' ran with the current. The fisherman tightened up the drag. The fish exhausted itself and was able to be reeled in like dead weight or bringing in a water log. I used my snare to bring the fish into the boat then thumped it good on top of the head, knocking it out cold. I cut its tail deep in the main artery then tied it off outside the boat. When the fish regained consciousness it would try to swim with the current, pumping all the blood from its body, leaving pure white, excellent, boneless meat while putting the scent of its own blood in the current and attracting other sturj'. We were lucky, catching two more fish. The sturgeon gods had shined on our fishing trip. The crew started drinking soon thereafter, and we called it a day.

Come Monday morning, these anglers would be heroes on the jobsite. I was cruising the *General* at low speed. Everyone was in good spirits from the successful trip plus the alcohol they were consuming. The sun was bright and warm. Now I was $600 richer before expenses, thinking about what happened the night before then the good luck on the charter.

It seemed like things were going my way, but I couldn't stop thinking about the large black box cars that I had marked on the bottom earlier that morning. I motored over to that exact same spot on the return trip home but saw no indication. Worse than that, I couldn't get it off my mind. It was starting to bother me. After mooring the *General* then some light cleanup, I headed home.

CHAPTER 5

CONCORD HIGH SCHOOL, 1979, THE COMPETITION

In every person's life there is always somebody that will be one up, a little faster or better looking, better in sports or smarter, or maybe they have a nicer car or more money. In my case, this person was Eric Zachary. Of course everyone called him E.Z. or "Eazy Money." It seemed like no matter where I went or what I did E.Z. was always one step ahead. Since the third grade, we were both in the program called MGM, Mentally Gifted Minors, where the requirements were to have an I.Q. over 125. It was rumored that Eric was well over 160. He was the same age as me, but he looked two or three years older. He was one of those guys that could grow a full beard when he was in the ninth grade, although he was close shaved all the time without ever having a single blemish on his handsome face. This guy was so far ahead of his time. When he was only seventeen, he dyed his shoulder-length hair from dark brown to sunny blonde with platinum blonde highlights. The dyed hair accented his naturally deep olive-toned complexion. He stood about six-two at 190 pounds with wide shoulders and good-sized guns for a guy who never went anywhere near weights.

E.Z. played all types of sports where he always dominated—a natural born athlete who excelled in gymnastics. His specialty was the horse and parallel bars. E.Z. was constantly showing off his strength on the rings, performing the difficult Iron Cross with ease. He had the straightest, whitest teeth, a narrow, perfectly-shaped, large but triangular nose, which he seemed to always have pointed up, looking down at everything and everybody. His jaw jutted out too far from his long neck. He always was smiling, that mischievous but handsome "I am better than you" grin. Eric's eyes were the color of black obsidian. You could barely tell where his pupils and irises began or ended. He was a hard guy to read because his eyes gave off a look of death like the eyes of a shark. He was always tan and no matter how cold the weather, he always wore a T-shirt with the sleeves cut off, skin-tight Levi's 501s with well-worn Roughout cowboy boots. Eric sported black Ray-Ban horn-rimmed gangster sunglasses, even at night, before anyone else knew what they were.

The way he walked with his arms sticking out, like he was carrying two full five-gallon buckets of paint, looked like he had a stick shoved up his rear end. Eric always had complete control over anybody he dealt with. It was like he could tell anyone anything, and they would do what he said. A complete loner who got straight A's without ever cracking a book. When we played Little League, we were both always picked for All Stars. Most of the time, I would be the second or third best player on the team while he was always the hero. If I was playing shortstop, he would be the pitcher. In football, I would be running back, and he would be quarterback. When we were younger, I got a Tote Goat minibike—he had a Yamaha 4-stroke Thumper T.T. 250-cc motorcycle. I drove an Impala. Eric had a Corvette. When I got a summer job as a welder's helper for a pipeline outfit, he was running his family's tanker truck fabrication company where he was one of the most talented, high frequency heliarc welders in the industry. His family's company specialized in fabrication of aluminum tanks that hauled fuel with tractor-trailer rigs on the highways, as well as design, fabrication, and installation of underwater fuel tanks for marina gas docks and the neighboring oil refinery receiving docks. This is where he learned how to dive, and excelled as an underwater welder. His father also held contracts on Mare Island in Vallejo, California located downriver from the shop—Mare Island being the first United States Naval installation on the West Coast, building over 500 ships in the last 150 years. Although Mare Island had not produced any ships since 1970, they still went on to repair, dry dock, and overhaul nuclear submarines. At an early age, Eric became infatuated with the history, design and fabrication of submarines. He made it a point to study the history as well as the latest innovations in submarine technology.

E.Z. seemed to have some kind of mystical, hypnotic power over everyone, especially girls. When it came to money, he had way more than he could ever spend, having worked at the family business since the age of thirteen, but he preferred the fast cash of selling street drugs. E.Z. was constantly scamming, pulling heists from auto theft to burglaries. He never even came close to getting caught. By the second week of our high school drafting class, he was teaching the instructor. This young man was so mechanically talented that the military had contacted him, wanting to train him to design weaponry for the civil defense. E.Z. wanted no part of this because he was addicted to criminal activity. He could afford anything or do whatever he wanted, but unless he could steal it, he didn't want it—all that talent, just going to waste.

CHERRY BOMB

My high school sweetheart, Olivia West, was the most gorgeous young woman that ever walked the planet. She came from a good family. Compared to all my other girls, she was solid gold. When I met her, she was riding her horse in a small corral on Bailey Road where her parents rented a stall. I was cruising by in my car, revving up the engine in neutral, showing off my brand new dual-exhaust, 36-inch Cherry Bomb glasspacks with chrome pencil tips straight out the back. The '68 2-door coupe was painted ultramarine blue with baby blue diamond tuck. The Cherry Bomb Glasspack muffler, being the third generation of the "packs" mufflers, was originally 36 inches long by 3 inches in diameter, with 3 x 2 concentric reducers necking down to the 2-inch pipes, creating an expansion chamber, producing the sweet sound of duels with packs. In the 1930s the first packs were filled with carbon steel metal shavings that rusted out the muffler. The second style was packed with red lava rock, the same used in landscaping, but this also failed. In the 1950s the third generation was internally wrapped with fiberglass resulting in the name "glass packs." The red Cherry Bomb was the most popular for decades, and still is today to the OG hotrodder, but has been replaced by an aluminized chamber.

When I built her I removed the bucket seats and replaced them with a front bench, relocating the floor shift to the column so the babes could sit next to me on the front seat. I had lowered the car by cutting one-and-a-half coils out of the front springs and two out of the rear. I was running 14-inch BR-78 Firestone Tiger Paw 721 Radials with one-inch white wall tires, outfitted with Tins Lloyds 14 x 7 fully reversed deep dish, the OG five-spoke rims, the same rims that were on the "Batmobile," the skirts covering most of the rear wheel—she was "dirted and skirted." I named her "The Pimpala."

Olivia's horse reared then pawed the air with its front legs. I think she must have been showing off as well because the beautiful black thoroughbred she was riding spun slow circles while standing on its hind legs. She played it off like she wasn't in complete control. The horse kicked up dust, throwing his head side to side. Olivia was fresh off the farm. She had recently moved here from Montana. Her family had lived on a large ranch where they had been in the horse breeding business for generations.

Doubling back in my car, parking next to the corral, I asked if she was alright. Olivia tried to act like she was mad, but she was holding back her award-winning smile, telling me it was OK, but not to ever let it happen again. I promised that I wouldn't and offered to take her for a ride and buy her some ice cream or something, to make up for scaring her horse. Olivia said that would be nice but she didn't know me well enough, that she didn't get in cars with strangers. She said with a smile that everybody knew I had a bad rep- utation, and she heard I had a girlfriend anyway. I ended up hanging out with her all day, helping her clean the horse stall where I was able to work my magic. Before I left we were making out, sitting in the barn on a bale of hay. I will never forget that big black horse throwing a fit inside the stall the first time I kissed her, that horse was jealous of any- body or anything that touched Olivia. I was thankful he was safely in his stall where he was pawing and rearing, kicking the back wall with his powerful rear legs, making a show out of stomping the ground with his front hooves, banging his massive black chest against the stall gait. He whinnied, snorting with mucus flying out of his nostrils with saliva foaming around his mouth. Of course I couldn't let on to Olivia that I was terrified of that beast. I think she got a big kick out of the situation.

It was our senior year. We had been going out since September. The senior ball was all set up, having made arrangements to use my dad's new Mercury Marquis instead of my 1968 ultramarine blue hot rod lowrider Super Sport Impala. Everything in my life seemed to be on track with no worries.

It was Friday night. I took Olivia to the Solano Drive-in movies, parking in my usual spot, the very back row. The sun was all the way down. Halfway through "Jaws," the blockbuster presentation, we were steaming those windows good. This continued through Intermission then into the second movie. The condensation dripped down the inside of my windows. Both of our young healthy bodies were completely soaked with sweat. Me being a young man with a lot of wind in my sails after three times at bat, scoring three home runs, I started the car, letting the defroster clear my windshield. I twisted the cap off my last bottle of Coors, giving her the first drink then we passed it back and forth between us. We drove home slow and easy, cruising the '68, Olivia next to me on the bench seat, my arm around her shoulder, blasting my tunes from the Clarion blue light high-power 8-track stereo with the Jensen 6 x 9 coaxial speakers: Wild Cherry's "Play That Funky Music." I thought to myself, *it just doesn't get any better than this.* What could go wrong?

When I dropped her off at her parents' house, she had

crocodile tears streaming down her angelic face. I was so shocked that I didn't even have a chance to react or time to think. She looked me dead in the eye saying she didn't know how to explain it, but she would not be going to the senior ball with me. Olivia asked me please not to call her, saying she was extremely sorry. Just at that exact moment, her front porch light came on as her father stepped on the porch. She opened the passenger side door then ran up the front walkway. Her dad held the front door open as she walked in under his outstretched arm.

I drove away with the transmission in low gear, the pedal to the metal, tach-ing out the small block 327 until I thought it would blow. Coming to the end of her street, I left the Turbo 400 Short Shaft Hydra-Matic transmission still in low gear. Letting off the gas, my 2-inch dual exhaust with 36-inch glasspacks sounded like a fully-automatic machine gun, back rapping as I let the rpm come down from the back pressure of the small block as it started to unwind. When I got home to my dad's house, I didn't sleep a wink that entire long night.

HOOD PARK

The next day I was standing in front of Concord Park, right next to Concord High. There was a sign in front of the park that read "Concord Neighborhood Park." Somebody had spray-painted over Concord Neighbor, so the sign read "Hood Park." A couple other guys and I had our custom cars parked in the front, all underage, all sneaking brews, when we heard a loud Harley-Davidson Sportster. It was a '69 Sporty with a rigid frame, a Narrow Glide front end with drag style handlebars, straight pipes cut off at 45-degree

angles right behind the foot pegs, and gloss black paint with
white pearlescent ghost flames. The first thing I noticed was
E.Z.'s evil grin, white teeth blaring, blonde hair blowing in
the wind. He was sporting the black Ray-Bans with Olivia
on the back, holding on tight with her arms wrapped
around his waist. Olivia's beautiful face was tucked in the
back of his neck, surrounded by his creepy, wind-blown,
dyed hair. We were all staring with our jaws hanging down
when Concord P.D. snuck up in a black and white cruiser.
There was no need to try to hide what was going on. We
were caught red-handed: minor in possession of an open
container. Well, just when I thought this day couldn't possibly get any worse, my dad came driving by in his El
Camino on his way home from work, rubbernecking, catching the whole scene.

We got hauled downtown where my dad had to come
get me out of jail. On the way home, I asked how much trouble I was in. He said I would get work details. He said it with
a laugh; he thought this was the greatest program of all time,
where kids had to get up with hangovers on Saturday morn-
ings then go work on the highways, picking up the beer bottles they threw out the night before. I told my dad about
Olivia, but I received no sympathy. The old man knew that
I would go after E.Z., telling me she wasn't worth fighting
for. I was a brawler with lightning-fast hands, but I was no
match for him. At seventeen years old, only standing five-
eight, weighing 135-pounds, Eric at six-foot-two, close to
two hundred pounds—even if things went my way and
somehow, even if I won the fight—I knew in my heart I
could never forgive Olivia, that I could never take her back,
much less trust her for the rest of my life. Dad told me since
I had already lost my girl there was no need to add injury

to insult by getting whipped as well. He told me the best thing that I could possibly do was find a new girl to take my mind off her, that I should go after one of her close friends to achieve the best results. One thing I loved about my dad, he always had the best advice.

When we stopped to pick up my '68 on the way home, it was long gone, so we turned around then doubled back to the Concord Police Station to ask where to pick my car up out of impound. They swore up and down that they did not tow it. I guess I could not have been more wrong about this day getting any worse. Now my cherry, fully customized car that I had sunk every dime into was gone. I had to fill out a stolen car report. That spring I seemed to go into a cold slump for a while, but as summer came around I pulled out of the dry spell. I went on a pretty good hot streak with the skirts. My young tender heart had been broken, but it wouldn't be the last time, of course. Somehow I managed to survive it.

E.Z. $

Eric's father had died in a mysterious accident at the shop. Eric had no mother or immediate family. He suddenly became extremely wealthy when he turned eighteen. He got rich the old- fashioned way: he inherited a very large sum of money along with the family business and fabrication shop. Eric became such a flamboyant showboat, wearing a top-of-the-line Presidential Rolex watch with heavy gold chains around his neck. He had a brand new Harley-David-son motorcycle as well as cars, boats and properties, includ-ing a house in Blackhawk, a high-dollar, high-end gated community in Danville. E.Z. was allegedly affiliated with a serious local motorcycle club, a counterfeiting ring, as well as the production and distribution of large quantities of hardcore street narcotics: LSD, PCP, and Eric's personal favorite drug of choice, crystal methamphetamine. He had a connection that was transporting raw cocaine from Miami, Florida through the fishing boat industry here into Half Moon Bay. Eric used a 28-foot Skipjack to transport between Half Moon Bay and his shop in Benicia. First, a 60-nautical-mile trip to the breakwater then 75 more miles straight out to sea to the rendezvous point, where a bale of the raw cocaine would be floating. The bale was outfitted with a homing device that allowed E.Z. to track the signal. This was easily handled by the common fishing boat, slow but steady, perfectly incognito. He had installed two 100-gallon auxiliary diesel fuel tanks to make the round trip without having to stop for fuel. He would transport the raw coke up the coast, under the Golden Gate Bridge, across the San Francisco Bay, around Point Richmond and then up the Carquinez Straits. Eric would offload at his shop in Benicia.

Eric was well on his way to becoming the youngest, most established and feared criminal in the Bay Area, if not the country. If anyone owed him money, no matter how small the amount, he would come after them personally, using fear and intimidation as well as threatening their families. He would force people who owed him to hand over personal possessions of value greater than the amount that was owed, or he would force them to sign over a pink slip, taking their car or preferably their bike. Eric and Olivia disappeared from my life after that summer, and that was alright by me.

THE STURGEON KING

Out on a date with Andrea, the good looking brunette with the Z-28, where I had taken her to Nantucket, a seafood restaurant downriver in a sleepy little waterfront town called Crockett. We were enjoying cocktails in the bar, waiting for our table when the older well-seasoned barkeep told the story of Joey Pallotta, The Sturgeon King. We sat back, enjoying the famous fishing tale that had been told again and again.

The barkeep started the tall tale: On July 9, 1983 Joey Pallotta went fishing out of Crockett, which is downriver from Martinez. He was in a 16-foot tri-hull boat. He and his girlfriend were enjoying the nice warm summer weather and some ice-cold beers, using live grass shrimp for bait, and fishing deep water. Joey was getting some good action after about an hour. Now, when a sturgeon pulls down hard, it's time to set the hook. You have to yank that rod back with everything you've got to set the hook deep into its leathery lips. Joey came back so solid that he thought he was snagged. Whatever was at the end of the line wasn't going to budge no matter how much effort he gave, so he was going to attempt to break it off when it appeared to rise off the bottom just a fraction. It felt as though he had an old submerged water log where his older short but stout rod with the pulley on the last eye at the end was bent almost at ninety degrees. He was outfitted with 60-pound cloth woven line, which was popular at the time. The reel was a large Penn 4.0 Senator, red plastic with chrome housing. The fish went back to the bottom then would not move at all. Joey tightened up his Star Drag and repeated, trying to break his line, forfeiting his steel leader and 16-ounce sliding weight when the fish started to swim against the fast-running, outgoing tide.

Joey was white knuckled on the rod, having the drag set tight. The fish almost pulled the rod free from his arms, nearly pulling him out of the boat. The big strong fish, which he assumed was a stingray from the way it stayed on the bottom, was actually pulling the boat from the stern and starboard—sideways against the current. Joey told his girlfriend he should cut the line. A stingray can swim with the power of a tractor because of the large flat wings. His lady friend replied that it would be fun to play the fish for a while. Joey loosened the drag as the fish played out line. The boat straightened out with the flow of the current when the fish changed course and headed downriver, using the tide to enhance its already super strength.

There are three classifications of sturgeon: shaker, keeper, and peeler. In 1983, the minimum length of a sturgeon had been 36 inches with no maximum length. This fish peeled 300 of Joey's 400 feet of line with the first run, swimming away from the stern with the line moving side to side as the fish kicked its tail. If it had been a stingray, it would have swum in a straight line. Joey had lived in the area his entire life. He was an experienced sturgeon angler. His father had brought him along since he could walk. He used to listen in absolute awe as the old timers would tell the tall tales of the legendary monster sturgeon that lie on the bottom. Joey knew this was a sturgeon. He told his girl to untie the anchor line then tie an inflatable fender to serve as a floating marker so they could hopefully come back later to retrieve their anchor. The mighty fish pulled the boat along with the natural force of the current heading downriver toward San Pablo Bay. His lady was at the the helm with the engine running, using the gears in forward then reverse to help control the boat so they could wait for the monster to wear down.

Joey was now sitting comfortably in the open bow of the tri-hull boat. As the boat was being towed along past the other anglers that were anchored along the way, pleasure boats that were motoring in the area, a group of boats started to follow. Some knew Joey, so they shouted encouragement and a lot of advice, adding to the hype. The battle wore on as the giant sturj' headed into the mouth of San Pablo Bay. As the tide was at the bottom of the outgo, the fish seemed to lie down, as though there were actual suction cups on the bottom. What the extremely smart sturj' was doing was getting rested up, waiting for the tide to change so it could use the force of the incoming tide to swim back upriver to familiar territory. The powerful sturj' was ancient as well as wise.

The tide now slowly changed from slack to incoming. The boat, now in tow from the sturgeon, was being followed by a fleet of boats of all different styles, everything from a rowboat with oars or small outboard engines to luxury cabin cruisers running up to 40-plus feet. The powerful fish showed no sign of fatigue. He headed upriver all the way up the Carquinez Straits, clear into Benicia—a good four miles from San Pablo Bay. There was an 80-foot hole just down from Dillon Point on the north side of the channel. This was where the fish apparently wanted to go. It was probably the home territory where it consumed all the food that accumulated on the bottom. A fish of that proportion required a steady supply of grass shrimp, clams, dead bullheads, mud suckers, and whatever else it could scavenge off the bottom.

By now six hours had gone by. It would be getting dark in two more. The boat was running low on fuel, and another boat pulled alongside. Joey jumped from his boat into the other, thanking his girlfriend who had been trading off duties with him, alternating between operating the boat and holding on to the rod to let Joey rest. The exhausted Joey turned the rod over to another fisherman on the new boat, and graciously accepted the offer of sandwiches and cold beer in return.

It was almost dark. The sun was setting on the black water, making the boat appear to be in a spotlight on a stage. The wind had stopped completely. Joey was back on the business end of the rod. Feeling revitalized from the food, he got a second wind. The sturgeon was too big to ever jump clear of the water and cut the line. It seemed to be circling, staying down deep in the bottom of the 80-foot hole. Joey wondered if the battle would go all night. He wished he could at least see the fish before the sun went completely down. The current was just beginning to lose its momentum with the incoming tide peaking out. The fish had begun to develop some kind of routine: running with the current in the deepest part of the 80-foot hole then heading toward the shallows to go against the current where there was naturally slower water, using this to its own advantage, conserving its energy.

Surrounding the boat Joey was on, there were a lot of very loud, very intoxicated fishermen and boaters alike. The whole scene was like a giant adrenaline-pumped party. Boaters are always a loud, rowdy bunch to begin with. Add large amounts of alcohol mixed with adrenaline plus the fact that most of these were indeed sturgeon anglers that felt somehow they were part of the biggest thing that would ever happen in their life, all this added to the almost magical atmosphere. The fish at last started to show signs of slowing down. The circles it swam were getting smaller and smaller, to the point where the 16-foot fishing boat was in fact just spinning lazily as though it was circling the drain in the bottom of a bathtub. When Joey felt confident that they could safely handle the fish, bringing the boat directly above it, he tried to bring the monster to the surface, and then finally landed the sturgeon. When a large sturj' is finally, completely exhausted it will come up just like a submerged water log. The sturj' had had all it could take. It was reeled to the back of the boat after a brutal eight-hour battle. Everyone saw why it had fought so hard for so long. Besides the fact that the sturj' weighed a whopping 468 pounds, measuring over 12 feet in length, the line had become wrapped around the sturgeon and basically lassoed its midsection as the fish had tried repeatedly to roll and cut the line with its massive armor that ran the length of its back, making it look like exactly what it was: a prehistoric dinosaur that hadn't changed for 250 million years.

The sturgeon was gaffed then tied off with a rope through its mouth and out the side gill, tied to the side of the boat, and taken to The Nantucket, where Joey had purchased the grass shrimp earlier that day. There were boat slips as well as marine repair shops, plus The Nantucket seafood restaurant, bar and grill, outdoor decks with Tiki Torches and candles lit on the top of empty, straw-covered fiasco red wine bottles, all adding magic to the carnival-like atmosphere. The people were shoulder to shoulder. So many people stood on the docks that in some places, the tops of the boards were actually under the water, getting people's feet wet. The sturgeon was documented, measured, and weighed hanging from the ancient dead-weight scale. It was then photographed for the local newspapers, and it appeared in dozens of different newspapers and languages all around the world. Somebody popped a cork and handed Joey a glass of champagne. There was a toast to the new North American record, the largest freshwater fish caught on a rod and reel; a toast to Joey Pallotta, known from that moment as The Sturgeon King.

From that day on Joey was a hero. Wherever he went, he was shaking people's hands and getting patted on the back. He could walk into any bar and drink until he was blind without spending a dime. Joey was smart and used his notoriety well; in no time at all he had his own charter boat, white with red trim, which he named the *Sturgeon King*. Joey ran a good, shipshape business for many years. His record will live in the history books for eternity, for in 1986 the rules were changed by California Fish & Game Commission so that the maximum length sturgeon that can be kept is 72 inches. The fish was sent to a local taxidermist where it was mounted. It is still proudly displayed today at the museum in Port Costa, California. The 12-foot, 468-pound monster is also in the *Guinness Book of World Records*. It turned out the fish was a pregnant, ripe female. Almost ten gallons of the dark purple, almost black caviar referred to as black gold was harvested from the fish.

Joey Pallotta is a card-carrying member of the Plumber's Union in Martinez, L.U. 169. Andrea and I listened to the tall tale and went on to enjoy a delicious seafood dinner. Then off to her place where my night really began.

CHAPTER 6

THE DINO

I was just plugging along with my charter business, hiring out the *General* a couple times a week. I definitely wasn't going to get rich, but I enjoyed being on the water as much as anything else. The sturgeon bite had fallen off and the striped bass run was still months away. Now, under normal circumstances I personally would consider a striper, or any other fish that messes with my sturgeon bait, to be a *pesticle*. I will eat striper if it is prepared right but prefer sturgeon over anything else. As far as catching a fish goes, once you come back solid on a keeper sturgeon, nothing else will compare. Sturgeon is without a doubt the big game of the sport fishing industry. A lot of people on vacation in Hawaii, Mexico, or other places close to the equator will pay handsomely for a single-day charter with a chance to catch a marlin or various other species of big-game fish. Shark fishing has always been popular as well.

To successfully catch a blue marlin (also known as a sailfish or swordfish), you have to be able to afford a charter with a well-seasoned captain as well as crew, You need a good boat equipped with the proper fishing gear, heavyweight rods outfitted with large Penn gold anodized international reels holding 1500 feet of 1000-pound test wire. A crew will cost $2500 per day, where you can only split that between four people max. The average swordfish comes in at 100 to 150 pounds. A blue marlin can go as high as 1200 pounds, but not very often. After the expenses of traveling by air, the resort where you would have to stay, the food with bar bill, and the fee to charter a boat and crew, you would be talking an astronomical amount of cash.

A good friend of mine's father, who could afford these fees, was fishing off the Big Island in Hawaii and got lucky trolling. The 500-pound blue marlin hit like a bolt of lightning, peeling off 500 feet of the 1000-pound test wire on the first run, with one of the deck hands pouring a bucket of water over the reel to keep the drag from overheating. They chased the fish with the boat in reverse, the waves breaking over the stern. My friend's father, Stanley, strapped into the fighting chair with a full four-point body harness. An experience like that would be absolutely priceless, no doubt, but your average Joe will only watch something like that on television. On the other hand, anybody can fish for sturgeon. All you need is five bucks worth of bait and a cold six pack.

The sturgeon evolved long before the dinosaur, 250 million years ago after their direct ancestors survived the Great Permian Extinction that killed nine out of ten of every species of large fish. The white sturgeon, or diamondback lives an average of a hundred years, reaching maximum lengths of 10 to 15 feet, an average sturj' approximately 4 to 5 feet, weighing up to 75 pounds, yet there are rare occurrences of much larger and heavier sturgeon. The mighty sturj' soon became the dominant big fish in every river system in North America and Eurasia. Lake sturgeon migrates back to its birthplace to spawn. The ingenious people who inhabited the Great Lakes migrated with the travels of the fish, much like the nomadic North American Indian tribes, traveling with the herds of buffalo for survival. In the Great Lakes the land-locked fish flourished.

Back in the day, the locals would take a 300-foot, 1-inch rope with a 6-inch treble hook baited up with a whole chicken, row out then drop the bait in deep water, with a team of mules on the shore, where the mammoth 10- to 15-foot sturj' were dragged out of the water for harvest. The grandpa would keep a machete handy to hack the rope in case the sturj' overpowered the mules. According to Potawatomi as well as Ojibwe legend, the rivers were so full of sturgeon that a person could walk on water across the backs of the fish. Throughout North American history the main population of human beings, the tribes of the Indians, actually survived extinction during droughts, harsh winters, disease, and famine by harvesting the fish then smoking the meat, as it would last indefinitely. If it were not for the abundant supply of sturgeon, the human race would have become extinct.

Initially the European settlers who pushed westward in the 1800s traded with the Indians for dried sturgeon meat, but the sturj' had not yet gained its popularity. The commercial fishing industry arrived, targeting herring and lake trout instead. With sturgeon ripping through and damaging nets, they were considered a nuisance, so the commercial fishermen just slaughtered them. They would cut the artery near the tail with the fish swimming away to bleed out. The abundant bodies were dried in the sun on the banks of the rivers then burned for fuel like wood logs to fire the boiler on steam ships.

In 1867 after the California Gold Rush, there were masses of Chinese laborers absorbed by the Central Pacific Railroad. A large portion found steady work with irrigation and reclamation, building the endless miles of levees to create the California Delta. These workers dug in along the river towns, recreating their rich Chinese culture in various historic towns from the Sacramento to the San Joaquin rivers. The sturj' was considered a pest as it slowed down work, but Chinese workers, being instructed to cut the tail of the sturgeon then let it swim away to bleed out and die, knew this was a waste. Instead they utilized the clean white meat, internal organs, and fins—no bones, scales, oil, or smell—boiling the head with its external skull for soups. Throughout the years, the sturj' has been harvested near extinction again and again. The size limit changed as the years went by in hopes of more reproduction.

You can fish for sturgeon from piers, the banks of rivers, oceans, bays and estuaries of the Columbia River in Oregon, the Great Lakes in Michigan, Frazier River in British Columbia, the Caspian, Baltic or the Black Sea. People fish for sturgeon every single day all around the world, although you have a much better chance fishing from a boat. There are more people in more places fishing for sturgeon every day, making it the most sought-after big-game fish.

THE LEATHER LIPPER

Hanging out at the Marina, I took a walk up to the bait shop to drum up some business, get the latest on any recent hot spots. Now, if you have ever walked into a real bait shop that's been around for a long time on a hot day, you will never forget the smell when you come through the door: the odor of fish bait, tobacco, alcohol, and bullshit, there's nothing like it in the world. Standing outside on the front porch near the corner of the redwood deck where the scale is set up for weighing in fish and taking photographs, just minding my own business, everybody else was saying the same thing I already knew: The bite was cold in the local spots with a small amount of activity down in San Pablo Bay, buoy number nine, the pump house and the rock wall at the outlet of the Napa River—most of those were good all year round. I overheard a group of three fishermen complaining in disbelief that their buddy, the one with the boat who was already 45 minutes late, had called the bait shop explaining he had the boat hooked up, ready to leave when he had a family emergency. He was extremely sorry, promising to make it up next time. The first thing I noticed was that these guys were dressed for success, sporting warm clothes for all-night fishing. The bait, food, various types of alcohol, all sat on the tail gate of a late model 4WD. I knew they had a little cash by the quality of the clothing they wore and their mannerisms, probably union construction workers. Apologizing for being nosy, I explained that I'd overheard their predicament and offered the services of myself and the *General*. They knew who I was and my reputation as a charter captain. I gave them a decent price, lower than normal for an all-night excursion. The usual fee for an all-nighter, up to six people, was six hundred, paid in advance. The price I offered them, three hundred cash, included me and the boat. They had their own bait and gear. We would get set up anywhere they wanted to go, dropping anchor and staying put until sunrise, then coming back in by 9:00 a.m. They agreed to my offer and we were soon underway, as I explained to the three-man crew that after we got set up at a fishing hole that they had their hearts set on I would try to catch some shut eye. There were 45 minutes of daylight left. The spot where we were heading was about 30 minutes out.

We were passing under the Benicia Bridge, the *General* gently eating up the small waves. The water had a slight chop, the wind not strong enough to present any problem. Just past the bridge the Hummingbird fish finder started to light up, the fish alarm indicating large black continuous blocks just off the bottom in the deep water channel, not far from where I had marked them two weeks ago, having scoped this same area a few times since first seeing the mysterious boxcars but produced no results. The three fishermen leaned with their backs against the stern rail enjoying the ride, drinking cold beers, reliving past sturgeon trips. One of the guys named Mark was busting his buddy Ron's chops on the boat ride out. Apparently Mark had a beautiful red-headed, pure-blooded, Irish girlfriend, a total Ginger. She was tall, extremely well built, talking about a real siren, her name was Karen. Her only flaw was she had extremely white skin where her lips looked almost transparent. Friday night after work and several beers, Ron had asked Mark what was going on over the weekend. It was loud in the bar and this is where Ron got confused. Mark said he had a date with Karen. They both agreed she was a babe, Mark pointed out the only thing he noticed was her lips looked leathery. Karen was pure class, nobody cared about what her lips looked like, but they were going to rip some lips on Friday night, with the loud music and the Friday night bar crowd. Mark was talking about a hot sturgeon spot, the trip was set up and they were going out on a friend's boat. Ron, already feeling the cold beers and shots, thought Mark was calling Karen "the leather lipper," and that he was going to rip some lips. Karen was referred to from that day on as the leather lipper, of course never to her face.

THE HONEY HOLE

Leaving the Martinez Marina, we headed upriver passing under the Benicia Bridge, the *Glomar* off the port side
when I saw the boxcars on the fish finder. I would have
loved to drop anchor and wet a hook but the spot they had
in mind was at the outlet of Port Chicago near Seal Island,
directly north of the Tosco Oil Refinery, maybe one mile
from the nearest unit in the plant. I had fished at the same
spot, producing sturgeon, on many occasions. The only
problem was that it wasn't safe to drop anchor in the shipping channel for obvious reasons where most of the area
was restricted naval territory. The hot spot, "the honey hole"
was on the edge of the restricted zone near the edge of a
sharp drop off the main shipping channel. There are at least
a hundred shallow places, sand bars which seem to move
from one location to the next due to storms, with overflowing
tributaries that channel into the swollen creeks. It's a good
place to run aground in the dark, so I was in a hurry to pick
a good spot before losing all the remaining daylight. Of
course, the *General* is outfitted with a large, 3 million can-
dlepower spotlight mounted on the whale point remotely
controlled from the wheelhouse, as well as spare recharge-
able, hand-held lights that I kept around for emergencies.

We dropped anchor, setting the *General* to where it would
shift 180 degrees with the incoming and outgoing tides, so
I would not be disturbed from my much-needed beauty
sleep. Going over the rules, if they needed any of my gear
they were welcome to borrow whatever they needed but
they were financially responsible for anything lost or broken. I set up a propane lantern that ran from a 10-gallon tank

mounted under the ladder behind the stern. The propane is soft piped to its mount above the hard lid where it illuminates the rod tips as well as the fishing deck—with the lantern safely on top there is no need to keep the required anchor light burning. I held a small safety meeting, giving them instruction on how to turn on the halogen spotlights near the back end of the hard lid, just in case they got lucky and got tied in to a peeler. Everything was gone over again until I was one hundred percent confident in the crew: # 1 rule do not fall in, # 2 don't overdo the alcohol, especially if you couldn't handle your liquor. And last but not least, rule #3, don't wake me up unless there was an emergency. These guys seemed to be competent, so I shut the cabin door then made myself comfortable in the small but cozy forward V-berth of the cuddy cabin. I was just about asleep; the time was going on 8:00 p.m. when they tied into the fish. Lying there listening to the building excitement, thinking that their fishing hole had paid off, the first fish was about 55 inches— I could tell without looking due to the amount of time from when the angler yelled *fish on* until it was snared then pulled into the boat. They were continuously getting action with the bite going strong when one of the anglers hooked a second fish. Smiling to nobody but myself, knowing there would be no sleep for me until the action died down.

CHAOS

Less than one mile away, Kenny Callaway had been working at the Tosco Oil Refinery for almost five years. He had recently been promoted from operator trainee to Number Two Operator. He was married with two young children, recently purchasing his first home. He ran his house on a tight budget where the pay increase plus the rotating shifts would add up. After dressing down with FRC's (fire retardant clothing), hardhat with goggles on the bill, clear safety glasses, leather gloves, 02 sensor, flashlight and hearing protection, picking up his heavy-duty aluminum clipboard, Kenny was making his first routine lap, gathering readings from a series of gauges and sight glass instrumentation when he felt the ground vibrating under his feet. Kenny was well-trained but was still a little green, making him wary about being alone in the part of the plant where he had been stationed. He was pulling a 12-hour night shift, 6:00 p.m. to 6:00 a.m. Noting the time at 9:15 p.m. then jotting down notations on his clipboard, he was focusing on a gauge and thought he had to be seeing things; either the gauge was malfunctioning or there was a very serious problem. The refinery had had a series of accidents recently. That was the main reason for his concern, especially him being personally responsible. But after five years of being in the live unit, Kenny knew he and his fellow workers lives could all depend on his reaction to the problem. Reaching into the back pocket of his company issued FRC dark blue overalls with reflective silver safety illumination, pulling out his vulcanized, 3-D cell safety flashlight, he moved in closer for a better look. The moment he hit the switch into the on position all hell broke loose.

The hydrocracker collector unit that funneled out of the bottom of the 80 x 20-foot vertical vessel had ruptured internally, creating a time bomb. What Kenny saw on the gauge was correct, the needle had gone past the green into the red danger zone with such force that when the tip of the indicating needle hit the stop it actually had bent the needle forcing its way past the stop. When the 24-inch heavy wall pipe, that should never have safely contained more than 750 pounds of normal operating pressure, burst from exceeding 5,000 pounds due to the meltdown inside the vessel, Kenny never had a chance to blink. The force from the explosion disintegrated him from head to toe. He was completely vaporized, the product blowing out of the rupture, a six-inch hole ripped in the side of the 24-inch pipe, the half-refined fuel ignited instantaneously, spraying high-pressure flaming product for hundreds of feet horizontally in every direction as well as several thousand feet straight into the dark sky. The only thing Fire and Rescue found the next day where Kenny had been standing were two footprints burned into the black asphalt from the neoprene soles of his work boots, some of his dental work and the change from his pockets, the pennies, nickels and dimes so hot that the coins had melted the asphalt and were embedded in the surface.

I was lying there half asleep when I felt the explosion. My first guess was the 10-gallon propane cylinder on the back of my boat had somehow exploded or my diesel fuel tank had ignited. My eyes now wide open I saw what appeared to be daylight outside the portholes. I grabbed the closest fire extinguisher then burst out onto the back deck. The three fishermen were standing on the deck staring in disbelief at the inferno lighting up the dark sky. The fire burnt with such powerful force that the light from the flames could be seen for hundreds of miles, the rapidly spreading fire from the burning oils along with half-refined fuels, that were now spreading to other parts of the surrounding facility, creating a completely out of control "Code Blue" situation. The smoke was spreading to the point where it actually looked like a mushroom cloud, creating dangerous breathing conditions. Yelling, "Reel 'em in," as I fired up the Cat's, already winching up the anchor and turning my navigational lights on when we all started to cough from breathing the toxic deadly smoke.

I headed away then brought it around hard, making straight for the shipping channel, my global positioning system showing me where I was. Plotting my course, knowing I could bring us home safely using my electronics, but I still followed the main channel using the red and green navigational channel markers, keeping the green buoy to my starboard side. When you are navigating downriver the green is always on the right. When you are coming from the ocean up the river the rule of thumb is "red right return." After getting the *General,* complete with crew, safe and sound back to the marina, the fishermen had two keeper sturgeon onboard. When we were safely on dry ground I offered them half of their three hundred dollars back, which they refused to accept. Telling them to book a charter at a future date, I would cut them a good deal, we all shook hands and went our separate ways.

CHAPTER 7

PIPE ON

The next morning I went to the union hall in Concord, taking a dispatch to go work in the refinery that exploded the night before. The demand for men to work $even-twelve$, 7-12$, double $hift$, both night and day, cleared the bench where we had several hundred unemployed men on the out-of-work list. I chose night shifts, where it paid an extra 15 percent. Taking a dispatch for B&W (Babcock and Wilcox), where I had to do an orientation that day then went straight to work that night at 6:00 p.m. That made my first shift double-time, already counting the cash I was earning as well as building up my retirement and getting my benefits back online. Union fitters scale is hard to beat. Despite the fact that I would be going into a dangerous if not deadly environment, by claiming 99 dependents on my W-2 forms with all the overtime I would be grossing $4,000 per week, taking home most of that. They say the difference between a stone broke and a wealthy fitter is one week of employment. At this rate I would be moneyed-up real fast. Hopefully I'd be able to work out any problems with the Internal Revenue Service with legitimate tax write-offs from the *Sturgeon General* at the end of the year.

Showing up wearing my customary work attire, fresh creased Cowboy Cut Wranglers, black cotton turtleneck under a Carhartt Hickory Stripe zip down work shirt, steel-toed Red Wing Pecos boots spit-shined to repel water, plus lookin' sharp wearing a custom-made cotton welder's cap with the creased bill folded to the side, Pipeline style— my custom-made caps are reversible with black on the inside, red with white polka dots on the outside—old school wire frame safety glasses with the wire net side shields, number two dark green lenses, best safety glasses ever made, and of course my black Carhartt Antarctic vest.

After orientation we all dressed down in FRC's, safety gear, hard hats, etc. We did a walk-through out to the area where the initial blast had occurred. What I saw will stick in my mind clear as day for the rest of my life. Every painted surface was scorched, the blast had blistered many coats of industrial paint and primer, the heavy mono-coat fireproofing, even the galvanized coating completely gone, leaving all the exposed iron burned to bare metal, already oxidizing an ugly red. There were pipes with diameters from two inches up to as large as forty-two inches running horizontal from adjoining pipe racks, hanging like long, limp spaghetti, sagging over 50 feet to the ground, everything melted from the intense heat. The pipelines that ran up and down the roadways surrounding the hydrocracker unit consisted of multi-tiered, I-beam constructed pipe racks with different sizes of pipe running parallel with the run of the rack. The force of the blast had actually moved the lines, welded angle iron guides and all, bending and stretching pipes like they were made of rubber. The fire had been extinguished earlier that day, but workers were operating the fire monitors, spraying the entire area with the plant water, keeping everything cooled down, also to aid in dust control. Some areas were blue-taped off, others red or yellow depending on the danger level of the exposed chemicals. Crews operating with Scott Air-Paks were attempting to contain the deadly, highly toxic products that were being refined.

My job description for the duration of the project consisted mostly of rigging, demolition of pipe and equipment working with chokers, shackles and tag lines, signaling the cranes, a lot of high rigging while tied off to a safety harness.

Working on a job like this there is always a lot of standby time. Catching up with a buddy of mine, Dave from Concord High, he told me that E.Z. was around. Rumor was he was broke. I found this hard to believe. My friend knew I was dying to hear, he stood there smiling until he made me ask about Olivia. The only thing he had heard was that she was still racked up pretty good. He hadn't personally seen her but heard she was still smoking hot. It was Friday, the day the eagle flies. While we were waiting to go to lunch, "Jungle," the union steward walked up collecting money for the check pool, where you take the net amount of your check, add it to the check number and this is played as a poker hand. Most of the workers on the job kick in 10 dollars each; a good fat pot usually goes around a couple thousand bucks. I had two twenties and a ten-spot in my shirt pocket. Dave wasn't playing so I kicked in another ten bucks, playing his check. Dave asked me if I won playing his check numbers did he get half the money. I answered, no but I would take him on a free charter. We all headed for the break room.

Now keep in my mind, some steamfitters are just like a bunch of overpaid carnies, traveling with the work, staying in trailer parks or motels. A big job being similar to a large tree full of fruit, where all the fitters, like a flock of birds will land in the tree, plenty for everybody, then as the fruit runs out, some will fly to a new tree but some will stay, fighting over the last hours. The meat eaters will work 7-12$ year-round, the true carnivores of the industry, but have dedicated their life to their careers. They "paid the cost to be the boss," some addicted to the money, drunk with power, true Alphas. Don't get me wrong, any one of these guys would give you the shirt right off their back, great leaders doing their jobs. It's no easy task organizing and supervising several hundred construction workers. Most steamfitters just put in their time, making good wages, living a good life, raising families, pumping up their 401s. A job of this magnitude is like a giant oak tree full of monkeys, hundreds of monkeys on every branch. When the monkeys look up, what do they see? A—ho!es, with one monkey on top.

The majority of people don't know the history of how plumbers back in the days of the Romans saved the world from disease with advanced fresh water supply, as well as the handling of sanitation. The pipefitting industry supplies water, petroleum pipelines as well as building power plants. When you take a shower, be grateful to a pipeliner for the natural gas that heats your hot water. When you turn on the light in your child's room, the power is supplied from a power plant built by steamfitters. When you fill your car up with gasoline, the gas came from an oil refinery, the gasoline transported safely and efficiently through our underground pipelines. The world would stop turning without pipelines, the cross country high pressure petroleum pipelines being the blood vessels of the world.

The break room consists of a large white tent, 250 feet long by 250 feet wide, lined up with large folding tables, surrounded with collapsible chairs filled with hungry construction workers. Refrigerators along with microwaves line the walls of the break room, the tent filled with travelers from other locals as well as local members manning their work, people selling everything from hot homemade breakfast burritos to colorful, custom-made welder's caps. "Bennie the Blade" holds daily raffles for very expensive, high end hunting knives, guys raffling off show cars, as well as firearms of every sort and style. In the corner, Robert Rodriguez running a street craps game, the table covered in Benjamins. Bobby the Rod talking loud and fast, holding court while dramatically rolling the dice, making his number, and snatching all the money off the table.

I wolfed down some grub: a peanut butter pickle sandwich with mayo on Wonder white bread, with hot black coffee in my chrome cup from the green Stanley thermos. I saw two of my union bro's playing a high-dollar card game called Acey Deucey, aka "spit in the ocean." There was L.T., an African-American all of six-foot-five-inches tall, in shape—thank God he was one the nicest guys you ever met—with another brother they called the Pipe Fighter, Carlos, who came from the Bronx, 100% Puerto Rican, at six-foot-three, two hundred fifty pounds, his street smarts sharp from growing up hard in the projects. One time Carlos was in line at the tool room when another worker from the Boilermakers Union made the mistake of starting a fight with the wrong guy. In self-defense Carlos had "one punched him," knocking the other man cold as a clam, earning his nick name.

ACEY DEUCEY

This game is played with only three cards dealt at a time, one on the left, another on the right, each player antes up five bones where the third card is placed in the middle, landing in between the other two cards. If an ace is dealt first card, it can be called high or low. If you call it low it makes the ace the lowest card, the best possible hand being the ace called low then the second card being another high ace. You can bet one dollar minimum or any amount up to the total in the pot. If you got good cards you can "pot it," but if you "match up" (get dealt the same card as your top or bottom card)—hard to do but not impossible—you have to double the pot. I had seen guys digging paychecks out of their pockets or signing over vehicles when they lost big or matched up on a big pot. Having thirty bucks left in my shirt pocket, I asked L.T. if I could sit in.

He answered laughing out loud, showing big white teeth with his deep, baritone voice, "Sure thing, Stoner, we'll take your money too."

Looking at my Seiko I noted there was fifteen minutes of our lunch break left. The Pipe Fighter was dealing to L.T. first where he drew a 5-Queen split. With fifteen dollars in the pot he maxed his bet, playing for the fifteen dollar pot. L.T. drew a 4 making the pot double to thirty dollars. My cards came next, where I drew a 7-10, no odds, no bet, I passed on my cards. The cards were dealt where I was betting cautiously only having thirty dollars to start with. The other two players were continuing to lose where I was slowly chipping away at the pot. The game heated up fast with L.T. and Carlos losing hand after hand, the cards were going my way where I was up over three hundred frog skins. It was my turn to deal when the Pipe Fighter potted on a six-hundred-dollar hand. He had been dealt a 3-King split but lost by being dealt an ace, tough break. L.T. looked at me saying this is getting bloody fast, the normally loud break room getting quiet as the game heated up. My cards came, a 2-10 split. I bet $250 of my $300, in case I lost I could stay in the game with the remaining $50. I held my breath as the five was turned over, the game went on with the other two players digging deep in their pockets, the break room now silent watching as the game got more intense. I'll say one thing, neither one of these players were scared to bet, repeatedly potting, losing hand after hand. I was dealing when the pot swelled up over $2,000.

LT said, "Nothing personal Mike, but please place the deck on the lunch table," where we would all draw our own cards off the top without touching the deck; it was a friendly game of cards but it was getting serious with the pot over a couple grand.

Up over $500 bucks and feeling good, the cards came my way again with two minutes of break time left to play. I drew a 4-K split and was all in with my $530, drew a 6 and collected the $530, now being up over a grand. Break was over, with over a thousand left in the pot. I told my two union brothers I was out and they could fight over the rest of the pot at the next break.

Among the group there was an older, well-seasoned welder, a Hawaiian cat called "Kanack" —where the legend was he was once the president of a world-famous motorcycle club and a Golden Glove boxer in his youth. In 1968, at the age of 18 he had fought George Foreman for 15 rounds, the winner to represent the U.S. Olympic Boxing Team. The fight ended in a draw. George Foreman sang in the choir at a Southern Baptist Church, the Hawaiian rode in a motorcycle club called "Sons of Hawaii" in San Francisco. We know who they picked for the Olympics.

He had been silently watching the game, but now he

stands up saying to L.T. and Carlos, "You two giants should be ashamed; you probably weigh 700 pounds combined. Mike is so small compared to both of you two. You let him manhandle you and take your money. Mike's arms are so skinny he could use a pair of Cheerios for Water Wings." The break room which had been silent now busted out laughing long and hard. Then break was over, with me a thousand bucks richer in less than fifteen minutes—had to be some kind of a record.

The foreman instructed me to get with another rigger named "Clay Baby." Clay and I were to rig out the piece of pipe that had ruptured. We set the rigging: two red, 20-foot Kevlar-wrapped nylon slings with shackles and tag lines. We used a two-way radio to communicate with the crane operator, who couldn't see our hand signals because it was dark. The pick went smooth where the ruptured spool was hauled out with the crane. We were waiting on the foreman for instruction on our next task when the Union Steward came walking up, pulling an envelope from his pocket. I asked with a grin if I'd hit the check pool.

He answered, "No, but Dave did. Here's $2100 for you, Mike." This day kept getting better. I paid the stew' $210, the customary 10% for running a union check pool. Knowing this job was over for me, I found my foreman, using the proper chain of command, telling him I was going to drag up (when a fitter quits his job it's called dragging up), stick a fork in me, I was all done, and asked for a layoff. My hours had beefed up my benefits. My quitting would do the other hands a favor where they could bank more of the precious hours.

Spending the rest of the shift walking the job passing out business cards, saying goodbye to my union brothers for now, my foreman and the stew' walked up handing me my last paycheck. This check is referred to as your A$$ - check. Sometimes when a fitter leaves a job it's the only money he has. He leaves the job the same way he showed up: broke, stoned and busted. When it's a fitter or welder—welders more often, busting a test or bad welds, get run off—they escort the worker off the property, because of liability. If the hand that is getting run off is "hot headed," he might damage a boss's truck—tires slashed or worse. Usually when they are escorting me off the jobsite, I'm kickin' rocks. This time it was all good. The stew' and the foreman were shaking my hand saying it was sad to see me go—Jungle and Benny were looking down when The Blade handed me both my check$ where I was ready to do a Mexican Hat Dance. I told them with a grin, "No worries, brothers, will see you on the big one," telling my boys I'd never seen a day where I couldn't use two checks.

Moneyed-up *Big Time* with not one but two fat overtime checks, almost $8,000 total, the Acey Deucey money, plus the check pool, I had almost $11,000 in my shirt pocket, telling the boys my ass is red, but my pockets are green, screw Tosco Oil and their money-making machine. The fever was coming strong. I was getting the urge to go fish. They gave me a layoff where I could draw my unemployment, running the *General* at the same time. So, I had to drag, saying goodbye for now to my union brothers. The sun was coming up as I let the cold-blooded big block warm up. I pointed the El-Co toward the house, cruisin' through the morning reverse-commute traffic, going home fat and happy. Lying in bed where I should have been asleep from exhaustion, I was just staring at the back of my eyelids thinking about the job I had just quit, the union, the *General* and yeah, I admit I was wondering what Olivia looked like.

ERIC SPINNING, CIRCLING THE DRAIN

After resting for several days, tightening up the *General* and the *Aquaholic*, topping off tanks, paying off all my bills: the fuel dock, my tab from the bait shop and local watering hole, I could only think about two things: the big fish I had marked and Olivia. It wasn't that I wanted to get with her, I was thinking about what her situation was, how E.Z. could possibly be broke. The last anybody had heard was that he was worth about five million, rolling hard running a motorcycle chop shop, selling custom choppers out of his family's old fabrication shop. He employed four older, well-seasoned men who were fully tattooed from the neck down, full sleeved, black jailhouse style ink. All four were Caucasian, all over six-foot and weighing at least 250 pounds, each sporting some style of beard or goatee, all four completely legit. Eric ran the business shrewdly: they wore uniforms with their names above the pocket, were top mechanics, earning top wages, keeping regular hours—very punctual and extremely organized—everything shipshape. They repaired motorcycles, fabricating the most intense, custom-construction chopper frames then assembled the bikes with his large supply of used parts from hot, stripped-down bikes. Apparently E.Z. had had a few too many run-ins with the law, even though he could afford the best and most expensive legal representation that money could buy, he had paid out millions in cash as well as forfeiting major liquid assets, losing a better part of his inheritance attempting to avoid doing any serious long-term, state penitentiary time. He had served six months here, another year there, losing all trust from all his connections. E Z was so paranoid of being ratted out that he could no longer trust his mules to make drops or deliver cash. Eric had signed over mortgage titles as well as the lavish vehicles and offshore cigarette boats that he had collected. He had borrowed against the family's fabrication shop property where he was deeply in debt, with the kind of people that make large cash loans then come around every Friday afternoon collecting cash payments with extreme interest. Now that's what I call straight up bad karma. All he ever had to do after inheriting his dad's business was to keep the existing contracts with the trucking companies and surrounding refineries, fabricating and maintaining submersible tanks. He would have been set for generations to come. Instead he'd gotten involved with all the illegal get-rich schemes, the narcotic manufacturing and distribution, he had nearly lost it all, any profits from the "blood money" he had given back ten-fold, justice served.

E.Z. and Olivia lived in a small but expensively furnished apartment on the second floor of the shop. Olivia served as bookkeeper; Eric designed then welded the unique chopper frames. The rear section of the fabrication shop was where the large aluminum tanks were laid out, assembled, then welded out and pressure tested. Eric would spend endless hours by himself, on many occasions going in the back area after shop hours, staying locked in secrecy the entire night. This part of the shop was off-limits to everyone, including Olivia. She had never stepped foot in the back area. When Eric went into seclusion, she was grateful to get a break from the possessive, highly jealous Eric, with his explosive temperament. After the first year of the relationship, she knew she was only a possession. Olivia was treated like a prisoner, not a mate. She knew one day she had to separate from the highly abusive toxic relationship. She had a little cash rat-holed away waiting for the right opportunity. Olivia knew when the time came she had better be ready to run fast and run far, because Eric had sworn she would disappear from the face of the planet if he ever caught up to her. Olivia was more fearful for her parents and siblings than for her own life, so she kept a tight lip, her eyes and ears wide open, waiting patiently for a way out, praying Eric would catch another beef then have to do some serious time. Not feeling sympathy, either for herself or Eric, she'd made her bed; she was the one who had to lie in it.

HAWG HUNTIN'

Not being able to book a charter to save my life, I was getting restless. Deciding that I would invest some time and go try to soak some shrimp, knowing that if I could some-how manage to bring in a larger sturgeon or at least a decent keeper the word would spread, business would have to come around. Going out solo in the *Aquaholic,* motoring out past the Benicia Bridge, running continuous grids past the *Glomar Explorer* looking for sign of the mysterious boxcars, it was about 3:00 p.m. with a strong outgoing tide. Checking my tide chart, I knew from the strength of the current that the outgoing was a minus red-letter low tide. According to my tide tables the outgo would bottom out at 8:00 p.m., reg-istering at one foot, eight inches below sea level. I couldn't believe my good luck picking this particular afternoon to fish. It was the rare occurrence of the minus tide, the ultra-low tide referred to as a "red letter" tide. Any qualified ship captain worth his salt has these tides memorized, needing to be fully aware and extra cautious about running aground. The tide comes in then goes out twice every day, usually an average of six hours each tide change. When the red-letter tide runs out seven or eight hours continuously, the sturgeon wait in the shallows, grazing from clam beds like cattle on the grass ranges. In theory the sturj' will come out of the relaxing shallows just like you or me lying on the couch, when the sturj' wakes up from its nap the fish will naturally be hungry. At the bottom of the outgo, when there is little or no current and the fish can swim to feed without wasting energy, with the slack tide, they forage for whatever baitfish has accumulated in the deeper holes as the tide slows, not having to fight the swift current. So at the end of a normal six-hour tide the fish is ready to feed, has a bigger appetite and will bite much more aggressively, resulting in stronger odds for the angler to have the opportunity to "rip some lips." After continuous scoping of the bottom the fish finder was silent, so I dropped anchor in the spot where I had last seen the boxcars.

The weather was fair, the time going on 6:00 p.m. with just a glimpse of the setting sunlight traveling across the smooth surface of the water like an endless freeway paved with bright gold bricks. The remaining ultraviolet rays burned bright, surrounded with florescent, pastel oranges accenting the pastel purples with a sky-blue perimeter. I said a small prayer thanking God for this blessing. He could not have created a more beautiful, picture-perfect sunset. I armed myself with one of my custom-made Hank Frys sturgeon rods. Hank had fished the Delta up around Pittsburg for the last sixty years or more and had caught more sturgeon than everybody I know put together. He is a living legend to say the least, with hundreds of pictures in numerous bait shops up and down the Delta and trophy sturj' up to ten and eleven feet, all from the years before the 72-inch maximum. Hank, now in his golden years, fabricated the best sturgeon rods money could buy. The particular rod I'd brought with me that afternoon had a stiff backbone but was equipped with an ultra-light tip, so you notice the gentle "catfish-style" bite of the leather lipper. The reel was a large Penn International gold anodized conventional baitcaster with a big crank, level wind with a four-to-one retrieve. The reel was tightly wrapped with 500 yards of state-of-the-art Kevlar Spider Wire, the diameter of the dark green 150-pound test miniature woven line was the same as 8-pound monofilament, resulting in less resistance against the current so your bait wouldn't float off the bottom. You have a better chance of feeling the bite with the lightest weight possible, so when the fish picks up the bait you hope he doesn't feel the weight of the sinker and spit your hook. A standard sturgeon leader is 30 inches of 150-pound test, stainless steel wire with two #5 hooks. Having rigged a custom eight-foot leader that I had fabricated myself with a heavy gauge stainless steel wire, a single #10 Gamakatsu laser-sharpened, curved bait hook, clipping a 16-ounce oval weight on a red plastic slider above a single eye-by-eye ball bearing swivel, eliminating a snap swivel, because when you're "hawg huntin'" you don't want the possibility of a spring snap opening under pressure. I tied a handful of live grass shrimp using elastic magic thread to keep my bait on the hook. The best method is threading the shrimp tail-first with the barb coming out of the head, then tying as many as it takes to make it the same diameter as your thumb at the 180-degree curve at the bottom of the hook, being careful to leave the barb exposed. This method works well for hawgz—comes in handy if you want to catch some Z's while overnight fishing.

Flipping the lever on the big Penn into the free wheel position I lobbed the heavy, oversized hook with bait gently behind the boat into the swift current, holding my thumb on the back of the spool for a few seconds to ensure that my leader would not tangle with my slider. Using pressure from my thumb, clutching the spool, letting the current carry my bait out away from the boat, I felt it hit bottom then put the big reel back in gear, cranking a few rotations on the handle to eliminate any extra slack, keeping a tight line. When it felt like my line was straight, true from my rod tip to the soft, muddy bottom of the channel, I eased back with the rod tip, feeling my 16-ounce lead weight lift off the bottom then eased forward again, feeling the sinker thud on the bottom.

Everything was in order. The Mothball Fleet was off my starboard bow, lying in anchor like hundreds of massive sleeping giants, the *Glomar Explorer* was downriver to my right, as the ultimate feeling of tranquility set in. I sat in deep thought about life in general, nursing a couple of ice-cold beers and chowin' down on Saltines with Vienna Sausages, aka "Pipe liners' filet mignon"—I keep a case on the boat. My eyelids started to get heavy. Making a quick inspection, making sure the Perko switch was set on the proper post, saving the number one battery, ensuring I had a fully charged battery for the ignition, reaching under the bow I pulled out my Carhartt Arctic lined coveralls, duck brown with the black insulated lining. These overalls had saved my bacon on more than one occasion. Now set to spend the night, I drank one more beer from the cooler, engaged the clicker, flipping the lever on the reel back to free wheel so if the "Big Daddy" came along while I was asleep, the clicker would let me know he was taking line. I clipped on a small bell, which is a sturgeon fisherman's alarm clock, clamping it to the tip of my rod for a second insurance policy. After that I positioned the *Aquaholic* so she could spin 180 degrees in case I was in a deep sleep and somehow managed to sleep straight through the tide. The channel was about 50 feet deep, having let out probably 100 of my 250 feet of anchor line. The bite was completely dead, not even a nibble. I was sleeping like a baby, occasionally waking to stand and stretch out, draining my bladder of the spent beer, focusing my eyes on everything I could see. It doesn't matter how many nights you spend on the water; your eyes will still play tricks on the brain. I was sitting with the captain's bucket seat spun around backwards facing the stern, my feet on a plastic milk crate, a black wool sock hat pulled down around my ears. The tide ran out and then came back in, peaking out at close to 2:00 a.m. with a 3-foot, 8-inch high, resulting in about a 5-foot tide differential. By my calculations that means the sturgeon had fed four or five hours ago. The next outgoing tide would bottom out at about 8:00 a.m., so I sank both hands deep into my warm pockets, knowing I would sleep until sunup. The sky turning colors as the sun light pushed through, just creeping up out of the east while the tide was splitting at the bow, streaming down the sides of the boat, running past the smooth lines of the gunwales, coming back together behind the transom. I was lying there with the pains and stiffness of a man who had worked hard his entire life. My spine felt like it had been spot welded, my shoulders, hips and knees screamed in protest as I stood stretching out, putting a small stainless steel percolator on the gas burner, nibbling on what was left of the food, waiting for a cup of the strong brew.

CHAPTER 8

THE TUG IS THE DRUG

Watching the sun rise, listening to the current racing past the boat, I pulled anchor then scoped several well-known hot spots, fishing the incoming, catching a shaker here and there. Going back on shore for fresh bait and bait shop breakfast burritos, talking to a few fishermen and bait shop "hang arounds" the word was the same: the sturj' bite was as cold as it had ever been. The boxcars still eating at me from the inside, driven by determination I fished all day, dozing off here and there, spending the whole day enjoying what I do best—being on the water, minding my own business, not bothering anybody. It was almost 7:00 p.m. when I went back to the lower end of the fleet, the tide on its way out. I dropped anchor upriver from the stern of the *Glomar Explorer*. With the outgoing tide I was positioned where my bait would be upstream from the stern with the outgo. Getting ready to fish until the tide stopped, maybe another three hours then I would call it quits, slipping off into sleep, I left the reel in neutral. Just as I was starting to saw logs, the clicker hit. Reaching out calm as could be, placing my thumb on the spool, turning off the clicker when a small sturj' or a shaker hit the bait. It's aggressive like a striped bass, but the big sturj' bites like a small catfish. When the tip of that rod pumps it is *show time*. There is no drug that compares to the adrenaline rush when you come back solid, setting the hook. Hitting a home run, scoring a touchdown, the first time with a new girl, knocking out the neighborhood bully or winning a big poker hand; nothing can compare to "The Tug." Now this was a different situation. I'd heard about the OG sturgeon anglers leaving the reel in neutral, letting a sturgeon run, similar to a striped bass, but I'd never tried it. The theory is that the bass will run slowly at first; then when it hits second gear and higher speeds you flip the lever, setting the hook. With a sturj' some of the old-timers swear by this: you let him run until he stops then rip some lips.

Watching the line rolling slow but steady off my reel, my heart was starting to beat pretty heavy as I thought all this through. It turned out I didn't have to set the hook. This type of hookup is known as a "suicide," where the sturj' has ingested the bait, hooking itself from the inside. Seeing a trail of air bubbles leading away from the boat I smelled a familiar scent, but I couldn't place it. Just then, before I had a chance to react, I watched in fascination as my line veered to the right.

I was off the stern of the *Glomar Explorer*. The *Glomar* being chained bow and stern, north by south, to weighted concrete mooring blocks on the bottom, presented the problem that the fish would surely get snagged on the chains, where I would no doubt lose the fish. Flipping the lever, cranking back the rod handle, for a second thinking that I felt the fish slow down but quickly changing my mind when it kept taking line, I tightened the drag, attempting to slow him down. I planted one foot on the stern, bracing my shoulders with the butt of the rod handle between my legs, but the sturj' was too powerful. Wondering to myself if this was in fact a fifteen to twenty foot fish, so large that it might not even feel the hook in its leathery lips, with my right hand I tightened the star drag a little more. Thinking the fish would pull me in the water because the Kevlar Spider Wire was not about to break, having no choice but to loosen the drag, the strength of this fish reminded me of a tractor. There was no indication of it slowing down whatsoever. Grabbing an old standby rod with a big Penn Senator reel, having my anchor rigged where I could hold the toggle in the down position with a twenty-four-inch by six-inch white inflatable finder attached, the end of my anchor line not being attached to the boat, if I ever hooked a "peeler" I would be prepared to leave my anchor behind, then give chase to a massive dino'. The sturj' running with the out-going tide, kept taking line, leaving me no choice but to but to drop my anchor. Holding the toggle switch in the down position, looking at the small amount of line I had left on my reel, the fish showing no sign of wearing down, in an act of desperation I connected the snap swivel of the second rod to the horizontal bars on the first reel, then throwing the rod in after the fish, I had three hundred more yards of line as an insurance policy. Now free of my anchor I could give chase to the sturj'. The fish was running with the current when it flipped a 180-degree turn. It was coming right at the boat. Reeling in fast, holding my rod way back behind me to not give any slack, I retrieved most of my line on the second rod. Now the sturj' was swimming against the tide. This slowed it down some but not much. Checking the time on my Seiko wristwatch, 7:20 p.m., the powerful fish headed upriver past row after row of the Mothball Fleet. Having the motor running, the gear shifter in neutral, using my rudder to control the boat, bumping her into gear now and then to keep her straight, we went past the west end of the fleet. The small town of Suisun came up on the left, then the entrance to Montezuma Slough, which is a bypass from Grizzly Bay. The mighty fish showed no sign of tiring, heading up Montezuma past the "Red Barn" and several well-known spots to fish from the bank.

Halfway down the slough are the locks, a hydraulically-operated set of control gates that control the flow of tidal fluctuations. The Suisun Marsh, being the largest estuarine marsh remaining in the United States, consists of over a hundred thousand acres of salty duck hunter heaven. There is an operator on duty from 8:00 a.m. to 8:00 p.m. to open the gates for boats to come through. The locks were coming up fast when I checked my time, 7:40 p.m. Having used this shortcut many times over the years, I knew the gate operator would enforce the strict 8:00 a.m. to 8:00 p.m. policy. I was about one hundred yards away, incredibly the sturj' was towing me, boat and all through the gates. The gate operator saw me coming. Recognizing my boat, he had the gates in the open position. When the big sturj' laid down on the bottom—this is common for a big fish when it's exhausted—I reeled in the line on my secondary rod, pulling the rod into the boat, then cranking in the primary rod until I was directly on top of the fish. Knowing my depth to be only twenty feet, I couldn't make him budge. Time seemed to freeze as I thought this through.

Remembering the old "Indian trick" I grabbed the Master padlock off the doghouse motor cover. Opening the lock with the key off my ring, I put the line inside the hasp, locking it around the line then dropping it down the fishing line to irritate the sturgeon, making him swim up off the bottom. Instantly the sturj' was on the move, it seemed to be moving at half the speed, half the power it had before. It was still too strong, there was no stopping him. The rod handle was being pulled from my grip like it was hooked to a tractor. Time check: 8:05. Thinking to myself, this is one smart fish, maybe a little too smart, I remembered the old joke: Why are fish so smart; because they live in schools. I looked up at the operator who had closed the gates and was already walking the gangway catwalk back to his car. Having never experienced anything close to this before, I kept the rod tip up, the slack tight, feeling a continuous vibration coming from the handle of my rod. The sturj' was already through the gates, leaving me no choice but to drop anchor where I was locked out. Tightening the drag up where it wouldn't slip, I pointed the rod straight at the water. Leaning over the transom I had no choice, I had to cut the line. In a futile attempt to let go of the rod with one hand, I reached behind my back, thumbing the snap to get my Buck 110 folding Hunter out of its well-worn black leather sheath. I tried to open the blade with my thumb but I couldn't hold the rod; it slipped from my grip. The line had stretched to the point that when the rod took off it shot like a rocket, straight as a laser and disappeared into the water like a bullet. When I lost my grip on the rod I went ass over tea kettle sprawled out. I banged into the dash of the boat landing hard on my rear. Sitting on the floor of the *Aquaholic* thinking the sturj' had to be bigger than anything I had ever hooked. There was no way I stood a chance with the power I had felt on the end of my line. My imagination was running with the magnitude of what had just happened, when suddenly my brain kicked into gear. The monster sturj' was heading out the other side of the slough. Guesstimating that it would take the fish 15 to 20 minutes to come out upriver in the open water at Pittsburg then cross to the main channel, still dragging my rod with about a hundred feet of line, my plan was simple: run wide open back the way I came, come out above the fleet in Martinez, take the shortcut across the channel. If I could beat the fish back to the other entrance of Montezuma, I could use my electronics to scope the fish on its way out. I thought with the rod plus the hundred feet of line it created a window of opportunity to cast over the line, then reel in my other rod, then figure out how to deal with the mighty sturj'. Everything was going as planned, the 409 wound tighter than a ten day clock, what could go wrong?

The shortcut was a tricky one that I could never forget. Once upon a time I was working the Clean Fuels Project. My fishing partners then were my two nephews, John and Dan, 12 and 14 years old. We had been fishing out of Martini town, picking up fresh bait on a Sunday morning. While inside the bait shop waiting in line for fresh grass shrimp I recognized an older guy I knew when he was bartender. Bruce, a typical bait shop hang around, was telling me he had the "hot hole." When I asked for directions, he explained how tricky it was to get in or out, especially at low tide. Bruce was slick, explaining that he couldn't give directions because it was very shallow, that he would have to show us, conning us into taking him with us. Now with Bruce onboard, the four of us went to a spot next to the restricted Navy dock at Port Costa. It sounded simple but was far from it: go up river until a water tank on the hill is on the right side of the river, when the boat is lined up with the Naval dock, turn left toward Ryer Island, as soon as you see a white piece of 2-inch PVC pipe sticking out of the water, turn right into the open water within casting range of the hot hole. The tide was on its way out; we caught shakers, then a nice striper. Heading back to the marina it was high tide where we could go straight in.

Going in to work on Monday morning I was rained out and sent home at 0600 with 2 hours show-up pay. The nephews were home from school for Easter vacation. I called my sister asking if the boys wanted to go back out on the water. She explained they were off school for Easter but had wrestling practice at 4:00 p.m. Promising to have them back by 3:00, off we went, back to the new honey hole, where we had a good day with plenty of bites, a few shakers, plus one slot fish. The Sturgeon Gods had shined, everything was in order. I pulled anchor at 1:30, not realizing the tide was on its way out. With plenty of time I was motoring through the way Bruce had showed me when we ran aground. Trying every trick I knew but I was running out of time. The outgoing tide still on its way out we were going to be stuck for at least six hours waiting for the tide to come back in and float us off, having promised my sister to bring them home by 3:00.

Thinking fast I raised up my out drive, just out of the mud, to the point where it was barely sucking in the river water, prop spinning clear of the bottom. Putting both nephews on the bow, placing the shifter in forward gear, in the trolling position, she was still stuck so I stripped off my boots, Wranglers and my shirt, leaving the boat in gear. With my nephew counterweights on the bow, sporting a pair of camo briefs I grabbed a rope and jumped into the murky Delta water. Tying the rope to the front tie down loop on the bow I put the rope over my shoulder and started pulling. We were lucky getting out of there in time. By the time my nephews told that story it had been slightly magnified, like all fishing stories, the two boys boasting that their Uncle Mike, wearing a camo banana hammock, had pulled the boat to safety getting them home on time for wrestling practice.

Getting my head back in the game, the sun was setting in the west, having limited daylight left I was running wide open, pushing the 409 to its limits until I tried the shortcut. The tide was pretty low where I was turning mud, feeling the bottom of my hull starting to stick hard on the bottom. I had no choice but to keep the boat in gear, put the trim tabs all the way down then power out. This would risk damaging my props as well as my impellor for the fresh water cooing system. Running on adrenaline, racing against time, using the power of the big block to push me out, everything was working fine until I failed to navigate the last turn because I was going too fast, sticking the *Aquaholic* high and dry. My props were out of the water, I knew I would be sitting there for at least 6 hours waiting for the tide to come back in. This didn't bother me for I still had bait. Losing my chance at catching up with the monster sturj' was another story. There was no need to worry about it. I tried to clear my mind but I couldn't stop the feeling that I was missing something about the whole scenario, from the first time I marked the big boxcars until what happened that evening, something was eating at me from the inside. I just could not put my finger on it.

CHAPTER 9

SURPRISE DINNER GUEST

I made the drive up into the hills above Martini town, where I rent a small, cozy mother-in-law cabin cottage that is the secondary property to an older ranch estate, having full use of the otherwise empty barn, where I keep my toy collection. The barn locks up tight with a security system. Nobody knows I live there, nobody comes by, I don't even bring women there; the "Lone Ranger Rides Alone." Pulling up to the remote-control wrought iron gate, my dog Apollo was waiting inside. He chased the El Camino up the half-mile palm-lined, single lane, cobblestone drive, his two-inch bobbed tail wagging so hard his back legs were barely touching the ground. Growling, showing his teeth, threatening to bite the tires, dodging in and out, throwing his head around in animated gestures showing off, he wanted attention. I drove up the hill past the main house, the elaborate landscaping complete with corrals and vacant horse stalls. At one point in time years ago the owners of the property studded thoroughbred racehorses. I parked the El-Co underneath the covered 160-foot carport area. Apollo was waiting when I opened the door, playfully attacking my feet, one foot then the other, tugging on the leg of my Wrangler jeans, letting me know he wasn't happy because I left him alone for two days. He has a doggy door in the back of the cabin, and I had left plenty of dry kibble and fresh water. I raised the dog from a pup, and he always has my back.

Apollo looked like a big black pit bull but he was half English Bull Terrier and half Chesapeake Retriever, weighing in at 90 pounds with zero fat.

I saw the landscapers on their way out, after a full day of maintaining the grounds with the seemingly endless hedges that lined all the walkways and property lines. The main house was vacant most of the year, the single occupant being an extremely wealthy, retired elderly gentleman who was constantly traveling around the world. The rent was fair, where I had the run of the place, spending most of my time in the barn working on projects or sleeping in the cabin, when I had time. Hosing down the back redwood decks, uncovering the spa and turning on the heater, I went inside. Noticing the answering machine blinking, the red light indicated eleven missed calls. This was well out of the norm as I rarely get messages. Wondering what was so important, there were no messages at all, just repeated hang-ups from a number I recognized off the caller identification as a phone booth down in Martini town. Having no clue I cleared the machine, hit the bathroom for a clean shave, and took two beautiful pre-marinated, one-and-a-half-inch thick, porterhouse steaks out of the fridge. I made a large salad which I devoured for a snack while preparing red potatoes with peppers wrapped in foil. Lighting the coals on the Weber next to the now steaming tub, I pushed in the 8-track tape, cranking up the tunes, blasting some of my favorite James Brown, "Papa Don't Take No Mess," thinking to myself it doesn't get any better than this. I was easy like Sunday morning, what could go wrong?

Drinking an ice-cold bottle of Coors, enjoying the sunshine on my olive skin, wearing white bikini brief underwear, I also sported my old school pair of dark welder's safety glasses, a red and white polka-dotted welder's cap with the bill flipped up in the front, with slip-on Rockport's. The potatoes were roasting next to the coals. J.B. was pumping from the speakers, with a pot of dark greens steaming on the stove. The dog saw me grab both steaks, he knew one was mine, the other one was his. He was so happy his hindquarters were ahead of him as he strutted proudly, jumping up, lying on the edge of the tub, never taking his eyes off his master. Apollo is solid black with a large white diamond on his "battleship chest." When I take him to the Delta he loves to swim for hours, as well as playing fetch forever. When I throw the ball down the hill of the long drive where he has to run back up, he never gives up, waiting with the ball in his mouth, ready anytime. The coals were ripe, as I was putting on the porterhouse steaks the savory scents filled the air and Apollo started to drool. Wiping his face, kicking off my slip-ons, I climbed into the steaming water. I turned on the jets and felt the force of the water massaging my muscles. The scenery from the deck is unreal. The view overlooks the Alhambra Valley, with the sun setting on the water that backs the tree line, surrounded by green, grass covered rolling foothills. Cracking a fresh beer I leaned back to rest my neck, when Apollo's ears stood straight up. James Brown was in between tracks. Apollo was already gone with the quickness, without making a sound. His hackles were up, running down the entire length of his back. His ears were laid back, his white teeth bared. He went left, the quickest way to the front drive.

Wasting no time, climbing out of the hot tub, slipping in the back door, I grabbed a 1913 model 12, nickel steel Winchester pump. The shotgun known as "The Breakdown" had been cut off at 18 inches before I got it, the stock shortened like a pistol grip. Operating the slide, I chambered a military green and black 4 x 4 high-base shell with a dual load, number eight birdshot and double ought buck—one shotgun shell covers up close as well as far away, two shells in one. Slipping out the back, I left the music blaring, pulling on the Rockport's. Staying low I circled around the right side of the cabin skirting the manzanita bushes for cover. What I saw next turned my blood to ice water. It felt like the earth was moving under my feet. Getting instant cotton-mouth, it felt like my heart was hooked up to 220 volts, making it beat in my chest like a pneumatic jack hammer.

Lowering the muzzle of the 12-gauge as I stood there staring, Apollo had a woman treed, standing on the rail of the front porch, balancing on her right foot with her left leg stuck out for balance. She was long-legged and heavy-chested, to where her breasts were flattened out against the wall. She was wearing tight, faded big bell Levis with the bottoms tattered, a faded blue Wrangler men's button-down denim work shirt with pearl snap buttons, sleeves cut off at the shoulders, tails tied in the front below her heavy chest, exposing a flat, tan, hourglass waist. Her slightly graying hair was in a braided ponytail down the middle of her back, reaching close to her beltline. The woman had her left hand on my porch light, holding herself steady with her right hand held high in a "hands-up" pose. Wearing well worn men's brown leather cowboy boots with riding heels, an oversized pair of big dark sunglasses, she didn't know I was there. Noticing she was extremely calm for a person treed on a porch rail with a big black pit bull-looking dog growling, but wagging his tail. Apollo sensed I wasn't worried so neither was he. The dog looked at me, growling a little deeper. Knowing he was enjoying every minute of it, I sat down in a rocking chair, trying to catch my breath and gain control of my rapid heart rate, slowly setting the 12-gauge against the wall. Apollo positioned himself between her and me, then gave me the "how do you want to play this" look.

When I first tried to talk no words came out my mouth. Regaining my composure, realizing I was still wearing wet, probably see-through white bikini drawers, Rockport's, safety glasses and a welding cap, when I found my voice the only thing I could say was, "You're lookin' good, Olivia, hope you're hungry, you're just in time for dinner." Apollo still playing the part, acting mean as a dog can, still wagging his tail, I asked Olivia if she had a car parked outside the gate and if she was alone?

First she asked me, "Who's this black dog?" as she spun around slowly bending her knees, extending her arm with the back of her hand out, palm down, letting Apollo sniff across the backs of her first knuckles. Apollo was always a sucker for a gorgeous woman. You can't hold that against him for I have the same affliction. Olivia answered she was alone, that she had no transportation. She said she had hitchhiked to the bottom of the canyon then walked the rest of the way. She took a chair next to mine then took a deep breath. Olivia sat still, silently looking at the ground. Asking her if everything was okay, I offered her a beer. Sensing everything was all wrong for her, giving her some space, I asked her to come inside as I went out back to turn the steaks and turn off the stereo. She accepted the beer, saying she wasn't being rude but didn't think she could eat. I told her no worries, just relax, I would make her a plate anyhow. Remembering I was only wearing briefs, not realizing it at the time but somehow this whole new situation had made me aroused, when we were walking to the rear deck she nodded at my now see-through underwear. Olivia said, "You're looking good too, Stoner." She kept apologizing for the intrusion. Out of the corner of her eye I saw her give me an appraising look. "Mike, I remember you having game sporting those silk boxer underwear. What's with the bikini briefs?"

I had to explain to Olivia that as I was getting older gravity was kickin' in and the briefs were more like a ball bra, the Man of Stone needed support, this answer seemed to make her wonder. Apollo acted like I didn't exist, staying at her side, soaking up the attention like a sponge. Olivia was carrying a shoulder bag when she showed up and had set it on the porch. She grabbed her bag, asking to use the bathroom to freshen up. Hearing her shut then lock the bathroom door, after a few minutes I heard the shower running. I went about setting the table on the back deck, pulling the cork on a bottle of Napa Valley's finest, Old Vine Red Zinfandel, aka "Dago Red." Letting the fine wine breathe as Olivia came out of the bathroom wearing fresh clothes, a plain looking flower sack dress with flat sandals. The first thing I noticed were dark fingertip bruises on her upper arms. A fat shiner around one eye she had been concealed with the big dark sunglasses. Olivia was combing-out her long wet hair, being as timid as a deer in the forest, walking slowly, looking around as she was taking in the modest but comfortable cabin. She said nice place as she sat down in front of a sizzling, fat porterhouse steak, dark greens with garlic salt, red potatoes topped with melted butter, grated cheese, sour cream, and bacon bits along with a fresh loaf of San Francisco's finest sourdough bread.

Apollo, seeing her about to eat his steak walked over and lay down with his head on her feet. That dog always knows what time it is. Olivia reached for the glass of wine with two shaky hands. I had a hundred questions but stayed quiet, forcing a smile to try to make us both relax. Crow's feet had started to show around her sea green eyes. I could have put my hands around her hourglass waist and touched my middle fingers to my thumbs. Her hips were wider than when she was young of course, but this added to the sexy curves. Her gorgeous smile was all but gone. I could tell her confidence was shattered. Seeing where she had tried to cover her tattoos without much success, one of a half-dressed Viking warrior queen with a horned helmet and a large sword on her left breast over her heart, with several others I couldn't make out, she caught me staring and I looked away as we ate in silence. The Dago Red did its job cleansing my pallet between each bite of the blood red porterhouse steak.

Olivia told me thanks, that she appreciated the hospitality. Her appetite must have made a miraculous recovery; she was cleaning her plate before I was done. Olivia immediately stood up and started clearing the table after I finished my plate. I told her to sit down and relax but she started doing dishes at the sink, trying to do something to occupy herself to get around the awkwardness. I sat at the kitchen table then asked how she knew how to find me, and who else knew about where I lived? She answered that she had always kept track of me, and nobody else knew about the estate. Olivia told me that she secretly stayed in touch with my mother through the years and had talked her into giving her my telephone phone number, when she explained she was in trouble. I asked how many calls she had made to the cabin. She told me at least ten but that she had left no message. Then she told me she had no choice; she was afraid for her life. I knew it had to be hard to bring up E.Z. Seeing her pause, searching for the right words, she started slowly easing into what she had to get off her chest. Telling me that Eric was so deeply in debt to some bad people, she thinks from the years of using methamphetamines, that he was going over the deep end. He was talking about some big move that would cover his debts, make him wealthier and more famous than he had ever been before. Eric was also leaving the shop every morning at the same time and meeting with two men from Russia, who she thought were Russian Mafia. The motorcycle business was all but gone because of problems with the Internal Revenue Service. It seemed like the rich and famous E.Z. had run out of luck. He owed everybody from the top down, from the government to the loan sharks. She knew Eric was desperate, that his time was running out. The rich and famous E.Z. was circling the drain.

Olivia asked if she could stay one night. She promised to leave in the morning, saying she had plenty of cash but would not feel safe even if she took a plane halfway around the world. Olivia knew Eric would find her. I could tell she was all done. Olivia could go no further, and I told her softly she needed to quit talking. She tried to speak when I saw her eyelids close in mid-sentence as she mumbled, falling off into a coma-like slumber.

By now I figured Olivia was in a deep sleep, so I picked her up with my left arm under her bent legs, right arm under her back like a groom carrying his bride across the threshold. In her sleep she instinctively wrapped her left arm around my shoulders. Her wet hair smelled fresh from the shower but was overpowered by the natural scents of a beautiful, mature woman. Remembering her natural scent reminded me of the fresh, clean air of a mountain morning, dew on the wet green grass, wildflowers, fresh laundry hanging on a clothesline, milk and honey. I could swear I heard angels singing from up in heaven, huntin' hounds baying in the hills. Her breath smelled like flowers. Olivia's skin was soft and warm to the touch. Her head fell gently into my chest. Feeling her warm breath on my neck, I put her in my bed then removed her sandals and tucked her in, taking a long hard look at her chest rising and falling with each breath, then walked out of the room locking her safely inside. There's no way I would be catching any shut eye with a woman of that caliber under the same roof. I headed straight into an ice cold shower to chill myself out.

PREDATOR OR PREY

I put on a pot of coffee using my old-school percolator, filling the basket to the brim for maximum caffeine levels with good old-fashion Folgers Coffee Crystals. I filled the green thermos as I took my first sip of the rocket fuel — "Christian Crank, Jesus in a Jug." After a half cup I could feel the caffeine coming on as I was putting on a camouflage hunting suit with lace-up Red Wing Irish Setter boots and grabbing some accessories that I use when I have to eliminate the wild pigs from the estate. I know it's illegal to hunt at night, but the pigs do too much damage rooting while they forage for food. This is called a C-1 tag: see one and kill it. I had outfitted an old hard hat with a chin strap and earphones connected to a *Sonic Ear* amplified listening device mounted on top of the hat. Sometimes when it is completely silent, when stalking a wild boar I swear I could hear even a tiny field mouse scurrying through brush. Add to that my night vision goggles and a 30-06 Springfield M-1 Garand. A quick inspection in the mirror: boots laced, pant legs strapped tight at the ankles, yes, I'm dressed for success. The world-famous M-1 used by the United States military as far back as World War II, being a gas operated, semi-automatic top loader, holds eight rounds. It is outfitted with open peep style sights where it is lethal at five hundred yards. Anyone who knows a lick about firearms considers the M-1 the finest self-defense rifle ever built. General Patton declared the M-1 the greatest battle implement ever devised.

Slipping out of the barn, double checking all locks and doors, activating the alarms as well as disconnecting the phone line from outside the cabin; not knowing Olivia's complete situation I was taking no chances. Apollo was on point as though we were going out for pig; his senses were on high alert. This dog is smarter than most people. He knows when to be quiet, starting down then around the property, coming out far below on the road leading to the driveway. Strapping on the night vision goggles, catching glimpses of nocturnal activity—a doe with a pair of fawns in tow, raccoons on the move—I set up where I could see anything that moved on the street as well as the front gates. I double checked the load in the carbine, making sure I had one in the chamber. Silently pulling the bolt halfway back, my fingertip felt for the brass shell casing in the slide. The magazine loaded with eight from the top, two extra clips in my front pockets, totaling twenty-four rounds of ammunition. Having reloaded this ammunition myself, I was loaded for bear: Sierra 180-grain, expanding soft tip, boat tail hunting rounds. The rifle was on my back with the sling across my chest, a handheld million-watt spotlight fresh off the charger in my right hand. Sipping the bitter strong coffee from the chrome cup, nerves on end, wide awake, running everything over in my head I figured if she could find me then he could find her. I knew he was coming.

Apollo was out roaming the nearby game trails with his keen nose to the ground. If he came upon a pig, he knew better than to mess with it. Do not get me wrong, he has plenty of heart. He does not know the meaning of the word fear, but he is smart enough to pick his battles. Hiking the surrounding hills slowly, quiet as a cat, I occasionally used a small Maglite from a side pocket on the sleeve of my camouflage overalls to check my footing, cupping the light with the palm of my other hand. Rifle slung on my shoulder trying not to give up my position, one thing I remembered, Eric was extremely intelligent. For all I knew he was probably hunting me instead of me hunting him. Not wanting the hunter to become the hunted, I refused to become Eric's prey.

I'd never beaten Eric Zachary at anything as far back as I could remember, but now we were grown men, knowing we were playing for high stakes, fighting for our lives, playin' for keeps. While I considered calling the authorities my stubborn streak took over. I was taking this personally, and after all I didn't know if Olivia was telling the truth. Of course I wanted to trust her, but why should I?

I walked the grounds until one hour after sunup, feeling confident that he would not come in daylight hours. When I got to the cabin I found Olivia, who had been awake for a while. Not recognizing my cabin, everything clean and in place, there were biscuits and gravy with fresh coffee in the pot. Sitting down at the table, trying not to look at her shiner, Olivia had tried to cover it with make up without much success. Wolfing down the breakfast, washing it down with hot coffee and a glass of milk poured over ice, I thought things through. Olivia was looking way better. I will be the first to admit, despite everything that happened when were kids, even though she had been with Eric the whole time, I still wanted her in a law of the jungle, animal instinct kind of way. Not having slept with a woman for a while, I was overdue. The only problem was my stubborn pride, because the way I looked at it she was recovering from whatever happened; I still had to get over my bruised ego from being dumped in high school. I figured the best plan was to let things play out and see what happened next.

TROUBLE

Olivia's physical wounds started to heal, the shiner barely visible with what remained being concealed by makeup, but the mental abuse she suffered would probably never go away completely. They say the human body is an amazing piece of machinery that can recover from almost anything; if whatever happens to you does not kill you it will make you stronger. I hadn't made any attempt to discuss the terms of her sudden departure from Eric, for it was not time for that conversation. Olivia's body language told the tale: she still had trouble making eye contact, avoiding any face-to-face interaction with me. Apollo, on the other hand, sensed her insecurities. He was never out of her arm's reach, enjoying a stranger's company in the house as much as the female energy. I swear that dog thought of himself as human. Olivia needed the security blanket of the big black dog, so they got along like they had known each other forever. I felt confident that I could go into town for groceries and then down to the water to check on the boats.

I ran my charter business from an old-school pager. Although I kept it clipped to my belt it was dead as a door-nail. Feeling the slight euphoria of being close to the water, I walked the familiar docks, pulling the mooring cover off the *Aquaholic*, checking the fluids, cranking over the 409, listening to the deep throaty open exhaust until I could idle her down with the manual choke. She idled to a purr. I hosed down the *General* and repeated the same procedures, opening the motor house, checking all the fluids in both of the Cat's, etc. Satisfied that everything checked out, I fired up both engines in the *General*.

While I was topping off the freshwater tanks I heard foot-steps coming down the dock, recognizing a young man I knew named Jason. He kept a 32-foot sailboat at the end slip. There was a rule against live-aboards at the marina, allow-ing no more than three nights a week. Jason, on the other hand, was a single, good-looking young man who was ex-tremely successful with the ladies. In Jason's case, his boat was known as a "F" aboard. It seemed like the music was playing from the sailboat every night. Jason came walking up with a cold pack in his hand offering me a beer. It wasn't Coors, but any port in a storm. Jason asked about the fish-ing. I told him it was completely dead. He was telling me about a girl that he had brought to the boat a few nights ago, a good-looking blonde who, when they walked past the *General*, had asked if he knew the guy that owned the party boat. Jason said he had asked her why, and she had told him about the barroom brawl and that her ex-boyfriend was looking for me. I asked Jason if he had seen a big gnarly biker sniffing around the marina, and he told me no, but he would keep his eye on my boats, and contact me on my pager if he saw anything suspicious.

Just being around the water working on the boats I could feel the urge building inside me to go back out to the Mothball Fleet and try my luck by the *Glomar Explorer*. The boxcars were still eating away at my curiosity, and I could really use a big sturgeon to drum up some business. But I knew that with Olivia at the house I didn't have the time to risk leaving her there alone. Besides, I still had plenty of cash from working all the overtime, plus my lucky last day on the job. Jason hung out a while, asking me what I thought about the girl named Cassandra, who went by Cassy. He gave me her version of the story, where she had said that the big guy's name was Russell. Cassy said I had tried putting a move on her right in front her boyfriend, that I had started the fight, and that it was the first time anybody ever got the best of Russell. She also said that I tried to force her into my car. I asked Jason what he thought about her story. He told me he knew she was lying, that he knew me better than that. Jason also told me he knew she was a real freak because of her reputation around town, but she was pretty hot. To Jason she was only another one-night stand. Russell and she had broken off their colorful romance because she was constantly getting him involved in some kind of drama; that night was the last straw. Jason said she told him that Russell was looking for me to even the score, I should watch my back. Russell knew about my charter boat being moored at the marina, but Jason felt that Russell wouldn't try anything stupid, like messing with my boats, because he thought Russell was a stand-up guy and wouldn't pull anything that low, telling me that Russell's bike was a newer Harley-Davidson Evolution Road King with ape hanger-style bars and dual Thunderheader exhaust. The bike had a custom black and silver paint job. With the Thunderheaders you could hear him coming a mile away. Jason said he had better get going because he had a date on her way to his sailboat. I thanked him for the information and asked him to page me if anything developed.

STAND OFF

After buttoning up the boats then driving the El-Co to pick up some groceries, I pulled into the Union 76 station in town—76 being the only gas available with 92 octane, the 454's favorite fuel. I parked at the pumps and was reaching for the gas nozzle when I looked up to see another guy reaching for the same nozzle. I could not believe my bad luck: Russell, getting out of a tow truck, glaring at me with flames coming out of his eyes.

He said, "You go first."

I answered, "No, after you"

Russell, raising his voice says, "I insist." So I guess we were going to fight over who went first. I took a quick side-step around the tailgate so I had room to maneuver, not wanting to be blocked in. I didn't want any damage to my truck. We were standing in the middle of the filling station in broad daylight having a standoff. Russell was used to re-lying on intimidation, using his size and the way he was dressed: black Red Wing, lace-up, steel-toed lineman boots, black Wrangler jeans with a large, Western-style belt buckle and a tight black H.D. T-shirt. He was in decent shape, but with a pretty good size gut. You could tell he worked out but probably no cardio. Staring back, looking him dead in his eyes while at the same time wishing I had an equalizer in the back of the pickup—but no such luck. When I didn't back down from his hard looks I could tell he was having second thoughts about making a move on me right there. The first thing he says is, the only reason he won't take care of me right now is because his company's name is on the side of his truck, and he was on parole, so couldn't afford another beef with the law. He said next time I wouldn't be so lucky, and that he was looking forward to when we meet again. I figured he would have been a lot more confident if his buddies had been around. Calling his bluff I asked him if we could go somewhere else right now, and get it over with. I looked at the scar I'd left above his eye from my dental impressions last time around. Russell said he was on duty for two more hours, and did I want to meet him at Shorty's at seven o'clock? I knew it would be best to meet the problem head on, get it over with, but I wasn't going to show up at a place where he had backup, me being by myself. I could tell he was gaining confidence, thinking I was scared. He got a call on the radio in his truck then growled something about this being far from over. He got in the tow truck, driving away flooring the foot feeder. I filled up then went inside to pay, grabbing a cold six pack, then drove away thinking about Russell and the Olivia/Eric situation, wondering to myself how I had so much drama going on around me all the time. Apparently I was addicted to chaos. I told myself I should be used to it by now, and that I would deal with it the same way I always have: one day at a time. I would have liked to tell Russell my side of the story, but I knew in my heart it would not do any good because I got the best of him last time around. If he ever took a step backwards he would lose face with his buddies.

Instead of going straight home I went north, taking Highway 680 across the Benicia Bridge then drove down into the industrial park that ran along the water, keeping my eyes in the rearview mirror, starting to get a little paranoid about who could be following me. While looking out for the law because I had an open beer between my legs, I drove to a spot where I could scope out Eric's building, parking where the pickup was partially concealed but I still had a decent view of the front of his shop. I didn't have a bunch of time with the groceries still in the front seat, but thought I would try to relax and get some kind of an idea what was going on at the shop. While sitting there I thought to myself what an ideal location for an industrial shop, with the large buildings, the rear access to the water—there is a dock as well as a decent size hoist where they used to send the underwater tanks out by barge. I thought about converting it to my own uses: mooring my boats, plus living quarters. I knew I could never afford it, trying to get my mind back on track with the matters at hand. The only thing I saw out of the ordinary was an insulated reefer truck parked inside the fence. No activity whatsoever so I headed back to the cabin.

BAD GUY

He couldn't believe, after all the years of having virtually unlimited amounts of cash, properties and all the toys he had accumulated, that he, the rich and famous Eric Zachary was not only broke but in debt so deep that his "gangster loan shark creditors" were one step away from forcing his hand to sign over his last possession, his shop with everything in it—little did they know that he had taken a mortgage out against the property as well. The creditors let everything go as long as he kept up with weekly cash payments of ten thousand, plus the ten percent interest. They didn't care how long it would take to get square. The bank note on the other hand, at five thousand a month, always a month behind, didn't seem like that big of a problem.

E.Z. hadn't heard from Olivia since she left but really didn't miss her in a physical kind of way. He was just starting to boil inside because it was one more thing he had lost control over. He hadn't slept with her in four or five years, just forcing her to do obscene sexual acts while tweakin' on speed, where he would watch while entertaining himself. Eric had everything else under complete control in his brilliant but twisted mind. He had every detail, all the material he needed to get back on top with one diabolical move. E.Z. knew once he put his plan into effect he would have enough money to pay off the loan sharks that kept him out of prison.

When he got in trouble the last time around, he would have been looking at 35 years for conspiracy to manufacture methamphetamine with his prior convictions, serving time for violence charges on one account, then selling and manufacturing hallucinogenic street narcotics the second time. They didn't catch him with a laboratory or glassware, but he was caught purchasing ten 50-pound kegs of hydrochloride pseudoephedrine, then transporting across state lines, making it a federal violation. "The Feddie," as it is known on the streets, is the main chemical used in manufacturing the popular street drug known as "crank" that was now more popular than ever. The ephedrine was purchased up north across the Oregon border, buying the chemical in 50-pound kegs. Eric was paying the low price of $200 per pound, being able to sell all he could deliver at the increased price of $1,000 per pound in the Bay Area. The money he made was astronomical: an investment of $10,000 would net him $40,000 profit per truck load. Not a bad profit for a two days' work.

Eazy Money had an accomplice, another guy his age. Tom the sidekick had dyed his own long hair blond and was clean shaven. He and E.Z. looked like twin brothers at a distance, fairly close when side by side, Eric much taller and more physically built. They both hit the tanning booth on a regular basis, both heavily tatted, wearing $300 jeans, Anaconda Cowboy Boots, brand new shirts with neck and sleeves cut out, with heavy gold chains. These guys were show boats, cruising a brand new Corvette convertible, black ragtop with red interior—two tattooed, long-blond-haired gangsters, bound and determined to draw heat. It was only a matter of time before Tom and E.Z. caught a beef.

They were "riding dirty" with a quarter pound of raw meth in the trunk. Eric noticed he was being tailed, where he made quick work out of giving the tail the slip. After ditching the chase car, Eric thought the people wanted to rob him of his product. High as a satellite, with the heart of a lion, Eric fell in behind the other car, coming in hot with the ragtop down, pulled the other car over then jumped out ready to do battle. Bad move; these were DEAs, Drug Enforcement Agents. This would be Eric's second strike, so he promised Tom if he took the fall, preventing Eric from doing time, E.Z. would pay his rent and hire him a high-end lawyer, promising that Tom had a lifetime job when he got of jail. Tom agreed to say he was driving—they looked close enough alike—also took responsibility for the product in the trunk. Tom pled guilty and received a 5-year sentence. Of course, Eric screwed him bad. At first Tom's commissary books were maxed out. Eric had been dropping off cash at Tom's girlfriend's apartment. She fell victim to Eric's magic. E.Z. ran off to Vegas with Tom's girl. He kept her on the side for about six months but when the fire went out Eric turned his back on her, and Tom. Three years later, when Tom got released he started hustling, gathering glassware and chemicals—right back in the game—when he heard about a guy who had a never-ending supply of raw ephedrine. Tom had a friend score several pounds of the Feddie for manufacturing.

One of Tom's regular customers was a single mom who was a "functioning junky," using speed on a daily basis but somehow holding her job, keeping the lights on. She got in a fight with her boyfriend, who she had the police escort out of her apartment. He was under the influence and on his way to jail but he snitched his way out, telling the police where the girl's stash was located. The police found her supply, and were calling Child Protective Services when she gave up Tom to keep her child. Tom got raided, and although they didn't find mass quantities they found enough manufacturing equipment to put him away. Tom used his get out of jail free card rolling over on Eric in a heartbeat. Why go to the pen when you can send your friend?

When Eric got busted he used his contacts from when he was a high roller. It cost him a pretty penny, but the higher-ups had the connections to keep him out of prison by making payoffs through the courts and the expensive lawyers. Shortly after E.Z. was bonded out, while waiting on upcoming court dates, Tom seemed to disappear off the face of the earth. Word was he was terrified of Eric's wrath and had gone back east to live with family. Eric knew better.

He knew he should never have gotten personally involved, but he couldn't trust anyone anymore to drive the semi-truck to Oregon and back, which Tom had been doing. Eric had made the trip several times, and he needed the money. As accustomed as he was to beating the system and buying his way out of trouble that in his own criminal mind he could never be stopped, he was now driving for himself.

ERIC'S TOY

When Eric was younger, he used his design and welding skills to build a miniature submarine in the private back section of his shop, having learned about subs from his experiences at Mare Island as a young adult, where his family's company had flourished for decades. The MINSY, Mare Island Naval Shipyard, the first United States Navy base established on the Pacific Ocean, made a name for itself as the premier U.S. West Coast submarine port, as well as serving as the controlling force in San Francisco Bay Area ship building, dating back to WWII. Eric became infatuated with the design and capabilities of submarines.

Starting with an aluminum tank leftover from a fuel transport for the fuselage of the mini-sub, he welded an eccentric reducer for the nose of the vessel, which reduced the six-foot cylindrical tank to four feet in the nose, with a pipe cap welded on the front end to seal it off. Designing fin-style flaps that came out each side toward the front of the fuselage for gaining altitude or diving, with a large rudder out the stern for steering, the submarine was powered by two Honda four-cylinder engines that came out of Honda Accords. Eric had adapted the engines to a pair of Honda watercraft propulsion systems, converting the gas-burning car engines to burn a mixture of oxygen and acetylene. He had installed the inline 120-horsepower, four-cylinder engines side by side, the oxygen bottles stored horizontally, running parallel from the back of the fuselage, where they could be removed then reinstalled without a problem. The acetylene, after being slid in horizontally, would be locked in vertical position. The submarine could hold six cylinders of 2500 pounds oxygen, five industrial and one medical grade to supply oxygen to the cockpit, plus three acetylene tanks that contained 1200 pounds each. The cylinders were all connected in a continuous inline manifold attached to gauges in the cockpit. The oxygen and acetylene cylinders were readily available. Eric could steal these in large quantities from any of the industrial docks up and down the channel. The fuel was safely contained, where it could be changed out quick and easy. The heavy cylinders also served as counterweights. The submarine could run continuously for up to twelve hours without refueling. The exhaust valves would burn after continuous hours of abuse from the higher-than-normal operating temperatures, but the advanced cooling system from the watercraft propulsion made the twin engines operable without overheating and cracking the aluminum engine blocks. When the motors were spent it was a simple matter of stealing two new Honda Accords then stripping the drivetrains. Hondas were readily available and he had spare engines in the back of his shop on standby.

His plan to get wealthy again was a simple but elaborate scheme. Eric was going to rig explosives underneath the surface of the water at the two columns of the Benicia Railroad Bridge in the main shipping channel. Where the ships went under the drawbridge, the ancient railroad bridge ran parallel with the Benicia automotive bridge. When a large ship went under the bridge the river pilot captain would radio ahead to the drawbridge operator to raise the section of the bridge so the ship could pass underneath. The drawbridge was designed in the configuration of the letter H, with the

middle, horizontal section of the railway elevated and lowered by a large ball bearing chain. The plan was to rig two
55-gallon drums filled with ammonia nitrate fertilizer combined with diesel fuel, attaching the drums to each end of a
500-foot length of half-inch carbon steel galvanized cable
rope in a V-shaped configuration, with the front of the V attached to a weighted, remote-control release upriver on the
bottom of the shipping channel. When a LPG (Liquefied Petroleum Gas) tanker ship came upriver heading for Port of
Stockton, 288 feet in length with a 36-foot beam that drafted
28 feet at full capacity, it was carrying 250,000 gallons of liquefied petroleum gas. When the railroad drawbridge was
raised for the tanker to pass underneath, Eric would operate
the remote control. The third, but empty, 55-gallon drum attached at the front of the V would rise to the halfway level
of the bow of the ship, dragging the explosive charges, snapping the cables below on the bridge columns. When the barrels were dragging down the sides of the LPG tanker Eric
would then detonate the charges with the remote-control
transmitter, resulting in the ship's liquefied petroleum gas
exploding with the force of a hydrogen bomb. Somewhere
in Eric's twisted, criminal mind the LPG ship explosion
would trigger a domino effect, the catastrophic chain of explosions would not only take out both bridges, but also the
Shell Oil Refinery and the two adjoining crude oil refineries,
Tosco and Exxon.

With complete disregard for life and the environment,
the explosions would create a disaster of Biblical propor-
tions. In addition to the thousands of human lives in the surrounding residential neighborhoods, the price of demolition
and reconstruction of the two bridges and the three major
oil refineries, the damage would be in the hundreds of

billions, plus the devastation to the environment from Martinez all the way out past the San Francisco Bay through the Golden Gate into the Pacific Ocean. Eric was going to use the terrorist type attack as a way of becoming world famous and as a warning shot, threatening the major oil companies that he would blow up any incoming crude oil tankers, cutting off the supply of oil, then target the Chevron refinery five miles downriver in Richmond. His plans were to create a gasoline shortage that would impact the entire country, driving the price of fuel to an all-time high. The price of a barrel of crude oil would go through the roof, from $80 U.S. per barrel to an all-time high of $240 per barrel. This would have an immediate effect on the consumer, having to pay triple for a gallon of gas at the pump. Where the average Joe would pay up to $50 for a tank of gas it would now cost $150. This act of terrorism would affect the entire country then spread throughout the world as the economy stumbled from the shockwave of monetary devastation.

E.Z. was going to contact the four major oil companies and force them to wire $500 million dollars to an untraceable Swiss bank account where he would have pre-arranged to receive the transfer and then have the money bounce electronically to different offshore accounts. After receiving the $500 million Eric was set to invest in a new but small oil company, West Coast Energy, the company selling stock for pennies on the dollar trying to compete with the existing Big Four oil companies. Eric would be on the board of directors with his large share of the company stock. His demonic plan was already in effect, just an old fashioned case of supply and demand. Right now WCE was losing money, having to sell fuel for as low as the Big Four. It was costing money to sell gas, the Big Four were the suppliers—simple solution:

wipe out the supply. Once the WCE supply was in high demand, he was going to show everybody who he was. Somehow, with his extraordinarily high IQ, even with the lack of sleep due the continuous use of various drugs, including nonstop steroid abuse, this was all a game to Eric. The bad part was, in his twisted mind he was winning.

REVENGE

E.Z. had never gotten past losing his business with the four neighboring refineries. He swore revenge when they terminated his contracts. After his father had passed away, Eric started using lower grade material and taking shortcuts, shaving off production cost to increase profits. His greedy move only produced a lower quality product. After several incidents, including high pressure petroleum leaks, Eric lost his family's bread and butter contracts. His plan was simple, with Shell, Exxon and Tosco out of the way—maybe Richmond Chevron if necessary—his stock would soar, putting him back on top where he belonged.

His mini-ultra sub was equipped with a laptop connected to the latest GPS technology as well as autopilot, course plotting and navigation systems with sound wave sensors. By setting a destination using the laptop the submarine could operate virtually on its own, ending up within three feet of a preprogrammed destination. A simple but highly effective periscope consisted of a telescoping stainless steel tube with a built-in focusing viewfinder lens. When and if he could, he always ran with the current for better fuel efficiency where he could also make a lot better time. The 22-foot sub could run on the surface of the water as well, with a thirty-six-inch diameter cockpit porthole manway located in the top of the reducing fuselage. The water propulsion systems were used for transferring water for ballast with the compressors to vacate the water ballast chambers making the sub rise. These were operated from an ingenious serpentine system, connecting an elaborate, single belt pulley configuration from the drivetrain of both four-cylinder engines. This in turn operated the generator system that supplied the 12-volt to 120-volt inverter. The front of the nose was equipped with a mechanical hydraulically op-erated arm that could clamp and shift side to side. Mounted next to the mechanical arm he installed a submersible wind-lass hoist. To get in or out of the top section above the cock-pit, the porthole manway was equipped with a hinged, hydraulically operated manway. The mini-sub could travel at 12 knots running with the current but only 3 or 4 knots against the tide. The sub could maneuver with ease using the thrust of the water propulsion systems, having capabil-ities of alternating forward or reverse throttle from either power bank. He could spin the sub on a dime utilizing the reverse and forward function alone, by operating one side in forward with the other in reverse.

Eric had been working on the mini submarine for years, experimenting with different designs, always updating the electronics as technology improved. The price to create his invention was relatively low considering he already had the main fuselage. He had stolen almost all the electronics from boats in the surrounding marinas, the drivetrains from the Honda Accords, then had adapted the water propulsion sys-tems from stolen Honda three-seater watercraft. Nobody had ever seen the project, which he kept under total secrecy, hidden in the back private section of his fabrication area. Once the sub was complete it was stored, submerged and moored in complete stealth to a HydroHoist located at the service dock behind his shop.

TROTLINE

While waiting to get the offshore banking set up with the fictitious untraceable accounts, E.Z. had to keep producing large supplies of liquid cash to keep the creditors off his back. Eric had the mortgage payment on the shop. He also had taken out a second against the property. Current real estate prices were down and his re-fi had put him completely underwater with the bank. On top of all this he owed the loan sharks big-time. It was costing him $25,000 a month for the first and second, then $10,000 per week cash payments to the people that kept him out of prison. The once rich and famous Eazy Money having to scramble, was working around the clock to make ends meet. Eric knew it would not be long until he was "back on top." His first mission with the submarine was setting up shop underneath the *Glomar Explorer*, a short trip from the shop to the 200 x 75-foot opening under the *Glomar*. This was used in 1974 when the *Glomar* was used to steal the Russian sub. Eric had installed a simple hydroelectric generator that ran off a paddle wheel in the never ending current. He used this generator to charge the ship's batteries to utilize the lights and equipment. The ship was loaded with every tool, rigging, etc. Eric had access to every kind of welding equipment, underwater welding set ups, shield-arc stick, heliarc, including diver's gear, cutting torches and a full supply of oxygen and acetylene bottles.

Using a side tie to moor his sub, Eric was in heaven. He spent more and more time under the *Glomar* in his own private playground, after numerous trips using the submarine to transport everything he needed: a complete rack of dumbbells from 5 to 120 pounds, a small refrigerator where he kept daily doses of his own personally-designed cocktail—by combining the HGH, human growth hormone, with the testosterone liquid, injecting directly into his massive biceps, he could actually feel his muscles accelerate only lifting the minimal weights. To keep himself on track, Eric would mix meth in a time-released capsule with benzodiazepines, an anti-psychotic drug used to maintain control of his schizophrenic delusions, his daily doses becoming less effective as his tolerance increased. No one in the world knew where he was or what kind of evil he had planned.

Back east in the southern parts of the U.S., poachers from the country will string a line across a pond or a slough with white plastic jugs every 20 feet, a leader with a baited hook every five feet. They come back every morning and harvest the fish. Eric rigged 5 trot lines underneath the *Glomar*, spanning the 75-foot width, one every 20 feet, taking a hundred feet of the 200-foot opening's length under the *Glomar*, leaving him half of the 200 feet for bringing his submarine in or out. Ten leaders with ten baited hooks, the bait, Oregon River Eel infused with a salmon roe paste, the salmon eggs being cured with an ancient Portuguese recipe. Eric called his bait "Death Roe." The trot lines were rigged similar to a clothesline, with pulleys powered by a simple 12-volt starter motor. By pressing a button Eric could rotate the lines one at a time, removing the sturgeon then re-baiting the hook. Eric had 50 baited hooks in the water, 24 hours a day, the Death Roe irresistible to the sturgeon.

Transferring his catch with the sub from the belly of the *Glomar Explorer* back to the shop, under the cover of his indoor HydroHoist, he would moor the sub then hoist the cargo net full of the fish straight into the reefer truck. When the spawn season began in the early part of the year, Eric would harvest the eggs from the "ripe" females, with their expanded dark purple stomachs, indicating a pregnant female, and sell the caviar to his Russian connections. They took the bootleg, black market caviar back to Russia, which was the largest exporter of caviar in the world but had frozen all harvesting of the massive Black Sturgeon for reproductive purposes, the embargo driving demand for and price of the precious "black gold" sky-high. The Russians selling the bootleg caviar for $250 per oz. once they smuggled the bulk containers back to their home country, were glad to have paid the black market price. Bulk rate for the black purplish eggs was $2500 per quart, an average four-to-five-foot ripe female producing five to six quarts of the delicacy. Harvesting an average 10 sturgeon per trip, where one-third were ripe females, equaled $30,000-$40,000 of the precious caviar, not counting the money from Chinatown, where they paid $20 per pound in cash for the whole fish. Eric only kept the sturj' that were an average of four to five feet long. Handling the fresh caught fish was a chore in itself, delivering an average of 500 pounds of sturgeon. He needed the $10,000 from the trips to Chinatown in San Francisco in his reefer truck 4-5 times a month. After all, he had bills to pay. Eric stayed low-profile so was able to stay ahead of his debts and supply his daily methamphetamine habit. He felt he couldn't trust anybody anymore. He had to cook small amounts using ephedrine-based cold medicine. The dope was of high quality but caused hallucinations if he stayed up more than three or four days. Eric went about his business staying above water, biding his time until he could initiate his big plan.

PLAYING HOUSE

Olivia wanted to stay inside the cabin when she was there alone. Apollo and she had become inseparable, she felt secure with the ninety-pound watchdog at her side. The only problem I had with it, she was sharing the only bed with him instead of me, leaving me no choice but to sleep on the couch. Olivia still wasn't ready to talk things out. It gave me time to work on my many projects in the barn, keeping an eye on the estate at the same time. She asked if she could go in the tack room off the side of the barn, where she spent endless hours working the leather tack with saddle soap and straightening things out. It seemed to have a relaxing effect on Olivia and she got a lot of pleasure from it, so why not. Olivia asked about the owner of the property, why he had gotten out of the horse business. I told her he came home occasionally but after his wife passed the horses and the property brought back painful memories of her, and that's why he traveled most of the time. She had a faraway look in her eyes as she took in the whole picture of how the 25-acre sprawling ranch must have looked in its prime, with the million-dollar studs in every stall, the ranch hands, all the activity.

The weather was getting warm, but the sturgeon migratory run was behind schedule. The ripe female sturgeon came upriver to lay their eggs in the shallows, which were then fertilized by the males. The charter business was picking up with *The General* going out once a week, but very little activity. When the spawn started every female from the San Francisco Bay and surrounding Pacific Ocean would come right up the channel with every male from here to Timbuktu following the scent of the ripe female. The water teamed with fish like an over-populated city. Under normal circumstances with the food becoming scarce the sturgeon bite was better than all year. The *General* earned its money, booking two charters per day, morning and afternoon, seven days a week, grossing up to $6300 a week, booked solid for up to six weeks, if everything went well as planned. I was looking at roughly $39,000 for six weeks of something I never get tired of, as long as the *General* didn't break down.

Thinking of the big fish I hooked at the *Glomar Explorer*, I figured if I saw the boxcars on my fish finder then so did some others. I tried to keep an eye on the endless number of fishermen going out, all of them with a touch of the fever, all waiting for the sturj' bite to get hot. Sturgeon fever is a funny thing; once you get the incurable disease you will have it forever. Some fishermen will fish their whole life without ever having success; sometimes a "virgin," who has never even *seen* a sturgeon and who was invited out with a friend or on an uncle's boat, will have beginner's luck, getting their cherry popped. The newcomer will hook a sturgeon by accident with a "suicide style" catch; the sturj' will take the bait then swim away with the green angler cranking the reel like a madman. Hooking into a keeper is one thing, but unless there is a well-seasoned sturgeon hand onboard, the inexperienced angler will lose the fish when it comes to the side of the boat. The wise, experienced angler knows that it's crucial that the fish becomes completely exhausted then floats belly up. If not, when you attempt to snare the sturgeon it will thrash then roll and almost always get away. Once this happens the fever kicks in for the life of the fisherman. Even when he gets too old to fish he will hang out in bait shops or marinas and talk for endless hours about the latest sturgeon drama, reliving tall tales about the legends, the folklore, stories where the fish get bigger every time.

GOT LUCKY

Having Olivia at the cabin was nice. She knew I was going into town and asked me how I felt about picking her up some female necessities as well as new clothes? When she made this request I thought it might be difficult to shop for a woman, but I got the hang of it real quick. I stopped at a high-end women's clothing store, the young lady who helped me owned the store, her name was Eileen, and she was about the same height and build as Olivia. She was rather enjoying the task of picking out items, as she was actually modeling different outfits for me, quite a few outfits as a matter of fact, business was slow that day. With me being the only customer in the store Eileen asked me if I was thirsty, offering me a cold beer; I answered why not? She handed me the beer, locking the front door as she asked how serious I was about the woman I was clothes shopping for and why she wasn't here with me now. To make a long story short, I explained that I wasn't involved with the woman, she was an old friend who I was helping out, telling her Olivia was going through a difficult period, mentally as well as physically. Eileen told me how lucky Olivia was to have a guy like me around and that if Olivia wanted no part of me then she wasn't going to feel guilty about what happened next. Telling me I deserved a reward for doing such a good deed and being such a nice guy, Eileen kissed me, then pulled away smiling, dragging me by my arms to the dressing room with the full-length mirrors. She looked at our reflection the entire time. Not knowing if this was a fantasy of hers or a common occurrence I didn't care either way.

When Eileen rang up my total, I had to hide the look on my face. I figured I would drop a hundo but was slightly shocked when my balance was over three hundred dollars. Apparently the outfits I picked out came in three different colors, where the quick thinking Eileen had rung up all three. Smiling to myself remembering what my father had told me when I was a young man: "If it's got wheels, propellers or wears a bra, it's going to cost you money." I didn't really care—we all pay one way or another, giving her one of my business cards on the way out.

When I got in the pickup, looking at myself in the rearview mirror, I couldn't help grinning as I drove away. When I got home Olivia sensed a change in me and asked what happened. I bent the truth a little, saying that it just made me feel good to help other people out, which had Olivia suspiciously concerned. It had her thinking. Olivia was looking at me with a new perspective.

She was an extraordinary cook. Dinner was ready with a beautiful baked chicken, salad and steamed vegetables. We ate dinner in complete silence again, drinking a nice white wine from The Napa Valley Vineyards. We drank the first bottle with dinner. I decided to open the second bottle with an attempt to loosen us both up to where we could talk things out. I heated the spa then asked her to look at the clothes I had picked out for her. Olivia read the receipt, insisting that I accept repayment, not taking no for an answer. She went to her bag and counted out the money from a thick sheaf of one-hundred-dollar bills. Olivia asked me to put the stack of bills in a safe place. I could tell we had passed a threshold where I was earning her trust. I asked her how much cash was there. Olivia told me it was over twenty thousand, offering to make a donation toward rent or bills. I said I wouldn't take her up on her offer but maybe later, for now we could just let things play out. I told her I appreciated the gesture, but not to worry about anything.

Changing out of my Wranglers, wearing only my briefs and climbing into the steaming spa, I was sitting in the tub enjoying the massage from the jets when Olivia walked out with a large beach towel wrapped around her body, covering herself from her shoulders down. Olivia asked me how I knew to pick out the bikini in just the right size, and why everything in three different colors? Answering with a crooked grin that I wasn't sure what she would like best so I got all three colors. How did I pick the right size? I just got lucky, that's all. I couldn't help but smile at how true that answer really was.

Olivia told me to shut my eyes as she dropped the towel, sinking until the surface of the water was up to her chin. Sneaking a peek through squinted eyes, the sight of her body took my breath away. Acting like a schoolgirl, skittish and shy, I was overwhelmed by memories of high school. The second bottle of wine was going down quite well. Hoping the effects of the alcohol would take the edge off, I asked her if we could just erase everything in the past and move forward to the present? Olivia answered that she thought that would be a good idea, but she wanted closure before we went ahead. She started out saying that what she did, leaving me in the manner she had that night in front of her dad's house, was inexcusable, and she knew that she could never hope to be forgiven in this lifetime. As I sat there just listening, as the words slowly came out, her eyes began to cloud.

Knowing there was no way to avoid the situation, thinking we better get it over with, Olivia told me through sobs that what she was about to tell me was going to be hard for me to believe, but she felt that Eric had somehow brainwashed her. Not only did she abandon me but turned her back on her family as well. Being raised in a perfect environment with the best family, the wealthy, handsome Eric had promised her the world on a silver platter, smothering her with expensive gifts. Olivia admitted that she knew he was dangerous but had been drawn to his "outlaw style attitude." Sitting there finishing the rest of the second bottle of wine, I listened as she explained that the first year E.Z. had treated her like a queen. But Eric was so deep into the meth that he started to think he was some kind of a supernatural god. The money he was making from the many avenues of his drug trade was pouring in. Eric was stacking money like bricks. Life with him was like some kind of rollercoaster. She had to admit, the lifestyle was like a fantasy.

After a while Eric started to have sharp mood swings resulting in outbreaks of violence. At first he was breaking things during his fits, but after that he became more obsessive, finding reasons to accuse her of different acts of betrayal. E.Z. kept saying, "If you would leave Mike back in high school, and run away with me, there's no reason you wouldn't do the same to me," having accused her of sleeping with any man that they had contact with. After a while he kept her in complete isolation, not only thinking she was cheating with men but women as well. She wanted to leave after the first year or two, but Eric swore she would be putting her own folks in immediate danger, where he had no problem going after her family. She was to the point of committing suicide to end her problems, feeling she didn't deserve to live. Olivia was holding herself personally responsible for the situation. That was when she started stashing cash and planning her escape. When Eric started getting busted for his many different crimes, he paid his way out of everything at first, but the money coming in started to slow. When Eric was incarcerated the first time, for six months, with no drugs clouding his judgment, his attitude was entirely different. He depended on Olivia to run the motorcycle repair business. Her first thought was to get away while the getting was good, but with Eric being so nice she felt she couldn't abandon him. Eric swore he'd stay clean once out of jail, promising her they would lead an honest, clean life from then on. Every time he got released he would go straight back to the dope, making the fast money he said that they needed. Olivia kind of fast-forwarded to when she ran away, explaining that Eric spent all his time in his private shop. He had told her he had a plan to get back on top.

Olivia got really quiet for a while. Telling her I would get us something stronger to drink, I didn't say a word or ask what she'd prefer. I just climbed out of the tub then came back with a bottle of Bertoux Brandy. I filled the wine glasses to the top and asked her if she needed a break. She said no, she wanted to get it all out and over with, downing half the glass with a single pull. Mustering up her strength, taking a deep breath, she now made full eye contact with me for the first time since she'd come to the cabin. Olivia spoke as if in a trance, in a voice so low I could hardly hear, without so much as blinking her eyes. Eric had repeatedly told her she had grown old, lost her beauty. Having convinced her that he or any other man could never find her desirable, they hadn't had a sexual relationship in over five years, that when Eric stayed up with no sleep for many days he would play pornography, making her watch while he made her perform unspeakable acts to herself while he would videotape her while taking care of himself. I wanted to tell her that was too much information and I didn't want to hear anymore, but I could tell the emotional dam was broken, figuring it was best for her to let it all out.

When Eric started doing business with the two Russians, who she figured were gay, it had been so long since Eric had slept with her that she thought Eric had become homosexual himself. She made the mistake of insinuating this to Eric — big mistake. He went into such a violent rage that he beat her senseless. The whole event took place two months before she left. It took a month before most of the marks on her face were healed as well as bruised ribs. The black eye was so bad she couldn't see for the first month, the swelling closing her eye completely shut. Eric had left the country to set up something that was part of his mysterious plan, leaving her with no details. That's when she made her escape, showing up at the cabin. I could tell she had a big weight off her chest because she was no longer crying. Olivia almost laughed out loud, a trace of her gorgeous smile almost surfaced when she told me about sneaking around the security gates, creeping up to the cabin. She'd heard James Brown bumpin' on the stereo and hoped she would find me alone, reliving Apollo treeing her on the porch rail, scaring the living daylights out of her.

Olivia got real serious then asked if I would take her to the airport, that she understood how I must feel toward her. I asked if she wanted to leave, or if she felt that she had to because of Eric. Getting out of the tub I dug out an old 8-track from the sixties, a multiple artist collection of *Greatest Love Songs*, trying to set the stage for romance. I told her she could stay as long as she wanted but she cut me off, looking me square in the eyes, saying that's not what she wanted to know. What she was asking was, did I want her to stay? Downing the rest of my glass of brandy, I told her if she wanted an answer to that I couldn't tell her, I would have to show her. Olivia stood up taking off the bikini top walking slowly across the bubbling tub. Time had been on her side where she was aging nicely, gravity gently taking its toll with her heavy chest slightly sagging, with large burgundy wine-colored, elongated silver dollar areolas. This was no longer a high school girl but a mature female in her prime. Olivia sat down on top of me looking directly into my eyes, straddling me with her knees bent as she kissed me, slowly, sensually. I could taste the salt from her tears but couldn't help thinking about what had happened earlier that day at the women's clothing store with Eileen. I figured "when it rains it pours" and just had to let nature take its course.

The 8-track clicked between tracks, with puurrrfect timing: Leon Haywood, "I Want'a Do Something Freaky to You." The sensuous, sultry music played on: *As my fingers explore your valleys of love, compatible or not, I'll hit that spot.* We stayed there like that for a long time, kissing long full romantic kisses; eyes shut, hands shaking, hearts beating like a jack hammer, exploring each other's mouths with our tongues. I kissed her long slender neck, nibbling on her ears trying to get Olivia heated up so she couldn't pump the brakes. Apollo was sitting on the edge of the tub acting like he was asleep, wagging his tail with his eyes closed. I picked her up in my arms heading to the bedroom, placing her gently on the bed, telling Apollo to take a hike then shutting the door. You could tell he was happy about the situation,

Apollo headed out the doggy door wagging his little stubbed tail. We stayed in bed making up for lost time the whole night. Not having a charter booked for the rest of the week, Olivia and I got to know each other quite well. This was no seventeen-year-old girl anymore. I had a strong feeling she was telling the truth about no sex in over five years. Once we got to know each other's physical wants and desires she was like a caged tiger, where I was the key to set her free into the wild. This kitty needed to go for a romp. I could tell she was still trying to hold back, but her sexual appetite overpowered the shyness. I knew the "Man of Stone" had met his match.

SHRIMP-FLAVORED MARGARITAS

As I woke up that morning about 5:40 a.m., watching the sun entering the dark room, I kept thinking about the last time the sturgeon bite was this slow. In the early '90s there was a long dry spell, the lack of rain had the time clock on the Delta confused. With no rain to feed the rivers the cycle of the sturgeon migratory run was behind schedule. I had a charter booked at 0900 catching the incoming tide, with Olivia now more comfortable being left at the cabin by herself. The *General* was chartered maybe once a week. Even running all the way upriver as far as Pittsburg I couldn't bring in the fish. When the fish aren't biting they're just not biting. The spawn had finally started, but it was still incredibly slow. After talking to the captains of the other charters it was the same story all over, the money was nowhere near what it should have been and the migratory run was almost over.

When I had a boat full of fishermen and the bite was

dead, I would tell a fishing story about the spot we were at, trying to "pump up the hype," making sure everybody was having a good time. Having the *General* anchored in a well-known sturgeon hole up in the Sacramento River, it was obvious the group was getting restless. As I stood on the deck amongst the fishermen, I told a story that I always enjoy.

Years back before I had the *General*, I owned a 1987 25-foot Bayliner Sierra Cabin Cruiser. She was more of a cocktail cruiser than a fishing boat, but two men could fish comfortably out the back. Now don't get me wrong, this boat was tip-top, with a full snap-on Delta canvas for fishing in the winter. A single brand new 350-cubic-inch with a four-barrel carburetor, the out drive was a Mercury Bravo with a stainless steel prop. She would run at almost 40 miles an hour on full plane. She had a full cabin with sleek lines. Her colors were white with black trim, with custom red, white and blue tuck and roll upholstery. I was working at a PG&E power plant on a job set up on 6-10$: $ix days a week, ten hour$ a day, with Sunday being my only day off. Living in a house in Concord, I came home from work on Saturday night and saw my good neighbor Ken on the side of his house working on a tri-hull boat, so I walked over to B.S. Hopefully he would offer me one of his famous vodka and lemonade cocktails. Ken would drink vodka like most guys could drink beer without ever getting a hangover. Ken said he heard the sturgeon were biting up on the Sacramento River, but his boat needed to go to the shop. He went into his house without asking me then came out with two large glasses of his favorite drink: Instant Crystal Light Lemonade and Stoli Vodka in a tall glass filled with ice—hard to beat after ten hours in the grueling summer heat. Ken asked if my boat was running and if I was interested in fishing the next morning. He said he would spring for gas and the bait plus supply the vodka and lemonade. Now that was an offer I couldn't refuse, with one catch, having a prior engagement that I couldn't get out of at 2:00 p.m. On Sunday afternoon I had to drive a considerable distance. There was no way I could drink early in the morning then show up at my girlfriend's parents' house when it was the first time I was to be introduced to her folks. Explaining this to Ken, we both knew that if he brought his cooler along that I would drink with him and mess up my day. We agreed to get an early start, leave the house at 0500 then drive to Lloyd's Holiday Harbor where I kept my boat moored. The name of the boat was on the stern when I bought her used from a retired couple: *My Obsession,* scrolled on the stern in red, white and blue. We hit the bait shop and purchased a pound of live grass which comes in a plastic bag with newspaper on top of ice. We dropped anchor at about 6:15 and were set up on a promising incoming tide. The temperature was supposed to peak out at close to a hundred degrees in the afternoon, but the morning was still nice and cool. There wasn't a hint of a breeze and the water was flat as could be. We were marking fish on the screen, everything looked picture perfect. We baited up and cast out our lines. The tide was coming in, pointing the bow west, the stern east. We sat back with the sun rising, a brilliant fire-yellow-orange ball creeping above the horizon into the blue sky. We sat there until close to 8:00, getting decent action, reeling in a couple of shakers, with a decent striped bass. The morning could not have been more peaceful, when all of a sudden there was a commotion 25 yards off the starboard side. A 700-pound sea lion was floating by lying on its back with a still live 6- to7-foot sturgeon in its mouth. The sea lion was biting chunks out of the soft white underside of the massive sturj', the fish thrashing as the jaws of the sea lion opened like a hippopotamus, biting out chunks as big as pie plates, the long sharp teeth ripping mercilessly through the soft tissue of the sturgeon's stomach. The mighty sturj' fought until the end, even as the vital organs spilled from the opening in its underside. There was an oil slick fifty feet wide from the blood and internal organs floating on the surface. Ken, fast as a cat pulling out his Nikon camera, caught it all on film. As soon as it had appeared it was gone. The sea lion was done with his breakfast, releasing the near-dead sturgeon, which floated away with the incoming tide and disappeared under the surface of the flat water.

We were pretty jacked up after our peaceful morning was broken up by the act of nature we had just witnessed. Having to use the head, I went in the cabin where I was using the Porta Potty when I noticed there was something missing, something very important: no toilet paper. I started looking around the boat and found an extra roll under the sink, where I also spied a half-full half-gallon handle of Cuervo Gold Tequila and a full bottle of Margarita mix. Climbing out of the cabin, holding the bottles in my hands I watched Ken's eyes light up. The first thing he says is he can't drink the tequila straight and we can't mix a Margarita without ice. At the same time, we both looked at the bait box containing the ice with the live grass shrimp on top. Ken says no way is he going to drink ice that has shrimp juice in it. I knew what I was doing was wrong and my day would be ruined, but I mixed a Margarita on the rocks, stirring it well. I took one sip. To my surprise it was the best Margarita I ever tasted. Ken saw the look on my face, letting out a loud, deep, rolling laugh as he dumped the coffee out of his insulated mug, handing it over to me, ordering one shrimp-flavored Margarita, please. Ken agreed with me, it was the best he ever had. By 12:00 noon we had finished off the bottle and were a complete mess. It was almost 100 degrees. The tequila was doing a good job on the both of us. Ken caught a keeper sturgeon, like he always does, then we tried to make it home by 1:00.

I put the Bayliner back in her slip, and then I was fading fast from working sixty hours that week in the burning sun and from drinking the shrimp-flavored Margaritas all morning. On the way home I pulled over at the liquor store for an ice-cold sixer of Coors bottles and nursed beers all the way home. Trying to get a second wind, I pulled the truck into the driveway where I was almost an hour late. My girlfriend was standing there all dolled-up, ready to drive to her folks' house for the barbeque. She took one look at me then threw a pretty good fit. Ken grabbed the sturgeon out of the back of the truck, slinging it over his shoulder and trying not to laugh as he walked away toward his house. Bending the truth, I told the girl we only split a six-pack on the way home, celebrating the successful fishing trip. Ken could no longer hold back, bustin' up as he walked up his driveway.

I took a quick shower then put on some nice threads. We were getting in her car when Ken walked up carrying some fresh sturgeon filets in a small cooler. He said, "You better hope her parents like sturgeon, because this is your only hope."

We showed up at her parents' house about an hour and a half late. She tried to make an excuse, saying it was her fault we were behind schedule, when her mom asked what was in my hand. I said "Well Ma'am, the truth is it's my fault we were late because I had been out fishing all morning. I brought these fresh sturgeon filets hoping y'all liked fish."

Her old man, who was watching all this without saying a word, leaned his head back and I saw the look in his eyes. He asked, "How fresh are we talking, young man?"

Telling him I had been fishing since about 0600, we got lucky hooking up about 10 that morning. His eyes started to glow and he tried to pretend he was mad. He said I must be out of my f - - in' mind, if the sturgeon were biting and I left to come meet him and his wife to have barbeque I should have my head examined. He put his arm around my shoulder, telling me I looked like I could use a cold one and inviting me into the air-conditioned house to show me his framed pictures of sturgeon that he had hanging on the walls. I could tell the fever was stirring inside him from the look in his eye, and we talked about fishing the entire day. We pan-fried the sturgeon filets to go along with the barbe-qued tri-tip steaks. I'm talking about surf and turf. Her dad and I bonded right off then drank the afternoon away. That ole boy was a real angler in his day, and gave me some good tips I didn't know. When I left we had plans to go out in my boat the following Sunday. The day ended well. I passed out in the car on the way home. The alarm clock went off at 0430. I had hell to pay, hung over like a big dog Monday morning at work.

MR. ONE

The *General* was riding along, mowing down a slight chop. We were on our way downriver to San Pablo Bay, with the latest reports were of sturgeon being taken on cured salmon roe at buoy number nine. It was a long haul, but I

had to get on top of the fish. The crew were some steamfitters I knew personally.

One of them says, "Hey Stoner, tell us about the time you
cut the guy's ear off with a fishing rod."

Laughing out loud I told him I didn't cut the ear completely off, just almost all the way. I told him it was a long
story and asked if they were sure they wanted to hear it. We
had at least an hour and a half boat ride so why not. One
time Don, a good friend as well as fishing partner, and I
were out in Don's 16-foot aluminum boat. The weather was
ice cold being dead winter. We got out early, the sun just
coming up. Marking some fish showing good sign and setting the anchor, my good buddy Don was sitting toward the
bow, I was near the stern. Now to backtrack a little bit, I have
to tell you that when we were teenagers Don had a moped
and rode it everywhere he went. We were all hanging out at
a party house on Concord Boulevard, an old retirement
home for the elderly, located on a two-acre lot. There was a
big pit bull tied to a 20-foot chain with a three-inch steel ring
placed over a two-inch pipe sticking out of the ground. Don
would ride his moped around in a 40-foot circle, where the
pit bull would chase after him. Well, that old dog out-
smarted him and had dug a deep hole as far out as its paws
could reach. The next time he pulled up on the moped we
were sitting around drinking some beers. Don started the
game with the dog as he drove up. Now Don was one of
those gifted guys who could ride anything with two wheels
better than anyone around. He could get on any bicycle or
motorcycle and ride a wheelie around the block no problem.
Don could beat anybody in any sport where he was a true
athlete. He was gaining speed, leaning the moped, having a
good time while we were cheering him on. When the front

tire went in the hole, he went ass over tea kettle. The moped flew over him. Of course, we were all laughing way too loud until the dog went after him. In a split second the pit bull locked on Don's crotch. That's when things got real serious. The owner of the pit bull had to wrap his hands around the dog's neck and choke him out before the locking jaws would release. Don was screaming like a raped ape, sweat was pouring from his terrified face. We got the dog off him then had to take him to the hospital where unfortunately he had to have one of his testicles amputated. Poor Don was left with only one ball.

Now he and I were marking fish on the bottom, sitting there bundled up good with insulated overalls. I was getting a slow but steady bite, my rod tip gently pumping as the big sturgeon was trying to suck my bait off the hook. The sturj' will suck the shrimp off the green grass and natural growth of the bottom. I was in position, waiting patiently for the fish to give a good final pull where I would set the hook then rip some lips. When he took the bait I was ready, yanking back hard. Keep in mind, when I set that hook I'm trying to break the rod in half. Then I set it a second time for an insurance policy. When I came back over my head with the rod, the tip hit Don right on the edge of his head, in between his skull and ice-cold ear. Somehow my line had broken, but I didn't know it just yet, reeling in slack as I brought the rod forward. I attempted to set the hook again, hitting Don in same exact spot.

I heard him scream, "Please don't hit me again!" He had both hands holding his ear, blood seeping through his fingers. I thought he was joking until I saw the blood.

Feeling bad for what happened, I jokingly told him, "Hey man, the first one's on me, but you sat there and let me hit you the second time. The first one was my fault but the second one is on you."

Don screamed at me, "First I get one of my balls bit off by a pit bull, now you cut off my ear with a fishing rod, you dirty SOB!" Of course, it wasn't very funny at the time but now it makes for a good fishing tale. After that I always called Don "Mr. One." Don is a great guy with a big heart and always tells me with a laugh to f'-off. We fished the whole day and caught shakers but no keepers, making it a long ride home.

1985 BUBBLE GUM

In the early '80s the United States was experiencing a cocaine epidemic. The endless massive supply of the highly addictive as well as extremely popular street drug was coming across the Atlantic Ocean from Peru, Colombia and Bolivia by the thousands of tons. The bales of the cocaine, being flown in small aircraft or smuggled in a variety of oceangoing vessels, were dropped at designated areas offshore from Miami. The runners would pick up the bales of blow at prearranged longitude-latitude positions using a lorans navigation system that were the state-of-the-art technology in their day. The highly expensive as well as high performance, offshore racing cigarette-style boats that could travel through any type of ocean conditions at top speeds would pick up the shipments of the cocaine under the cover of darkness, then transport to Miami. Even after the authorities became aware of the drug trafficking, they were only able to intercept one out of ten of the shipments. The city of Miami was also flooded with Cuban POWs who were released by Fidel Castro then exiled from Cuba. The released

POWs were practically swimming ashore, coming the short distance from Cuba in every kind of boat imaginable. The Cuban movement supplied endless labor for the cocaine trade. Many prospered with instant wealth. The city of Miami with its major tourist attractions flourished. The money was outrageous for everyone involved, from common smalltime dope peddlers to the kingpins who made millions upon millions in illegal profits. One crafty smuggler figured out a way to make a bigger profit by using light aircraft to fly under the radar to Half Moon Bay, off the coast of California, selling kilos at an inflated price, much higher than the going market rate in Miami. The cocaine was dropped offshore, then received by a fleet of commercial salmon fishing boats and brought ashore at Half Moon Bay. The authorities were not aware because their focus was concentrating on Miami, where they already had their hands full with the ongoing, seemingly endless drug busts. The commercial fishing boats were going broke due to the banning of all salmon fishing on the West Coast. Poachers had done damage, causing the industry to go almost completely out of business. When they were approached with the illegal smuggling proposition, they jumped on the opportunity of the fast cash, where they made an extremely large amount of money, more than they ever dreamed of from commercial fishing.

Eric made a connection with one of these distributors where he was purchasing ten kilos a week at the low price of $10,000 per kilo. Eric would transport from Half Moon Bay using an incognito older boat that he had outfitted with brand new, turbo diesel Caterpillars. The old commercial fishing trawler looked exactly like the dozens of other fishing boats and was never looked at twice. The skipjack is known as the "Jeep of the ocean," ideal for rough conditions. Eric had installed large auxiliary diesel fuel tanks in the boat and could make the long voyage from Half Moon Bay up the coast, motor underneath the Golden Gate Bridge, across the San Francisco Bay, then come up the Carquinez Straits to Benicia without ever having to refuel. Eric would pay for the cocaine with counterfeit hundred-dollar bills that he was exchanging at the price of three for one. The counterfeit bills were not yet suspect in the Bay Area. Eric was buying these by the shoebox full then washing the money through the drug trade. E.Z. would buy the "funny money" through his motorcycle gang affiliations. The people supplying the seemingly endless supply of raw, uncut cocaine accepted the "play dough" then passed it up the line, no problem. Once the cocaine was safely transported Eric would take the product to his shop. Starting with the ten kilos of pure, raw cocaine, he'd come out with thirty keys of product by mixing the ingredients in a large vat, to the consistency of typical exterior house paint, then spraying the white batter through a common airless paint gun onto a ten-foot by six-foot sheet of glass in thin layers. These layers were cured in between each coat with infrared lights. The finished product looked just like pure, uncut Peruvian Flake. The coke had a slightly peculiar odor of regular pink bubble gum from the chemical process. When snorted or freebased the user would recognize the flavor, thinking they were getting pure coke.

Eric's mules were supplying the nightclub circuit in the San Francisco Bay area as well as moving the product down south to the L.A. market. The present market value of cocaine was $21,000 per kilo, which made Eric the kingpin of the Bay Area. Everybody who was involved, from the street hustlers to the numerous "ounce men," was suddenly rolling in the dough. With the endless readily available quantities, Eric would front his dealers all the product they wanted, reaping unbelievable profits. Eric was literally spinning gold from wheat, where he was soon on top of the world. Drunk with the power and influence from the mountains of cold hard cash, Eric made big mistakes, thinking there was no way he could be stopped. When somebody owed him that couldn't cover their debt he would collect personally, taking personal possessions ranging from cars or motorcycles to jewelry. If anybody resisted, Eric had to inflict violence to keep his reputation, so no one would think he was weak. He loved intimidation, and always got his money.

This is where E.Z. made his giant mistake. If he hadn't been so greedy, such a flamboyant showboat, always traveling in a chauffeur-driven stretch limo and attracting attention everywhere he went... Once he had gone into a violent rage over a large debt someone failed to pay, administering a near-fatal beating to one of his mules. When the man recovered and was released from the hospital he went to the authorities, ratting Eric out. When his suppliers got wind of the incident Eric was too hot to continue doing business and was completely cut off. The money stopped dead and Eric had to forfeit millions to avoid a long-term prison sentence. The only charge was assault, where he served just six months in a minimum-security county jail.

This was the beginning of the end for the rich and powerful Eric. Making friends with a cellmate while doing his time in the county jail in Clayton, California, known as The Farm, they developed a relationship of trust and financial interest. The new acquaintance, who was doing time for manufacturing LSD as well as PCP, was a student at UC

Berkeley with a major in chemistry. The chemist had a market for the acid around the college campus and the surrounding inner city. He was also connected to the heavy Hispanic population of San Jose, where the notorious Latino-based street gangs ran the streets. The PCP was a popular drug of choice for the Hispanics. The chemist had been born and raised in San Jose, where he was well connected. He said all he needed was financial backing and people he could trust to distribute, promising quick returns from the small capital invested. Eric was impressed with his intelligence. Going into a new market where the police wouldn't suspect him, this was another mistake. After getting released Eric went straight to work with the chemist making some decent cash. But again greed took over and Eric wanted to produce bigger quantities. It didn't take long before one of Eric's customers, who was on parole, turned Eric in. He still had properties and vehicles, which he signed over at much less than face value to his underworld connections to keep him out of long-term state prison, so had to serve only one year. It was only a matter of time before all his connections considered him too big a risk, closing their doors to any business transactions.

EL NIÑO

A storm had rolled in, the rain coming down was "socked in steady." Using this time to maintain the boats, I stopped in at Eagle Marine in Martini town to pick up some parts. I knew the kid Eric, running the counter. He asked me when I had ever heard of the bite being so slow. He explained to me that his grandfather told him the best time to catch a sturgeon was when the water was muddy after a big storm. I told him he was exactly right. Eric asked me if I ever got a chance to fish during El Niño, a weather system that poured water on the West Coast for ten straight months. Answering yes, that was during the big "clean fuels" boom. He broke out a couple of cold ones as I went on with the story. The four major oil refineries in the Bay Area were re-engineering the gasoline blending process with a multi-billion-dollar job called "The Clean Fuels Project." There are numerous oil refineries as well as power plants up and down the banks of the Delta due to the demand for large amounts of fresh water needed for steam, which is vital for the refinement process of crude oil. Endless amounts of water are needed for power plants as well as cooling the different products during the many different refinement stages of the process.

The crude oil is transported from all over the world using state-of-the-art supertankers. The Delta waterways are ideal for the large ships to unload the precious, raw crude oil at the receiving docks. Every pipefitter, iron worker, boilermaker and industrial electrician was working steady due to the demand of skilled labor. The boom lasted four years with travelers coming from all parts of the U.S. as well as from other countries around the world. The only problem was the weather, where it started to rain and didn't stop. This weather system was named El Niño, the relentless rain causing major floods filling all the lakes and reservoirs to maximum capacities.

When the boom slowed down the California Delta waterways were flowing at record levels, causing the ancient levees to break in numerous locations, resulting in catastrophic flooding along the banks of the San Joaquin River. The rich fertile farmlands were flooded. The San Joaquin

Valley, otherwise known as the "Fruit and Nut Basket of the World," which starts as far north as Sacramento and runs south down to as far as L.A., is one of if not the largest agricultural producers in the world, and suffered the most from the impact of the flooding. The river, as well as the swollen creeks and tributaries, flowed with water that was so thick with the washed-out, precious topsoil from the farmlands that the river itself seemed to be filled with mud the texture of thick chocolate milk. The natural force of the water overpowered the incoming tides, although the level of the water would rise on the incoming tide, then go back down a few feet on the outgo. This resulted in the continuous current going downriver around the clock for weeks on end. When the water is muddy and brackish the sturgeon can't smell their food. Their instinct and feeding habits go into a frenzy, and they will feed aggressively on any food they can find.

We were off work for a while with the boom ending. It was time to fish, the only problem being the California Delta system was closed to boaters because of the risk of the boat wakes rupturing the already weakened levees. The boat ramps were closed, forbidding the fishermen from launching. We had to find a way to get on the water. My good friend, working and fishing partner, Gary Bean, who I met on the Clean Fuels Project, was a traveling welder from LU 364, the steamfitters union in San Bernardino. Gary was raised in a marina down south where his grandfather was the harbormaster. He had fished his entire life and was a natural sturgeon angler right out of the gate. Gary had the fever as bad as anyone, game to fish anytime. The water levels were dangerously high, threatening the ancient levees, boat ramps closed.

Three of us were hanging out in my garage drinking a

few and watching the continuous pouring rain when we decided how to get on the water. Gary had a 1973 Bayliner fishing boat moored in a berth at Mac Avoy's Marina in Pittsburg. We devised a plan to wait until 10:00 p.m. then sneak his boat out under the cover of darkness and try our luck. We left the marina geared up with frozen bait and supplies. Right away the older boat experienced mechanical failure. When Gary started the engine it ran perfect. Backing the boat out of the slip she still ran fine, but when he shifted from reverse to forward gear the engine died. We didn't know it at the time but the neutral lockout safety device that enables the ignition to start in gear was malfunctioning. The Teflon gear was worn out, causing the engine to fail when shifting. We were too stubborn to give up, partly because of the effects of the alcohol clouding our judgment but mostly because of the desire fueling the fever, with the chance to fish the muddy, ideal conditions.

Somehow Gary and I, along with another welder who happened to be named Gary—Gary Easley, who was one of the best anglers I ever knew—managed to get the boat started to the point where once running in forward gear it would operate fine. Gary was cruising along with great care, barely above idle, running without navigation lights so as not to attract any attention. I was positioned on the bow of the old gray hardtop boat with a spotlight in my hand, turning the beam on the water ahead of the boat, only using the light for brief periods, when needed. When you run at night under normal conditions it is already dangerous to begin with, but due to the flooding the river was as hazardous as I had ever experienced. There were complete docks floating down the river and entire trees, uprooted from the continuous flooding, adrift in the main channel. All the major shipping was prohibited from the dangers in the water, seeing everything from dead cows with their bodies swollen up as big as a Volkswagen to derelict boats torn from their moorings by the flood conditions as well as the high winds from the previous storm. The entire surface of the river was covered with flotsam.

We had dropped anchor on the north side of the river directly across from Pittsburg, setting up on a fishing hole called "the dolphin," where a tripod of twenty-four-inch diameter Douglas fir, creosote-treated timbers were positioned in the water, serving as an old channel marker. This was a well-known hot spot. We chose it because we thought we were safely out of sight from anyone, plus it was only a short distance from the marina, straight across from Pittsburg. The wind was blowing from the south, causing everything on the surface to end up on our side of the river, making it impossible to fish without debris floating past and snagging our lines. Even when we tried dropping our lines straight down behind the stern without casting it was still impossible to fish without getting snagged. We decided this was fruitless and a waste of our time. The fish finder was indicating so many fish under the boat we had to turn it off because the continuous beeping of the alarm was driving us crazy, fueling the fever, hyping up the desire to fish even more. We pulled anchor, trying to take the boat into the mouth of nearby Montezuma Slough for safety as well as hoping for improved fishing conditions. This is when the trouble began. The boat, stalling repeatedly, was soon adrift in the swift running current. Floating down the channel with Gary trying to start the boat, the battery soon drained and failed to turn the starter. The boat was equipped with a Perko switch but unfortunately the second battery was soon dead as well. We were drifting toward Middle Ground, which is an island that was a whaling cannery in the early 1900s but was now just a very low rise in the channel. The island's highest point is only four or five feet above water level at high tide. Many boats have run aground here through the years.

Gary had a brand new fully-charged spare battery in the cabin. He was in the middle of changing it out when we noticed where the current was taking the boat. I threw the anchor out to keep us from drifting into the shallows while Gary changed out the battery. The third fisherman onboard figured out the problem with the neutral knockout switch and was able to jerry-rig the ignition, hot wiring the coil, making the boat temporarily operable. Gary E. completed the battery exchange, I heard the boat ignition catch then we were ready to be on our way.

By now it was 2:00 a.m. The wind had lain down, the river as quiet and eerie as I had ever seen it. Everything was spooky and I had a bad gut feeling. I waited on the bow to operate the windlass to retrieve the anchor while Gary warmed up the engine. My eyes always play tricks on my brain when I have been on the water at night. Thinking I was hallucinating when the boat started to list to the port side, I heard Gary scream, asking what I was doing to cause the boat to lean. I swear I couldn't believe my eyes: around the anchor line directly in front of the bow there had accumulated a massive floating pile of grass, tree branches, hyson and flotsam, being forced up the anchor line. I saw what started out as a single branch but to my horror realized was in fact an entire submerged tree at least one hundred and fifty feet in length with a trunk of five or six feet in girth. The current forced the continuous branch up on the bow, knocking me off the boat, to dangle from the bow rail with my heavy Arctic boots in the water. The end of the four-inch diameter tree limb broke through the windshield, going five or six feet into the cabin. When the current forced the trunk of the tree to the opposite side of the boat, acting like a giant lever trying to capsize the old Bayliner and sink the boat, I pulled myself back up on the bow, throwing my legs up over the bow rail. I pulled a Buck knife, folding Hunter Model 110, from the sheath on my belt, the Buck knife with the brass cases, rosewood handles and razor-sharp stainless steel blade.

The boat was listing so bad the water was beginning to pour in over the starboard gunwale. Both of the other guys were standing on the portside trying to level out the boat, screaming at me in complete panic. Holding the bow rail with my left hand, using my free hand I flicked the knife blade open switchblade style, then cut the anchor line yelling to Gary to hit full reverse and crank the steering wheel to starboard, the opposite direction of the tree.

We were extremely lucky. Gary was able to maneuver the boat with the prop turning mud. With the force of the current the large tree would have capsized and totaled the boat. We would have spent a long night on the island.

We decided to call it quits after the narrow escape and headed back into the marina. We got to the south side of the river with me on the bow using the spotlight guiding our way home. Noticing that the surface of the water was relatively clear of debris, we came up with a new plan to try our luck at place called the "yellow can." The large floating yellow can is upriver from a naval dock near Port Chicago, on top of a well-known clam bed, a favorite hot spot producing sturgeon for as long as I can remember. Gary pulled out a spare anchor and we set up the lantern then cleaned up the glass from the broken windshield, rigging a tarp to temporarily replace the glass for protection from the wind and rain, when something happened that none of us could believe. I cast out but before my weight even hit the bottom of the river I hooked a "suicide sturgeon." This had never happened before. While I was playing the fish Gary B already had a fish on as well. This is known as a "double header." When one man is fighting a sturgeon there is enough chaos just trying to land one fish, but when two guys are each playing a sturj' it gets pretty crazy, with the lines crossing as the sturgeon fights for its life.

Remembering back to a night at the Ozol Pier my nephew and I got into 'em. We had two sturj' on, where the younger, Derek, probably twelve years old, was not used to the conventional reel with no level wind. He got the line wrapped around his thumb, back then using 20-pound mono, it would either break the line or cut off his thumb.

Derek lost his composure screaming, "Uncle Mike, I'm hung up! What do I do? "

I yelled instruction but he was not listening. I had to fight my fish plus save his, screaming at him to pay attention where I slapped him across the face. This was effective as he was now fully focused. We were lucky, landing both sturj'. Gary B and I both managed to bag two hawgz, plus many more. Before the sun came up it started to pour rain. We were prepared with rain gear and suited up. We caught at least fifteen sturgeon that we were able to catch and release, keeping only three hawgz that were all 68-72 inches. The limit is one sturgeon for each angler onboard. This is called upgrading, throwing back the smaller sturgeon.

After calling it quits we went back to the marina, where

we saw there was nobody around due to the heavy rain. McAvoy's Marina was completely deserted, not a soul in sight. Instead of taking our prized catch and going home we tied the still very much alive fish through the gills with a rope, then tied the fish to a boat cleat, putting the three fish in the water under the dock, then headed straight back out to the yellow can. We knew this was risky, going out in daylight, but we couldn't resist the temptation to take advantage of the once-in-a-lifetime opportunity. We went back to the exact same location and didn't see one boat. Apparently, we were the only people crazy enough to be on the water in the hazardous conditions. We fished until 12:00 noon, catching fish almost every cast. We caught so many sturgeon that after a while it became monotonous. We ate all our food, drank all our beer plus a bottle of Kessler's in celebration, keeping three more hawgz.

Heading back to McAvoy's the relentless rain never stopped. Although we had sufficient rain gear we were all soaked to the skin, exhausted from the long night plus we were out of alcohol, losing our buzz. We secured the boat and were taking the second catch of three hawgz out. The first three that were tied under the dock were fully rested, and when they felt our footsteps on the dock they went completely berserk. The rickety old ancient dock was rocking side to side with the sturgeon thrashing below like an earthquake. Whenever I have been on a boat for a long time my legs are always wobbly when I step on a dock or dry land. My sea legs have to take time to adjust. The three sturj' under the dock were like a hippopotamus trying to destroy it, causing us to almost fall in the water. We decided to leave the three under the dock so if Fish & Game checked us out we were still legal.

After going home, enjoying a hot shower and hearty lunch we went back to retrieve the other three sturgeon. When we arrived at the marina, walking down the dock we noticed an old-timer who was checking his boat from the storm. He had his eyes glued to the three of us as we walked past. The dock started to wobble again from the thrashing sturgeon. When he saw us pull the three monsters out of the water he was scratching his head in amazement. As we walked past his boat carrying the three giant sturgeon he said he thought he was losing his mind. All morning he was trying to figure out what all the movement under the dock was about. We went back home, which is when the work began, filleting the six hawgz. All of our freezers were full of the massive fillets, as well all my surrounding neighbors.

JOHN WAYNE

I couldn't book a charter to save my life. I knew there were only a couple of jobs at the union hall. Both were over-time jobs. I could not leave Olivia alone that long. Not being quite broke but getting close I drove to Concord, stopping off at the union hall, asking the business agent about up-coming projects. We were talking about possible pipeline work coming up in the spring and he asked me if I still had a welding rig. Telling him my rig was up at the ranch and would probably be ready to go with a little work, one thing led to another. When we started talking about a job we'd had in Napa at a place called the Double Joint Rack, the agent asked about a sturgeon he heard I had lassoed with a rope. Steve poured coffees as we sat down and reminisced.

In 1992 there was a 42-inch high-pressure natural gas pipeline being laid from Ontario, Canada to Bakersfield,

California. At the time the cross-country pipeline project was the longest line laid in the United States since the world famous Alaskan crude oil overland pipeline that started in 1975. The Alaskan pipeline, 900 miles of 36-inch, had to be laid on top of the ground because of the extreme cold temperatures. The pipeline was insulated and equipped with steam tracing lines to keep the sweet Alaskan crude oil warm enough so that it would flow through the pipeline. With the new 1400 miles of 42-inch pipe, Pacific Gas and Transportation were expanding their capacity to transport the large volume of natural gas to meet the demands of the East. The abundant gas from the Canadian wells is a simple matter of supply and demand. Canada has more natural gas than they can use. They sell the product at such a low price that by transporting through the Transcontinental Pipeline, Pacific Gas and Transportation can pay for the million-dollar-a-mile price of installing the pipeline within a couple of years of operation. After the first few years the transportation of the product is all profit.

This project was known as the PG&T Pipeline Expansion Program because the line was laid parallel with two smaller existing pipelines, the first a 12-inch line installed in the late '30s, the second a 24-inch line installed in late '60s. The fabrication of the pipe consisted of flat sheets of carbon steel plates that were unloaded from the flat railroad cars then flattened with hydraulic rollers to the desired wall thickness of the pipes. After the flat steel is pressed with a series of pipe bending machines, the long seam is welded robotically with a continuous wire feed submerged arc weld, then coated with state-of-the-art, epoxy coating to insulate the carbon steel pipe and protect it from electrolysis, once backfilled in the ditch.

I got lucky landing a job at the Double Joint Rack. The job was set up on $even days a week, twelve hour$ a day. With all the overtime I was rolling in the money. After the first week, it was June where the weather was hot. After work, four other hands from the job and I were going to help a guy named Dice, who was living on a houseboat in the Martinez Marina. The houseboat needed the frame in the motor compartment rebuilt where it had rusted out. We replaced this with three-inch carbon steel channel iron. Dice had offered the five of us a dinner of pizza with cold beer so we all showed up and pitched in. After we fabricated then welded out the new frame, Dice offered to take us all for a cruise on the gorgeous water. I told Dice if he'd take us all fishing that I would put a sturgeon in the boat. Dice said he didn't have any fishing gear on the boat but agreed to this, promising a future fishing expedition, as he had been fishing for sturgeon many times with no success.

Dice was warming up the engine while we were rolling up the mooring lines, preparing to get under way. One of the mooring lines was a 50-foot rope. I was rolling it up neatly to leave it on the dock when one of the welders named Doug told me to bring the rope in case we might need it. I coiled it tight, leaving it on the bow. We were out of beer when Dice produced a half gallon bottle of Kessler's from the bar in the cabin, and we were passing the "handle" around drinking straight from the bottle. We were pretty well lit by this time. The water was flat with no breeze, the sun on its way down with the hot temperature starting to cool off.

Heading downriver out of the marina we went about a mile when I saw what I thought was a large dead striped bass floating in the water, drifting lazily in the swift running outgoing tide. The dead striper looked like it was forty inches long. There was a seagull pecking the fish with its beak, enjoying its free dinner. Doug asked me what kind of fish it was. I told him it was a striped bass. It was common to see a dead striper in that part of the Carquinez Straits. Doug was a big time freshwater, largemouth bass angler who lived back east. He wanted a closer look at the striper, saying he had never seen one before. Dice spun around in a big circle for a closer inspection of the fish but it was gone. Doug asked me if I was sure I saw it. Telling him I was absolutely positive, the guys were giving me a hard time in good humor, saying I'd probably had enough to drink. We all were enjoying a good laugh when we noticed five or six seagulls circling the surface of the calm flat water off the bow of the boat. There were the four of us standing on the bow with Dice at the helm on the fly bridge. We were really not paying much attention when out of the corner of my eye I saw the biggest seagull of the group dive at the water. The head of a monster sturgeon popped up out of the water, scaring the you-know-what out of us.

Doug says to me, in his country accent, "Mike, that ain't no bass, son." He exclaimed it had to be a shark!

I told him it was not a shark but a sturgeon. The seagull took a quick peck, stabbing its beak in the open flesh of the sturj'. As suddenly as the sturgeon appeared it was gone again, back under the surface of the water. We were all in shock, deciding to follow the seagulls, waiting for another glimpse of the massive sturgeon. There was no way of knowing this at the time but the big sturgeon had been hit by a propeller or had been bitten by a shark, leaving a large gash behind its gills. The sturgeon had lost its buoyancy and could not stay under water although it was still alive. A sturgeon is an amazing creature that can endure all kinds of punishment. You can catch a sturgeon then leave it out of the water, where it will stay alive for many hours. We came up with a plan to lasso the fish with the rope.

Doug said, "I told you guys we might need that rope."

We were following the seagulls with the houseboat, which was no easy task, for a 42-foot boat is difficult to maneuver in a fast current. By now we were feeling the effects of the twelve-hour workday plus the alcohol, but we wanted that sturgeon bad. We weren't ready to give up. I was hanging out over the bow with two guys holding the back of my belt with the noose at the ready in my right hand with five or six rolls coiled up in my left. We were armed with a six-foot frog gig and a carpenter's framing claw hammer. The sun had almost completely set with limited daylight remaining. I tried to lasso the fish but repeatedly missed. After several tries, I was getting the hang of throwing the rope, getting closer every time. Dice produced a handheld spotlight, saying we were low on fuel and would soon have to give up. We talked him into giving us one more attempt. The sturgeon surfaced again. Giving it my all, timing it just as the seagull dove at the fish, I threw the rope. Miraculously the sturgeon swam into the noose as I yanked back on the rope. When I pulled the rope tight, cinching the noose, I couldn't believe the weight of the fish as it tried to dive. If the two guys holding my belt weren't holding on tight, I would have had to let go or would have ended up in the water. Somebody speared the tail with the frog gig. As we pulled it close, Doug sank the claws of the big framing hammer into the skull. We pulled the seven-foot, eight-inch, 150-pound trophy into the boat then tied it off on the deck.

When we returned to the marina and secured the houseboat in the slip, we hung the prize fish from the upper deck where we took photographs of the five men proudly showing off the catch.

Doug put his arm around my shoulder saying, "Well Stoner, you weren't kidding when you said you would put a sturgeon on the boat!"

I told Doug that he wasn't joking when he told me to bring the 50-foot mooring line, that we couldn't have done it without the rope and the help of the entire crew. We called Fish & Game, bending the truth a little bit saying the sturgeon was near dead. We asked if we could keep the oversized fish. It wasn't far from the truth, for it was only a matter of time before it would have died anyhow. They told us it was okay to keep the monster sturgeon.

After we filleted the monster we were rewarded with over 75 pounds of clean white meat. We all ate sturgeon for days, preparing it many different ways with recipes from soaked in egg batter, rolled in flour with spices then pan fried—which is my personal favorite—to baked or barbequed. We made fish tacos and burritos then smoked a majority of the fish. If you have ever tasted smoked sturgeon that has been prepared with good brine you can appreciate this delicacy.

The next morning at 5:45 a.m., I walked into the break room at the Double Joint Rack with a bad hangover. Never forget true pipeliner law: "Don't call in, crawl in." A real good friend of mine named Scotty Too Hotty had already heard the story from Doug. He was sitting on the lunch table rotating his outstretched arm up above his head imitating throwing a lasso.

Scotty says to me with a big smile, "Goddammit Mike, you John Wayned that mf'er.

HOBO

I couldn't stand just sitting around waiting for something to happen, so I came up with plan to take Olivia and my faithful dog Apollo out fishing from the bank of the river, next to the railroad tracks in a spot known as the mud flats. I talked it over with Olivia, to see if she was comfortable with a small fishing trip and leaving the cabin for the first time. Olivia wanted to know why the famous captain Mike Stone would fish from the bank when he had two perfectly good boats sitting in their berths ready to go. I explained my plan: we could see Benicia across the straits from the mud flats. I would bring my binoculars and my night vision goggles with a spotting scope I use while hunting big game. We could watch Eric's shop to get a better idea about what he was up to. She wanted to know if I thought this idea was a safe one. Telling her there was no way he could see us from there, I thought it was a great idea to get her away from the cabin, where she had been like a prisoner for months on end. We packed a small portable propane-fired grill, some wild boar sausage, a fresh salad, a loaf of San Francisco's finest sourdough bread, a cold case of Coors bottles and not one but two bottles of Napa Valley's world-famous Merlot, loading the back of the El Camino. Apollo had already jumped in, making sure he was going. I brought along the ice chest, the surveillance equipment, a couple of folding lawn chairs and a load of seasoned firewood to build a fire on the riverbank, and a 12-foot spinning outfit with a small tackle box.

We stopped at a bait shop on the way where I picked up one dozen of the larger crawdad, like mud shrimp, so I could tie the bait on then leave the rod unattended while I tried to spy on Eric's shop across the water, plus enjoy the company of Olivia. She didn't think it was smart for her to go inside the bait shop, but was also wary of staying outside alone. Leaving the dog with her in the cab of the El Camino for protection as well to make her feel secure, I promised to hurry back. When I walked into the bait shop there were a few older fishermen hanging around, the strong sweet smell of tobacco, the cigar smoke was as thick as fog. I was recognized immediately by the gal behind the counter, having known her for many years. Her family-owned bait shop had been in the area as far back as I could remember. Her father was in a wheelchair as he had lost both legs in an automobile accident, but it didn't stop him from operating their shrimp boat, having had his trawler customized with a ramp and a small elevator to bring him, wheelchair and all, to the wheelhouse where he could still captain-ize.

Annie said to everybody that was sitting on bar stools drinking beers, smoking stogies, "Hey everybody! Look who just walked in, the famous Mike Stone, biggest 'hound' in the valley, captain of the *Sturgeon General*. To what do we owe this pleasure, Captain Mike? Are you chasing skirts or sturgeon today?"

"Long time no see, Annie. Can you fix me up with a dozen mud shrimp? I hate to be rude but I'm in a big hurry."

Making small talk asking Annie about the bite, she told me that all the charter boats were having trouble getting business but heard there was a little action up in San Pablo Bay. Annie and I had been involved at one time, she handed me my bait making contact with her hand on mine.

She came around the counter giving me a hug pushing her heavy chest up against me, whispering in my ear, "When you get this sturgeon mess figured out, Mike, you come back and take me for a boat ride in the *Aquaholic*."

Her hug was lingering where, still smiling, I had to push her away. Annie walked me outside the bait shop and was looking at the El Camino, where she noticed somebody sitting in the passenger seat. Smiling ear to ear she said, "Who's the 'flavor of the month,' Mike?"

I said "C'mon Annie, I learned how to share in kindergarten," laughing out loud answering truthfully, "You know me; I'm just helping out an old friend."

Driving out of Martini town the back way, we followed the railroad tracks downriver to the mud flats. Backing the El-Co up to the water's edge, first things first I rigged the 12-foot surf rod, my dad's old rod and reel, and got my bait in the water. The sun was on its way down, the weather was gorgeous with no wind whatsoever, with the tide on its way out. Olivia seemed a little nervous but occupied herself opening the wine and pouring two glasses. We set up the chairs, then I got out the binoc's, handing them over to her. I mounted my spotting scope with the screw-down clamp on the passenger side window of the El-Co. Focusing the scope, trying to take advantage of the remaining daylight, I had a bird's eye view of the back of Eric's shop, where at first there was very little activity. Leaving the scope I checked on Olivia, who I could tell was apprehensive, being a little nervous about our stakeout. Apollo was working the immediate area, running with his keen nose to the ground, making bigger circles each lap. When he grew tired of his scouting he jumped in the back of the pickup, where he scanned the water for floating driftwood. Apollo would swim out and drag anything he found floating to the bank. A never-ending free supply of fuel for a small bonfire, this was a routine of his. As long as he didn't interfere with my fishing line it was all right with me. It provided him with a good workout, supplying us with firewood.

Apollo was stockpiling driftwood and Olivia was preparing our dinner. I had to admit it was quite relaxing being able to fish without having to worry about a boat or crew while doing what I loved the most, just plain old-fashioned fishing. The mood was romantic as well as relaxing. I rigged the spinning rod with a sturgeon fisherman's alarm clock, clipping a bell on the tip of the rod. Then I went back to observing the shop with the spotting scope, still not a soul in sight with the gates securely shut, no one going in or out.

The sun was setting in the west with the temperature dropping pretty fast. The outgoing tide had almost slowed down with ships cruising lazily by: a tugboat en route to assist a crude oil supertanker on its way to the receiving dock at the Shell Oil terminal, the tugboat pushing six or seven feet of water with its oversized bow, throwing a massive wake causing waves to break on the riverbank. I moved the ice chest to the front of the truck, safely out of the way in case the waves came too close. It was so nice just relaxing, enjoying being at the water's edge. I helped Olivia lift the portable grill then set it on the tailgate of the pickup where Olivia set her folding lawn chair so she could cook the wild boar link sausage, watching me fish at the same time. Helping myself to another glass of the hearty merlot, I poured for Olivia as well. Lighting the gas-fired grill, setting the flame in the low position, I heard the alarm clock sound with a slight but distinct jingle. I got in position then unclipped the bell. Sure enough, I was getting a good bite. I could tell it wasn't a sturgeon because the rod tip was tapping instead of tugging. Waiting until the time was right, I set the hook. When I came back solid the long rod bent in a decent arc, where I figured I had hooked into a 15-pound striped bass. The exhilaration of catching any fish is always good, but nothing compares to coming back solid on a leather lipper.

A slow-moving train was leaving the Martinez Railroad Station where it was lurching and grinding with cars banging as the couplers were engaged, the three electric-powered locomotives pulling the freight cars dug in with their powerful 15,000 horsepower electric motors, the diesel-fired generators blowing black smoke, gaining momentum. I wasn't paying attention to the train because the whole situation was completely normal for the mud flats. I asked Olivia to come down to reel in the fish. Setting the lid on the grill, obviously excited about the chance to play the fish, just for a moment I saw the high school girl come out of her. She dropped her emotional guard. It was the first time I recognized the most beautiful smile in the world as she briefly forgot all her problems. Right there and then I knew why I had loved her so much when we were kids. Standing behind her just a little too close, giving instruction to keep the rod tip up, not letting the fish have any slack, I could tell how much fun she was having so I told her to loosen the drag letting him run to extend the fight. I also wanted this moment to last a little longer. Apollo was in the water waiting to see the fish, being as quiet as a mouse. He was staring at the line when the hair on his back stood on end. In less than a millisecond he was out of the water running toward the train. At first, I thought he had heard or seen an animal of some sort, so I let him go without paying much attention. Apollo's powerful paws were throwing gravel as he lit off for the train. Olivia never stopped playing the fish, doing a good job, her feet planted in the soft dirt with a look of determination on her face.

I was proud of her, for she was patiently fighting the fish, now calm, wanting no more help, telling me she had it under control, wanting me to leave her be.

Just about then I heard a bloodcurdling yell. As I looked in the direction of the train, Apollo had latched on to the seat of the dirtiest pair of pants I had ever seen, belonging to a grizzled old hobo that looked like he had never once had a bath, his Carhartt jacket completely black with grime. As the train was slowly leaving Martinez he had jumped from the boxcar, snuck up to the front of the truck, stolen our ice chest and run back to the train. For the filthy old rail rider an ice chest full of food and liquor was probably better than robbing Fort Knox. If it wasn't for my trusty watch dog, he would have gotten away clean.

Apollo ripped the back pockets off the seat of his hideously dirty pants clean off. Down he went, the ice chest scattering its contents. I called Apollo off but couldn't help laughing. The hobo made it to his feet, showing no fear as he hissed at me, eyes completely crazed. He swore through what was left of his yellow rotted teeth that he would take us both on. This was all too much for me to stand, busting out laughing, admiring his courage as well as his unsuccessful attempt to steal the ice chest, I picked up the bottle of wine and tossed it to him, telling him to enjoy the wine and get his butt back on the train while he still could. He caught the bottle, letting out the wickedest laughter I ever heard as he ran back to the train, bottle in one hand, holding up his pants with the other. He took off with his one inch escape sticks, his skinny legs like broom handles, and no socks in worn out work boots. Turning around I saw Olivia standing on the bank with her foot holding the striped bass on the ground, looking at me like I was insane. She said I must be crazy, giving away our last bottle of twenty-five-dollar wine. I told her he needed it more than we did, and that I had to give him credit for attempting such a bold maneuver. I made a joke saying, "the grizzled old rail rider was a retired pipeliner, you could tell from the Carhartt jacket—just another retired welder, "broke, stoned and busted."

We talked about what had happened, with Apollo playing it off like a hero, he was rewarded with fresh cooked sausage. After a good hard laugh then a good hot meal we both started to relax. Olivia told me I had a reward coming myself for being such a good guy. I threw some wood on the dying campfire then I took Olivia hard and hot right then and there on the bed of the truck.

The sun was completely gone. As the night went by, we stayed there and fished, looking at the three oil refineries across the surface of water, the darker it got the more they looked like metropolitan cities, with the brightly illuminated structures looking like skyscrapers. We both fell into an exhausted slumber on the hard bed of the truck. When I woke up Apollo had snuck into the bed of the truck with us. When I opened my eyes he licked me in the face, staring at me as he was cuddling up closer to Olivia, stealing her body heat, wagging his stubby little tail.

Now wide awake, I checked the time on my Seiko diver's wristwatch: 3:45 a.m. Rigging the spinning outfit with fresh bait and casting out, I resumed the surveillance operation. My first attempt with the spotting scope was fruitless. Out of range with the night vision goggles, but the binoculars were light collective, I could see fairly well even at that distance. Lying in the bed of the El Camino with my back against the cab, Olivia on her side, sleeping like a baby, Apollo snuggling up close in a sitting position, fully alert, on point as usual. The fire had completely died. The tide was still coming in fast with light, lapping waves coming nearly to the back tires of the pickup. Thinking my eyes were playing tricks on me when, across the channel I saw what appeared to be a boat materialize under the covered berth. I pulled the binoculars away from my eyes, blinking to clear my vision, and took another look. The boat was disappearing into the water. I thought I was seeing things when a shadow seemed to slip across my scope of vision, then the boat disappeared as quickly as it appeared. Although I watched for another hour I saw no more movement, writing it off as nothing. I fished until the end of the incoming tide, watching a spectacular sunrise with the tide now slack, at its full height.

Reeling in the spinning outfit and gathering all my gear, careful not to wake Olivia, I fired up the big block with the dual exhaust pipes pointing directly over the water's edge. The throaty growl magnified, it sounded like two grizzly bears circling each other getting ready to fight. Olivia sat up looking at me. Even though she had slept on the hard bed of the truck she was smiling, looking at me with bedroom eyes. So naturally I had to turn off the engine and take her one more time, the sun rising in a crystal clear blue sky with a slight trace of white stratus clouds lining the perimeter of the skyline like a white lace border. Across the water a tugboat operator was getting a free show, letting off a powerful blast with his air horns. I raised my right fist in a half salute, half rodeo rider gesture. Olivia asked what I thought I was doing with a devilish grin. Afterwards we lay there together, no words needed.

The surrounding river started to come to life, the sun was almost all the way up, everything warming as the golden

California sunshine dissipated the morning dew. Wasting no time I was back on the binoc's, glassing the shop until the sun was completely up. Thinking things through over and over, looking at both sides of the coin, E.Z. had messed up Olivia, bad. As much as I wanted to trust her, or believe in her, it was still hard for me to completely swallow her whole story. Considering all this information the only thing that truly bothered me was what Olivia had told me about Eric's big plan to get back on top. I would enjoy nothing better than to see the guy put behind bars permanently. It would be a lot easier to call the authorities but what could I tell them, having no evidence or knowledge of illegal activities?

After giving the situation deep thought, looking around at my immediate surroundings with Olivia and Apollo close at my side, I decided to let things work themselves out for a while and try to take care of some personal business. The sturgeon fishing was still extremely slow where I was running low on cash. The seasonal migratory striped bass run was still months away and the halibut season was not an option for another six months. Deciding the only way to get the ball rolling was to invest some time in myself, go out again and try to catch a large sturgeon, getting the word around the bait shops to get the *General* back in business. The way things were, my charter boat was costing me every month instead of making me money. Having the monthly note for the *General* as well as the rent for both slips added up. We drove back to the cabin. After a big breakfast then a long hot shower I went and opened the barn, where I decided to spend the rest of the day working on my projects.

FLH

When I purchased my motorcycle in 1977, it was one year old, with 3,000 OG miles showing on the odometer. The root beer brown '76 Harley-Davidson was an FLH, Fully-Loaded Harley, with hard saddle bags, front faring windshield, the oversized white king and queen seat, rear cargo box, Wide Glide front end with Appleton spotlights, swing arm suspension, wire spoke wheels with white wall tires. For nearly a hundred years the Harley-Davidson has been famously called a "Hog," which goes back as far as 1910. The Harley-Davidson motorcycle racing team was known as the "wrecking crew" because they had been winning every classification. The most popular of the tracks was the one-mile oval referred to as the "Miler," still a nostalgic race where motorcycle enthusiasts compete to this day. Back in the 1910s a competitor used to take a victory lap with a real live, pet pig named Johnny sitting in front of him, riding passenger on the tanks. He won enough where the world-famous nickname stuck—hogging all the trophies, the loud pipes and oversized tanks earned its nickname for eternity. Harleys have been called Hogs ever since.

When I bought the bike the first thing was to take it home where I was renting a room from Jerry, a guy I had been friends with since the seventh grade and who also owned a similar, even more custom bike. With Jerry's help we quickly stripped off all the excess gear, removing the front faring, the saddle bags as well as the oversized king and queen style seat. This gave the bike a much sportier appearance as well as reducing the overall weight. When we took off the front faring it left the large zeppelin-style, aerodynamic, soft polished aluminum shroud that surrounds the big six-inch headlight with the two smaller four-inch Appleton-style spotlights on either side. This gave the bike the look of the traditional 1936 Harley-Davidson, removing and replacing the seat with a smaller black, single, tractor-style seat that was mounted directly to the frame giving the bike a lower, sleeker look. The twin fuel tanks held 5.5 gallons of gas at full capacity. Back in the old days, one tank held gasoline, the other was the oil reserve. The oil would feed down through the top of the engine by gravity. I had made a lot of mechanical as well as cosmetic modifications throughout the years, upgrading the older technology to keep up with the newer bikes, including changing out the stock carburetor for an S&S high performance, changing the cam to a high lift, upgrading the front and rear sprockets from a nineteen tooth to a twenty-four in the front, from a fifty-four to a forty-eight in the rear, resulting in taller gears with more top end. The FLH came factory with true dual exhaust. Removing the stock factory mufflers and replacing them with Fish-tail straight pipes produced the OG sound from the old steel block. The older models were originally designed for police or military service. They carried heavy equipment where they had a lot of lower end power, but reached top speeds quickly, topping out at around 75 mph. These modifications helped the older bike, with only the four-gear ratchet shifter, to compete with newer models that came equipped with five speed transmissions. I replaced the standard ignition points with a H.E.I., high energy ignition system. I had to customize and modify as the technology improved. The original factory paint job was replaced with a custom black cherry lacquer job. When the bike is in direct sunlight or at night under bright fluorescent lights it looks fiery red, but in the dark she looks "inkwell black." The tires were up-graded from hard rubber, old-school tread design to Dunlop Touring Elites with two-and-a-half-inch "gangster white-walls," as well as changing out the majority of the parts for chrome and polishing all the aluminum, giving the old bike its own personality. I kept the bike plugged into a small bat-tery tender, the trickle charger only put out 2 amps where it stayed fully charged. She would usually start when on the rare occasion that I would take her for a ride, blow the dust off her and grab some wind.

Pulling the bike cover off I gave it a quick inspection, checking tire pressure, fluid levels, leaning the bike side to side listening to how much fuel was in the tanks, making sure it had enough to get to the Union 76 filling station in town where I could top off both tanks with fresh high-oc-tane gasoline, I started the engine feeling my pulse acceler-ate as I depressed the starter button. The engine caught on the third try. With the manual choke restricting the flow of the cool air causing the bike to idle extra high, the pipes put out a higher pitch, shaking the interior of the barn, disturb-ing the peaceful morning.

Apollo was waiting patiently to chase me down the long driveway on my out. Olivia was working in the flower beds and came into the barn, admiring the bike, complimenting me on the old-school paint job and originality. I asked her if she was game to go for a ride, where I already knew the an-swer would be no considering her history with Eric and all his bikes. Olivia loved motorcycles but she wasn't ready quite yet. Wearing an older, well broken in, soft and faded pair of my blue denim bib overalls with a wife beater un-dershirt, a blind man on a galloping horse could see she was not wearing a bra underneath. I had no choice but to turn off the motorcycle engine. Sun shining, birds chirping, right in front of God I had to mount her one more time before I left. After three rounds last night then one more this morning, I was starting to get full control of myself where I was "riding high in the saddle," the barn door wide open with my faithful companion standing guard half in the doorway with his big black head outside where he could see anything moving, his large white teeth showing with his lips curled back in an alligator grin.

I rolled off Olivia, catching my breath when she said with a seductive grin, "Three rounds last night, then twice again this morning. They call you Stone 'cause your stone to the bone."

Cocky and beaming with confidence, trying to be humble at the same time, I acted nonchalant while I strutted around the barn, not talking but feeling it. Olivia said, "Well Stoner, we're right back in a barn where we first started, only this time my horse isn't here to make sure you behave yourself."

We didn't reminisce too long because we both knew the conversation would lead back to Eric, so to avoid an awkward situation I went ahead with taking the bike for a ride, coasting down the long private driveway, Apollo trying to bite my pants leg. Lifting my feet off the floorboards I pulled in the clutch lever and revved the engine, hitting him with exhaust to make him back off. On the open road I grabbed a "handful of throttle." The power of the big V-twin, the sound of open dual exhaust, there is only one bike in the world that produces this sound. It is often imitated but never duplicated. Feeling the wind in my face I realized it had been a long time since I had felt this good, if ever. I knew I had better keep my guard up because when things get going too good for me something usually goes wrong.

Driving into Martini town I filled up with Union 76 ninety-two octane premium unleaded then hit the highway heading east. It was a weekend and traffic was light, with clear skies to where I didn't need a jacket. It felt pretty good to be on two wheels again. I headed east on Highway 4, crossing the Antioch Bridge, running parallel with the Sacramento River then turned right on the Delta Loop. I was going to turn around and head back when I felt dehydrated. Dying for a cold one I pulled into a waterfront resort called The Outrigger, where you can drive in from the road or come in from the water to tie up a boat where the back deck faces the river. If you're ever on the Delta with a hangover The Outrigger serves the best Bloody Mary in the Bay Area.

The scenery around the resort is typical of dozens of marinas/resorts up and down the banks of the Delta Loop. There are marinas every couple of miles on the loop with thousands of boats in regular slips, with plenty of covered berths as well. You will see every kind of boat from a 9-foot rowboat to a 42-foot Fountain offshore-style cigarette boat, even a 1930 ancient yacht barely afloat with paint peeling and water pouring continuously from the bilge pumps. There are house boats that are barges converted to live-aboard with trailers set on the top of the barge, and there's every kind of "River Rat" living in these marinas. Parking the FLH then locking the forks with my big Master lock, I walked into the resort. There was music playing, a Hank Williams Sr. original classic, "Your Cheatin' Heart," go figure. I ordered a Coors Draft, wishing I could see my bike from where I was sitting but having my lock on the fork lock I wasn't too worried, not planning to stay that long, maybe just one beer—famous last words. One thing I always keep in mind: a Harley-Davidson motorcycle can disappear into thin air.

FREAKY IN THE LEAKY TIKI

Sitting at a table on the back deck of the bar, looking at the water when the first beer went down way too well. I was considering just one more, when the bartender brought me another. With a puzzled look on my face, she explained that the second beer was sent over by a lady sitting inside at the bar who asked if my name was Stone and thought she knew me from a long time ago. I told her to tell the lady thanks. The barmaid's name was Bernadette, a tall African American who was definitely easy on the eyes. She was grinning at me like the cat that ate the canary and asked if that was my Shovelhead out front. She said if I was ever in the neighborhood to come back and take her for a bike ride. Of course I gave her my card as she left with a grin, shaking what she had as she walked away. I never ask the ladies for their number, always giving them my card, that way if they call I know they are interested in me, so I'm not wasting my time.

After a couple minutes the woman came out, wearing large black-framed sunglasses with her chestnut brown hair pulled back tight in a ponytail. Not recognizing her in the least, I just sat there smiling to myself, thinking about how many times I had been with Olivia in the last twenty-four hours—three times last night, two more this morning counting the one in the barn. If this had been a normal day with me being single it would have been a nice score, but what can I say, feast or famine. No matter how this current situation played itself out it was going to be an interesting afternoon.

The tall, attractive woman held a wine glass, walking

with a confident dominating gate. Her stomach was flat, she was evenly tanned, obviously having spent long hours of dedication in the gym and the tanning salon as well. I was trying to convince myself that I had made no commitment to Olivia as I was looking at the lady who walked up and stood opposite me across the table. Hesitating before sitting, I could tell she was used to being pampered. As I got up and pulled out her chair the first thing I instinctively noticed was the lack of ice on her left hand, no wedding ring, but plenty of expensive jewelry including rings, necklace, piercings, bracelets and earrings. No tattoos whatsoever. She didn't say a word as she sat staring at my face. I smiled, deciding to play her game, and waited for her to talk. With her already knowing my name and me without a clue as to who she was, feeling I was at the disadvantage from the start, I was racking my memory banks wishing she would remove her sunglasses, so I had a better chance of remembering her face. Wondering if I had priors, from what I could see I could tell she was very attractive.

The barmaid broke the silence asking if she could bring another round. By now I had completely forgotten wanting to get back home, smiling at the server telling her yes please, one more Coors Draft and another glass of wine for the lady across the table. The juke box started with Johnny Cash, "A Boy Named Sue." I waited out the situation. The young lady introduced herself as Cassandra, thanking me for the wine. I told her she didn't have to say thanks because now we were even, as she already sent me the beer earlier. Lifting off her glasses and extending her hand—natural, manicured nails with clear gloss—her handshake was firm. She made intentional, full eye contact with me, smiling, revealing perfectly straight, dazzling white teeth.

She told me that I could call her Cassy, telling me to quit racking my brain trying to figure out who she was, because the last time I saw her she was only thirteen, and that I was going out with her older sister at the time. I remembered right away. Her sister's name was Tammy, a good girl from Discovery Bay whose father was extraordinarily successful in the computer chip industry. Having dated Tammy for a while, we were too young for a committed relationship, things didn't work out and we had gone our separate ways. It wasn't messy, we had remained friends. I told Cassy I remembered her, giving her a compliment on what an attractive lady she had grown up to be. Cassy told me I looked exactly the same with the exception of the graying hair. The last time she saw me I was still a slim, trim, black-haired dude. She thought the upper body weight with the gray hair was a good look on me. I asked her what her sister was doing. Cassy said Tammy was on her third marriage with as many children but was doing well besides having gone through two divorces. I asked about her: had she ever been married? She told me no but she was seeing some guy with no attachments. I smiled and nodded, acknowledging the green light. Studying her body language, figuring to myself the big sister verse little sister scenario, I knew if I wanted I had this in the bag.

The crowd increased as the time went by, the old rickety deck was half full of people as well as the bar inside. We were on the sixth or seventh round when I decided to order appetizers of crab cakes with popcorn shrimp. After eating the delicious entree I knew that if I stayed with the beer I would start to feel too full. Deciding to switch over to something a little stronger and less filling I ordered a double Stolichnaya Russian Vodka with grapefruit juice (Stoli Grape) in a tall chimney tumbler filled with ice. Cassy followed suit ordering a Dirty Martini with double olive. The time went by as the drinks went down. I knew in the back of my mind I had to ride my motorcycle home in the dark down the winding river road, but I was enjoying the company of the young lady who carried herself so well, remembering back when I was seeing her sister that we had always gotten along.

Tammy was one hundred percent class, the fact that her father was extremely wealthy I must admit, made the whole package more appealing. If a guy falls in love and the girl happens to be rather well off, I could see no harm in the situation. As it turned out with her older sister, we were both too young. I would have been number one on her list of past divorces. Cassy was telling me the reason she was at The Outrigger Bar & Grill was that her father kept his 52-foot yacht in a slip in the neighboring marina. When she knew he wasn't around she used the spacious boat as a weekend getaway and playhouse, explaining to me that the boat was older and she was having problems with not having any hot water, asking me if I could come take a look. I knew it was on, telling her I would love to help her out.

Right about then the jukebox was completing its last song when a two-man band started up. They had an electronic keyboard and back up music, with each musician playing more than one instrument. The whole scene looked ridiculously Mickey Mouse, but to my surprise when they started playing requests, they actually did a pretty good job. They played everything from Chuck Berry to The Beatles. Although the back deck of the restaurant was worn, old with peeling paint and weathered wood, the whole atmosphere was lively. Despite me having to ride the bike home down the river roads, running the risk of getting in a wreck or going to jail for drunk driving, I couldn't help but enjoy myself with the company of the younger lady, feeling the alcohol, the buzz from the crowd and the music. When the band played one of my favorites, James Brown, "Papa's Got a Brand New Bag," there was not a single person sitting in a chair. Cassy grabbed my hand and we tore it up. She had the body, looks and little sister had soul. My well-worn Western-style welding boots sliding across the floor. After numerous drinks I could "let it all hang out." Pee Wee Herman couldn't have kept up in his Big Shoes. I caught Bernadette checking us out, I just grinned and kept dancin' harder, paying full attention to "Classy Cassy."

Good people, good music, good times; it was all good. The song ended then the two-man band went straight into Elvis Presley, "Can't Help Falling in Love." The next thing I knew I was slow dancing with Cassy. The other brain was trying to take over. With her hands on my hips she pulled in close. Cassy was a couple of inches shorter than me and her head was comfortably snuggled in the side of my neck. I couldn't help but notice how good she smelled: a combination of expensive Chanel perfume, sun block and just a trace of coconut oil. I gently eased one hand down the length of her back as the romantic song played, running my hand up her spine, my fingertips lightly touching her soft, warm skin. Pushing my fingertips into her hair, reading her body language, I felt her react with accelerated breathing, goose pimples rising on her skin. Feeling the moment, taking a deep breath as I was thinking things through, time seemed to stand still and just for one single enchanting moment, Cassy and I were the only two people on the dance floor or in the world for that matter. When she moved in for our first

kiss, she came in slow with her eyes open. When our lips
met I felt her entire body relax, the whites of her eyes showing as they rolled shut. We kissed slowly at first. As the song
came to an end I backed her into a corner, still standing, but
off the dance floor out of the way. The kiss heated up, with
light touching, a little bit of grinding, my head was starting
to spin from the drinks and from the heat of the moment
when I told her we better go for a walk, get some fresh air
while going to look at her father's yacht.

I paid the tab, leaving Bernadette a fat tip, a big seXXXy
smile on her face as she was winkin' one eye at me. Cassy
and I were walking past my bike holding hands, asking her
if I needed to move the bike closer for safety she told me no,
explaining the boat was moored in the first row of slips. She
was checking out my scooter as the sun was lying down
across the horizon. The lacquer paint looking wet, Cassy
asked if she could sit on the bike, saying she had ridden dirt
bikes and wanted to feel what it would be like to sit on the
big motorcycle. I got on first, bringing the bike upright off
the kickstand then had her strategically sit in front of me
where I could keep the bike from falling over in case she accidently dropped it. She asked me to start the bike so she
could hear the engine. Reaching around her, removing my
big lock from the forks and hanging it on my belt loop, I
turned the chrome ignition switch between the gas tanks in
the middle of the dash to the start position, lifting the manual choke on the front of the S&S carb', shifting the transmission into neutral then depressing the starter button. The
straight pipes with the Fishtail exhaust sounded sharp and
loud, disturbing the peaceful serenity of the Delta setting. I
let the bike warm up then lowered the choke lever allowing
more air into the intake. As the bike idled down I felt the

vibration of the engine, knowing it was having an effect on Cassandra as well. Taking Cassy's right hand, letting her operate the throttle it was obvious by the look on her face she was enjoying the moment. I turned the ignition switch off then locked up the bike.

Having a good buzz going and knowing I was distracted by the lovely young lady, being this far from home with the sun going down, I thought I should be careful and try to gather my wits. Cassy led the way as we walked toward the covered berths past the bar and grill down an older dock, where she opened the security gate. Taking in my surroundings, admiring the scenery of the sun going down across the endless agricultural fields to the west with the boats moored sleepily in their slips, there were low voltage sodium lights illuminating the covered berths that were filled with mostly older cabin cruiser style boats. Cassy told me the Chris-Craft was a 1963 Explorer. She was called *The Leaky Tiki*. Her father had bought her years ago in original, factory condition. Although the boat was many years old it had never been used. The low hours are great but sitting without running regularly is hard on the boat—a "dock queen" to say the least. Since then the new owner had invested endless hours as well as a boat load of cash to restore her to her original beauty. The teak and mahogany were reflecting the overhead lights, magnifying the many coats of hand rubbed clear. Cassy stepped up into the Chris-Craft, standing there watching me admire the pristine cruiser.

She asked me with a smile, "What are you waiting on sailor?"

I replied, "Permission to board, ma'am?"

She told me permission granted, we both took off our shoes to get onboard—one step in the right direction. Cassy

took me on a tour of cruiser. The wheelhouse was completely restored as well as the rest of the boat. The steering
wheel was wood-spoked with highly polished brass, the
dash was equipped with two of everything for the starboard
and port side engines, the motor house holding freshly rebuilt twin diesels leading to direct drive brass propellers.
We went down the stairs into the cabin area where there
were fore and aft cabins, a full head and galley where everything was fresh and new. Her father was a wealthy man and
he had spared no expense outfitting the gorgeous, classic
cabin cruiser.

Cassy produced a bottle of Smirnoff Blue Label 101-proof
Voddy, setting us both up with Vodka Martinis. She explained that she wasn't sure if she had the shore power
switch in the correct position, thinking she was running the
batteries down on the boat resulting in no hot water for the
shower. I took a look to make sure everything was in order,
finding the only problem was a tripped breaker. After reset-
ting it and inspecting the recently installed battery tenders,
figuring everything was in order, I told her she would have
hot water in an hour or so. Cassy dimmed the lights, lighting
candles and incense, putting some music on the stereo,
Diana Ross and the Supremes, "Baby Love." Of course I was
thinking about Olivia. I was still a single man, trying to convince myself this was justifiable when Cassy moved in on
me and kissed me full on the mouth, a three to four minute
long, pulse accelerating, eyes shut romantic kiss. Although
tall she was still feather light, maneuvering in close, already
on my lap. I had to admit she was passionate, without hesitation she was going right after what she wanted. Holding
the back of her head with my fingers lightly grabbing the
hair on the nape of her neck while running my other hand

with my fingertips down the ripples on her flat, washboard stomach, I had cotton mouth. My breathing was irregular as my heartbeat increased. It was time to get Freaky in the Leaky Tiki.

It should have been all net, when I did something I couldn't believe, as I stood up, following my gut feeling telling her I had to go. The Man of Stone was walking away from a slam dunk smoking hot young lady. She asked if there was a problem and I told her I could not explain it if I tried. But some inner instinct inside my head told me to get up and go so I got up and went, telling her I was sorry but I was out of there, giving her one of my cards and promising to make it up to her someday, kicking myself in the rear as I walked down the dock. Normally I would have been "on it like Blue Bonnet."

TRY HARD OR DIE HARD

Knowing that Olivia had her hooks set pretty deep in me whether I would admit it to myself or not, I got back to my bike thinking I could smell gas and figuring it had to be from running the engine earlier. Sobering alarms were now going off. I realized my instincts were reacting to the gut feeling as I unlocked the fork lock. Setting the petcock to the on position as I was bringing the bike upright I thought she felt light, writing it off to adrenaline and alcohol. Starting the bike, sitting there for a minute gathering my senses, looking around for the law for I'd had way too much to drink, I reached under my seat pulling out a pair of clear lens safety glasses and a pair of goatskin heli-arc gloves I use for riding. While I tried to convince myself the logical thing to do would be to shut the bike off then go back inside the boat with Cassandra, the longer I sat there the stronger my instincts became telling me to start the bike and go home.

Not having ridden twenty feet with the wind in my face, the feel of the powerful motorcycle between my legs sobered me right up, knowing I would be all right to drive home. I could usually ride better than I could walk after excessive drinking. I knew if I got pulled over I was going downtown, do not pass go, go straight to jail. The last thing I needed was a Deuce, so I drove as reserved and conservative as possible, obeying speed limits, trying to keep the noise from the straight Fishtail, dual exhaust to a minimum. Turning left off the Delta Loop getting on the highway I heard the engine miss with the carburetor starving for fuel. My first thought was that I had forgotten to open the petcock. Coasting as I shifted into neutral, my left hand dropping off the handle grip going instinctively to the petcock, I found the valve in the on position. Knowing I had only driven 30 miles at the most since filling both tanks earlier that day, and that my total range was at least 150 miles without having to rely on switching the petcock to reserve, I pulled over and rocked the bike side to side listening for the sound of almost full tanks. But I could tell that both tanks were near empty. Figuring some River Rat must have needed my gas pretty bad, I turned the petcock to reserve then started my bike.

The night was exceptionally dark with little or no moon, my big headlight illuminating various types of flying insects I operated the toggle switch behind the headlight to turn on the Appleton spotlights for extra light on the dark winding river road. The closest gas station was 3 or 4 miles on the other side of the river in Antioch, figuring it would be close but I thought I could make it, shifting from first to second on up into third gear where I would conserve the most fuel. I noticed a familiar "box style" truck off to the side of the road, but couldn't place it so I kept going, making a mental note.

Now within a couple of miles of the filling station I still had to make it over the Antioch Bridge, spanning a thousand yards over the San Joaquin River. The truck with the box on the back was following me with no headlights—a chill went up my spine. The bridge was only one lane in either direction; the truck was behind me blocking my only way out if I ran out of fuel. My first thought was that someone was trying to steal my bike, but I realized it was me the truck was after. Whoever it was had planned this out hoping I would run out of gas on the deserted part of the river road or, even worse, crossing the Antioch Bridge. At first Cassy was a suspect in the conspiracy, but I realized the whole situation might have been coincidental. I was probably getting paranoid. Maybe the truck forgot to turn on his headlights, maybe the bike was losing fuel while it was running, possibly the jets in the carb' were sticking, where fuel was leaking out the overflow tube. I remembered smelling gas back at the parking lot—but not five gallons.

Before long the carburetor was starving for fuel. Downshifting from third gear, bypassed second into first, I leaned the 750-pound bike on its left side to make the precious remaining drops of gas gravity-fill the fuel line as the engine was sputtering, barely pushing the bike over the remaining one-eighth mile of grade. Once at the top I could coast down the other side taking the off ramp at the bottom of the bridge then hopefully coast into the Chevron station. Still watching my rear-view mirrors the truck that was laying back was now accelerating trying to catch me before I made it safely to the top. When I was maybe 25 feet from the top, with the bike leaning over so far the floorboards on the left side were scraping the pavement with me leaning my body the opposite way to counterbalance the motorcycle, as the engine coughed its last breath of life, I left the transmission in first and engaged the starter button trying to use the 12-volt battery to rotate the starter to push the bike over the remaining 20 feet of grade. I was almost there when I smelled the plastic insulation of the starter wiring beginning to overheat. Worst-case scenario, if the truck tried to run me down I could jump from the bridge into the river, but I wasn't ready to give up without a fight.

Jumping from the bike to push with only a minimum of momentum remaining from running the starter, I hit the ground running knowing I had no choice; "Try hard or die hard." I had a bad case of cotton mouth from drinking all day, my legs felt like they were solid lead. Making a mental note to myself that I had to get back in shape, as my head was about to explode and my lungs felt like every breath I inhaled was going to be my last. Somehow I managed to grab a second wind as I barely crested the top of the bridge, swinging my right leg over the bike, trying to keep control of her I nearly passed out from the head rush. I could feel my heartbeat behind my eyes pounding like a drum. Taking deep slow breaths through my nose I tried desperately to control the speed of my rapid heart rate while looking in my mirrors for the truck I knew had to be coming. I had my bike in neutral, turning off my lights to preserve what remaining juice was in the battery.

In spite of the present situation being far from over, I laughed out loud in celebration of making it over the crest of the bridge. Gaining speed my head was almost cleared up when the truck came barreling over the top of the bridge, headlights on high beam. The truck was shifting gears as it too was struggling up the steep bridge. Just then I saw the most beautiful thing I'd ever seen: a pair of California State Highway Patrol Cruisers sitting at the bottom of the bridge next to the toll crossing entrance. Never in my life had I ever been so happy to see a lawman. Whoever was in that truck must have spotted the CHP at the same time, as I heard him let off the gas then keep going on the highway. Turning on my headlight and rolling right past the two CHP Cruisers with my motor off, the only noise coming from the rear chain, I took the off ramp and coasted right up to the pump, filling both tanks with premium unleaded. Keeping my eyes peeled for the truck, I tried to start the bike but was unsuccessful with the battery being dead and the starter wire burned out. So I pushed it over to the bathroom area then put the bike on the kickstand, where I put my big lock on the forks.

Washing up, splashing plenty of cold water on my face, slicking back my graying hair, combing it with my black oval-shaped "Jailhouse Rock" fingertip comb, I took a long hard look at myself in the smudged gas station mirror. My hair was a lot grayer than I remembered, the crow's feet around my eyes seemed to be "branded" into my skin from endless hours of exposure to ruthless ultraviolet rays from fishing as well as working outdoors in the pipefitting industry—back to reality. Inspecting myself for lipstick or signs of another woman, I couldn't help but smile at the narrow escape. Trying to rehydrate, cupping my hands to gulp plenty of water from the sink faucet, now I had to push start the bike. Scoping the parking lot looking for the truck, the law and any kind of downhill grade, ignition in the on position, petcock on with the transmission in second gear I pulled in the clutch, pushing the bike toward the downhill grade. If you have ever push started a 750-pound bike, you know this a chore in itself. After drinking, it's even harder to do without dropping your bike. Gathering speed then jumping with my rear hitting the seat at the precise moment I let the clutch out, the back tire barked and the ignition caught—sweetest sound I ever heard.

Driving home in deep thought, my relaxing ride had turned out to be a heck of a day. Thinking about the events that had unfolded with this new information, over and over in my head, Apollo was waiting for me in the drive. I could tell Apollo was worried and was glad I was home. Putting the bike away in the barn I inspected my melted wiring, letting the bike cool down so I can put the cover on it. Then I went inside, where there was a note from Olivia that my dinner was in the fridge. I popped the plate in the microwave and wolfed down the food. I filled up a big glass with ice water and took a couple of aspirin getting ready for the hangover I knew I couldn't avoid. After taking a long hot shower, when I climbed into bed with Olivia she woke up, asking how my ride was. Bending the truth, I told her I had a little bike trouble but did not tell her the whole story because there was no need to worry her. Olivia rolled over and for the first time slept with her back to me.

As I lay in bed I could not sleep because something was bothering me about the scene that had taken place on the bridge. I was exhausted from the long day with the narrow escape and the alcohol. Trying hard to put my finger on it, the truck seemed familiar. I lay awake in bed for a long time, finally my mind gave in to complete exhaustion and I fell into a deep but troubled sleep.

CHAPTER 10

STONE TO THE BONE

After the Antioch Bridge incident I told myself it was time to get back in shape, digging out a Universal workout machine I had covered in the back of the barn. It was an older machine, a dinosaur called "The Iron Worker" but with the cable rigs, adjustable bench press plus the free weights and heavy bag it was all I needed for a complete workout. Starting gradually with the weights then the heavy bag, jogging the surrounding hills where it served two purposes: getting my wind back while conditioning my lungs and heart, plus taking off a few extra inches and pounds. After the weights I split and stacked firewood for the upcoming winter, using the old-school "sledge and a wedge." I always figured why waste all the energy on weights or road work when swingin' the "eight pound beater" was a work out on its own, that would produce firewood for the winter.

Having forgotten how much I enjoyed working out on the seventy-pound canvas bag, it wasn't long before the snap came back. The power of my punches seemed stronger than before because even though I had recently lost ten or twelve pounds I was still at least forty pounds heavier than the last time I had hit the heavy bag. Standing in the barn after a good workout on the bag, trying to catch my breath, the weather was a little overcast with the coastal fog dropping the overnight temperatures. Apollo was sitting at the door of the barn on point as usual when I noticed Olivia taking a long look at me. Figuring I had dropped a good fifteen pounds, I felt pretty close to being in shape — still heavy for where I wanted to be but running five miles every other day, feeling confident — wearing faded, soft worn out sweatpants, no shirt with sweat running down my chest, I knew I had Olivia`s attention as she came up handing me a bottle of cold water.

As I was wiping down the sweat off my chest and arms she said she had something she had to tell me, that I had to promise not to get mad. Telling her it sounded pretty important so let's hear it, she told me she noticed there were a lot of bills piling up. Olivia knew they were overdue, I knew right away she was talking about the note for the *General*, the monthly fees for both slips down at the marina and also utilities at the cabin. The *General* had been sitting for over three months. There was no work at the union hall and my unemployment had expired a month ago, where I had no real money coming in. The rent on the cabin was well overdue but the owner / landlord knew he would get his in good time, where I could easily "work off rent around the spread." Olivia started out by saying it was only fair if she paid her own way because the money she gave me to hold was just sitting there not doing anybody any good. Knowing where she was going with this I started to protest. Olivia was smart: she hadn't given me all her cash in case she needed a way out — can't blame her for having survival instincts.

Asking me again not to get mad but she had already opened the bills, paying all the overdue balances. I couldn't do anything but swallow my pride, telling her thanks and that I would make it up to her. Olivia smiled that "bad little girl" smile, telling me I could start right now if I wanted to. So the way I saw it, I didn't have any choice. We spent the afternoon in bed, and during our third time around the bases I was looking down at Olivia and her eyes were rolling in her head like the wheels on a slot machine, and I knew I was doing my job. Olivia was making me feel like a man and I know I was making her feel like a woman. Rolling over, trying to catch my breath, we were both soaked in perspiration. I looked at Olivia as we were laying there in complete relaxation, where I have to admit sometimes life can be really rough.

Later in the day, after a long hot bath and a big lunch, Olivia explained that the money she gave me to hold was over $20,000 in cash plus $5,000 in pocket money, asking me if I wanted to invest it or if I had any use for the money. I told her that the sturgeon would have to return someday, where I was fairly content with the way things were going. I wasn't worried about life in general. Being able to work part-time as a union steamfitter and operating the *General* during the fishing season was all I ever really wanted. I didn't plan on getting rich but the more I thought about it, having been alone with only myself and the dog to worry about, maybe if things continued to go well with Olivia I would have to rethink everything. Olivia might want something more. I asked her how she felt, what were her thoughts? She answered if I was happy she was happy; for now we should just let things work themselves out. I knew she was holding something inside but instead of trying to dig it out, I let it go for the time being.

Olivia asked if I would take her shopping, telling me that since I had lost a little weight she wanted to buy me some clothes that fit a little better. I said I couldn't say no to an offer like that so we got ready then went to town. The spring weather was warm but not too hot. Having recently rubbed out the paint job on the El Camino, when I pulled off the car cover the deep cranberry red color looked better than ever. I fired up the big block, the noise from the open exhaust with the pipes reverberating off the enclosed carport. It seemed to make the El-Co come to life, the carport felt like it was shaking when I tapped the foot feeder, releasing the choke and letting her idle down. Apollo knew he wasn't going, trying to act mad but I knew as soon as I had it in gear he would be chasing me down the long drive.

The "fresh" look on Olivia's face told me this was a good thing, figuring it was due to the fact that she was going shopping for clothes, which I wrote off as a women's thing. We drove into town where she insisted we shop for me first. When I looked at the clothes I had on it wasn't hard to figure out why. My white T-shirt was so worn you could read a newspaper through it, my faded, tattered Wranglers hanging off my hips with my worn slip-on Red Wing welders' boots ready for the "through crew." After a couple hours, standing in front of a full-length mirror looking like a new man, sporting honey-colored lizard skin boots, black Wranglers, a light, black mock neck sweater with a silver and black hounds tooth light blazer, I hardly recognized myself but Olivia was smiling. That's all that counted at the time. She tried on several dresses, modeling for me then settling on a cocoa brown outfit that was split high, a gold belt wrapped around her hour glass waist, showing off her heavy chest and her gorgeous oversized hips. She picked out gold pumps then did some quick magic with her hair and produced some jewelry from her bag, telling me she was ready to go to dinner.

Olivia put on her makeup in the car as we headed across the Benicia Bridge, the *Glomar* sitting silently with the majestic Moth Ball Fleet in the background. The water was a little choppy with the southeast prevailing wind working against the incoming tide. I could see the marina where my two boats were just sitting collecting dust. Olivia saw me looking toward the marina then scooted over next to me in the seat. She tried to start a conversation to take my mind off the fishing business being so bad. Just the sound of her voice made me feel better, after all we were both dressed to the nines in brand new threads. The El Camino was lookin' sharp, the sun was shining, it was beautiful day plus I had a smoking hot, heavy-chested babe sitting next to me with a pocket full of money. What could go wrong?

GUN BARREL

Stopping at the toll crossing, Olivia insisted she pay even the ten-cent fee because the whole day was on her. As we drove through the toll plaza a motorcycle pulled up two lanes over to my left. I knew from the sound it had to be a Buell, a high-performance "crotch rocket" manufactured by Harley-Davidson. The bike was black on black with a highly polished aluminum frame, the rider outfitted in a black and silver full leather riding suit with knee high racing boots, a knife big enough to row a small boat tucked in his boot, the Buck Woodsman, with its seven-inch blade always at the ready, a full-face Shoei helmet painted like a life-sized, robotic skull, the bike having had a lot of work done to the already notoriously fast machine.

When the bike passed me he was "bangin' gears," speed shifting with no clutch, the front tire coming off the ground every shift. Looking at my speedometer, we were doing 50 miles per hour when he passed me like I was standing still. Losing sight of him, he had to be doing 150-plus. For some reason everything got quiet. Alarms went off in my head. Olivia grabbed the inside of my right leg with her left hand, pulling herself up closer to me in the seat. Looking at her, with her sea green eyes, tan cleavage exposed in the new cocoa brown dress, trying to watch the road at the same time, Olivia gave me a short but nice kiss then told me to watch where I was going. Putting my arm around her shoulders I tried to concentrate on the road when out of nowhere the bike materialized on my left. The biker must have slowed down as he hid behind a big rig, enabling him to sneak up from behind. He stayed right beside me for a full minute. There was a lot of custom work, with a polished aluminum frame, the coolest custom paint job, inkwell black with hundreds of white and silver pearlescent skulls in a hundred different formations. The rider was looking dead ahead, holding my exact speed. Something wasn't right. The whole bike was entirely trick, but the right handlebar end was exposed metal instead of being covered by the end of the handle grip. Anybody that meticulous would have fixed the damaged grip. My mind started to work, but I could not figure what was bothering me. Speeding up to seventy the bike stayed with me. Then I braked down to 55 when the rider of the motorcycle hit the gas and again disappeared.

I don't know why but my mind drifted for a minute to a job I had been on a few years back at Moffett Field in Mountain View, California, at the NASA Space Research Center, where the space shuttle was tested in a large dome, purged with nitrogen to simulate conditions in outer space. The air jets provide hypersonic flow techniques for testing material breakdown in support of aerospace research. The Space Shuttle was tested for re-entry of earth's atmosphere with the high temperatures due to friction from traveling at re-entry speed. The presence of the nitrogen purge plus lack of oxygen eliminate the risk of the space shuttle bursting into flames upon re-entry. The nitrogen is piped in through a series of high-pressure manifolds where from the incoming six-inch pipeline source, which leads to an ultra-compressor the nitrogen is squeezed then forced through a manifold. Paul, the foreman and friend as well as "union brother" had dropped the tailgate to unload the truck, pulling two Black and Decker Wildcat 7,000 rpm angle grinders and a new full box of Norton Blue 9-inch x 1/4-inch grinding discs but only one power cord. Asking the boss where the second power cord was, Paul answered he was sorry, but he had meetings all week where I was on my own. The job consisted of fabricating a super high-pressure manifold capable of continuous operation at 7500 pounds of operating pressure.

The U.S. Navy is a frugal bunch. They were recycling the barrels left over from numerous outdated battleships. The 40-foot by 6-inch inner diameter, 10-inch outer diameter, with 2-inch XXX heavy wall thickness, high carbon steel barrels were running horizontal in a group of six. My job was to grind 37-degree bevels on the ends of the square cut barrels. Paul said there was no hurry; I had all week to fabricate. I told Paul to bring me another power cord in case I burned out the only one I had. I remembered the old timers on the job, talking about the good old days, having to handle the old pipe with the heavy wall thickness, the old slicks referred to it as "gun barrel."

Not knowing why, I was thinking about this when the bike came up fast on my left hitting the front brake hard as he was standing on the front foot pegs and leaning over the handlebars, the back wheel coming almost two feet off the pavement. He was in complete control. In less than a millisecond I knew who was on that bike: the same guy who sabotaged my motorcycle then tried to run me down on the Antioch Bridge. I realized in the same instant why he was elevating the height of his handlebar: he was taking aim, and now I was staring almost point blank into a gun barrel.

Eric had installed a .410 shotgun chamber in the right handle grip; the 3-inch high base shotgun shell loaded with double ought buck shot, eight 3/16-inch pellets. I had my foot on the brake pedal as he was lining up his handlebar with the driver's window. All in the same moment I saw the muzzle flash from the handlebar, with catlike reflexes tapping the four-wheel disc brakes as the blast from the sawed-off style shotgun chamber hit directly on the driver's side post of the windshield, taking out the driver's window and the windshield. If I had not tapped the brakes when I did the shotgun blast would have killed us both at almost point-blank range.

The cab of the truck exploded in a cloud of powdered glass. Looking at Olivia to make sure she was okay, I floored the foot feeder to the fire wall, yanking the steering wheel hard to the left trying to take out the bike and rider, but he was already three car lengths in front, throttle wide open, banging the gears as he screamed away. Checking my gas gauge I had a half tank, telling Olivia to buckle up and keep an eye out for the law. Having installed a four-point restraint system in the El-Co along with a two-inch stainless steel roll bar behind the bench seat, I wasn't that worried if things went wrong. We crossed the bridge at speeds well over a hundred miles per hour, dodging in and out of the light traffic. Eric, standing the Buell on its back tire, was shifting gears while riding a wheelie most of the way across the bridge, his gloved left hand held up flying me the bird. I will say one thing, that dude could flat ride a bike.

After crossing the bridge then turning right heading east on Highway 680, the bike's custom exhaust was screaming as he hit the gas hard. The wind is notorious in this part of the valley. As I was gaining speed, using the air bag system I lowered the suspension for better handling with the high winds and slight curves. The bike was doing 160-plus, Eric lying down across the gas tank in the tucked position with his back feet on the rear pegs, café racer style. The wind was coming through the low spots in the rolling foothills so strong that watching E.Z. hold a track on the farthest left side of the highway, the wind was sweeping his bike across the two lanes. This side wind was causing the bike to go into a high-speed wobble if he went over 160, otherwise the 200-mph bike would have been long gone.

The El-Co was feeling the wind as well. As I would keep edging over close to the K-rail divider on the left, when the force of the wind hit the driver's side it would literally wash the El-Co over to the right shoulder. Using the Air Ride System I had the front end as close to the pavement as possible with the rear slightly raised, Pro stock style. The wind under the nose coming in at over 150 mph, plus the side wind coming in from the south, all it would take is a little air underneath the chassis to flip the 4,000 pound El Camino end over end. As we came out of the curves there was about a four-mile straightaway left before the freeway ended. Knowing once he could hold the bike in a straight line it would eliminate the high speed wobble, when Eric hit top end the bike would be gone, so there was only one chance, I had to make it or break it.

Flipping the switch on the nitrous injection system, when I put the hammer down the acceleration jerked with such a violent force that our heads bounced off the rear glass. The big block was wound tighter than a ten day clock. I knew the 454 could not handle this kind of abuse for too long but it didn't matter, I had to go for broke. Olivia never said a word. She looked like she was in a trance, her face drained of color. The shotgun blast alone wasn't bothering her, or the high speeds; it was the fact that Eric had been stalking us. Now we were chasing him down the freeway, she was obviously petrified; I understood why. Closing the distance between the back of the bike and the front end of the El Camino, less than ten feet from taking out the bike with the front bumper of the truck, as the road straightened out the El-Co was hitting uneven road surfaces. I couldn't adjust the Air Ride for fear of flipping over. The Hooker Headers were dragging, throwing sparks, when the turbo-mufflers tore away. The 454, now with wide open headers, sounded like a dragster coming down the highway, the deafening noise like a freight train running through my head. With only two feet of exhaust left, straight headers, the big block was blowing fire, with flames feathering out from underneath the front fenders. The El-Co coming down the highway over 150 mph must have looked like a "rocket sled from hell."

As I straightened out the front end, the rear of the El Camino was drifting off the soft shoulder, the independent Jaguar rear end pushing the 4,000 pound truck dead ahead with the BFGoodrich Radial T/A's digging in, throwing a rooster tail of gravel. The tires were rated at a maximum of 120 mph. I had pushed them well over that speed before, but never for this long. The right rear tire, repeatedly slipping off into the soft shoulder, started to come apart, the soft rubber compound coming off in chunks, exposing the wire of the steel belted radial. When the tire blew the right rear of the El-Co dropped down, causing the pickup to power slide out of the corner into the straight away, the beauty ring and center cap coming off the rim at 150 mph rolled past the El-Co. Eric was less than five feet from my front end and I was closing when the Radial T/A disintegrated and the chassis dropped, tearing off a high-pressure line from the Air Ride system. The frame of the El Camino now slammed on the pavement, throwing sparks from underneath in all directions, the rubber stripped from my right rear steel rally rim now spinning on the road surface throwing sparks like a "Pinwheel."

Less than two feet away from the bike, pushing 7,000 rpm, I could smell the lubrication starting to breakdown as the bearings started to burn; the valves starting to float, solid lifters were screaming in protest. Praying that the double roller timing chain and four-bolt main would last one millisecond longer, the pressure gauge on the nitrous cylinder showed I had less than one pound left, but I had Eric in my sights. I was all in, trying to force the foot feeder through the fire wall when I heard a noise like a fork in a garbage disposal. The bearings spun on the forged stainless steel crank. When the connecting rod gave she threw a rod still attached to the piston, leaving a hole in the side of the block like a stick of dynamite had been detonated inside the combustion chamber. The freeway was filled with black smoke plus the steam from the cooling system, as the big block self-destructed from the inside. The timing chain stripped as the valves clattered and bent. Before I could react we went into a high-speed slide. Somehow I managed to gently pump the brakes as the rear end locked up. Shifting into neutral we went into a spin, still moving at over 100 mph. As the pickup spun around its first rotation the hinged, padded Tonneau bed cover came apart, not designed to go in reverse at high speeds, the wind ripping it from its mounts as the truck spun around it blew off the back scattering shattered fiberglass all over the highway.

On the left there was a K-rail divide with the open marsh land on the right. The El Camino hit the concrete K-rail rear-end-first with the impact caving in the rear quarter panel. The tailgate ripped away from its hinges on one side dragging behind the El Camino. After five or six rotations the pickup came to a halt with the front end halfway in the marsh, the chassis sitting slammed on the asphalt. There were truck parts strung out over a mile down the highway.

There she sat, windows blown out, smoke and steam rising from what was left of the big block, tailgate on the ground, rear quarter panel caved-in, trails of fluids leading to what was left of my 1970 El Camino. Even with the motor blown, body and paint destroyed with the frame on the ground and barely able to read my "Praise the Lowered" license plate frame I couldn't help but think the El-Co still looked bad as he!!

Sitting there for a few seconds taking in long deep breaths, praying out loud thanking God that we were both still alive, Eric had vanished into thin air with no sign of him or his bike. Olivia just stared straight ahead. We heard the sirens; first California Highway Patrol then several Solano County Sheriffs. I told Olivia not to say a word about Eric to the authorities because now this was personal, where I was taking it to another level. The CHP repeated the same questions over and over, where we kept repeating that we didn't know who fired the shot or that it was a motorcycle at all, wanting Eric for myself. For all I knew he would beat the charges in court then come at me again. The Highway Patrol officer asked me what was under the hood.

They explained they had me on aircraft radar at speeds over 160, which I knew was a felony violation. Knowing I was on my way to jail I still couldn't stop from grinning at the performance of my beloved hot rod, SS El Camino.

The officer asked me if there was a motorcycle involved, which I denied. He knew I wasn't telling the whole truth, the officer having a sneaking suspicion I would take care of this matter on my own. He told me if I didn't give up more information he had no choice but to arrest me. They cuffed me, putting me in the back of the sheriff's car as a tow truck showed up. Olivia was taking information on how to get me out of jail as the tow truck was backing up to the rear end of the El Camino. When the driver got out I could not believe what I was seeing: Russell steps out, looking bigger than life itself wearing his customary two-sizes-too-small black Harley-Davidson T-shirt, his Wranglers so tight they were cutting him in half.

Walking up to the sheriff's cruiser he looks me dead in the eyes saying just loud enough for me to hear, "Looks like you're having a pretty bad day, Stoner." Russell took a long look at Olivia, reminding me of a hungry lion looking at a lost baby deer then he got real serious, telling me, "Hey man, no hard feelings. I give you my word as a man this is strictly business. I'll make sure to take good care of what's left of your beautiful SS El Camino."

Silently nodding, I had to take his word. Olivia was standing on the side of the freeway in her brand new gold pumps and the brown dress with the split up the side, with the wind picking up everybody's eyes were on her, including mine.

They asked her repeatedly what happened. She said over and over she heard a bang then we got in the wreck. A cab was pulling up as I was hauled away, cuffed in the back of the sheriff's cruiser, a plan forming in my head.

VACAVILLE SHERIFF'S STATION

I was booked and fingerprinted by two "corn fed country boys." The two deputies were brothers, clean shaven with thick black short hair, both over 6-foot and a good 200 pounds each they were dressed in matching dark blue coveralls with the pants tucked into their black lace-up combat-style steel-toed boots. They looked like two bear cubs, both wearing sheriff's riot gloves with the lead sewn into the knuckles. I asked when I would have an opportunity to make a phone call but was denied. One of the rednecks smirked, telling me we could get to that later if I really wanted. During processing they were rough. After fingerprinting then profile pictures they manhandled me into a holding cell that was occupied by three other men. There were four cots with thin mattresses where I caught maybe five hours of sleep. When they woke me up and moved me to a bigger cell, by now it was past midnight, the cells filing up with men who were being detained. The intake cell, which was designed to hold 10 people at maximum capacity, had 22 full grown men: a few drunk drivers, routine traffic warrants, no hard-core criminals — the normal Friday night crowd. The floor was covered with trash from brown-bag-style lunches of cold, moldy, stale cheese sandwiches, warm sour milk, and empty cartons covering the floor. The only toilet in the cell was clogged, filled to the rim with vomit, feces, urine and toilet paper. Three or four of the men in the cell had been beaten senseless. One of the men let out a long whistle at me standing there all dressed up.

I said with a grin, "If you're whistling at me I'll put one of these brand new five-hundred-dollar size ten lizard skin boots right up your ass." A few of the older guys laughed, as all was well for now.

The two young rednecks came down the hall dragging an African American gentleman with his arm twisted so high behind his back I don't know why it didn't break. There was fresh blood dripping from his mouth and nose, and from the way he was breathing I could tell they had done a number on his ribs as well. It was obvious the young jailers had beaten the man and were enjoying every minute of it. I knew I shouldn't have said anything, but I asked what happened to him. One of the bear cubs answered that the man had to make a phone call, and then asked me if I still wanted to use the phone. Telling him no, I would have to pass on that, he told me good answer. I walked over to a corner, pulling a passed out drunk away from the wall then backed into the corner where I squatted down in a sitting position with my back to the walls. I faded out with one eye open.

In the morning the jailer told me a good-looking gal had posted my bail. But when I got outside the waiting area, Olivia was not in sight.

Eric, thinking quickly, had found the first Hispanic landscaper with a van, asking for a business card then taking the landscaper prisoner at gun point. He had locked him in the back of the van bound and gagged, pulling into the sheriff's station donning the landscaper's hat, jacket and a respirator to hide his face. He put on the backpack-style blower then started working the landscape, blowing down the walkways.

His plan had been when Olivia and I walked out together he would gun us down. He had planned on killing us both in cold blood under the disguise of the landscaper, but when Olivia walked out alone to check on the cab Eric thought, *even better*, he would kidnap Olivia then drive off with her in the van. E.Z. would use her for bait, knowing I would come looking for him.

Walking out of the sheriff's station stretching my stiff legs, not seeing Olivia at all, I looked around outside in the parking lot where there was an irate cab driver who said some nice girl had stiffed him for a fat fare all the way from Martinez, I knew right away that Eric now had Olivia. I could feel the black rage building.

RECON

I took the the cab home, promising the driver he would get his money when we got back to the cabin. When we got there he tried to make a joke, saying if I didn't have the money he would take my brand new boots instead. Shutting him down with one glance in his rearview mirror the cab driver knew right away I was not in a joking mood. Finding the stash spot of Olivia's cash, I paid the taxi driver his fare. After getting out of the stiff clothes then showering off the stench of the holding cell, I ate a big breakfast of grits and Jimmy Dean sausage with eggs. Next thing I got geared up for the first part of my plan.

I was dressed in an old pair of dark blue coveralls with big pockets. In the back of the carport I had one more vehicle left: "Old Yeller," a 1973 Ford F-350 one-ton dually, four-wheel drive welding rig—canary yellow with a custom black bed. Pulling the tarps off the rig, knowing all the batteries were dead, I grabbed a full 5-gallon gas can kept behind the barn. I put a couple of gallons of fresh gas in the tank of the welding machine then cranked over the Lincoln red face, old-school welding machine—copper wound SA-200, the old-fashioned way, with a hand crank in the front just like an antique Model T automobile. After a good warm up, I flipped the toggle switch from high to low idle, switched the amperage setting to the lowest minimum position. I opened the hood then strung out the welding leads, connecting them to the big Group 31 DieHard battery, letting the battery charge while checking the fluids under the hood then checking air in the Michelin tires. The Ford came stock from the factory with a 22-gallon saddle tank behind the seat, but any pipeliner worth his salt has an auxiliary 40–50 gallon tank behind the cab with a 12-volt electric fuel pump. The drag up tank is fabricated in the bed where you can get free gas from a contractor. It's known as a "drag up" tank because the day you quit your job you make sure to fill the drag up tank full of the company's free gas. The drag up tank was dry as a bone so I poured what was left of the five gallon can into the saddle tank. The cold-blooded Ford came back to life after turning the key three or four times. I let the truck idle to charge the battery, checking the gauges and letting the big block 460 power plant run a while to get the bugs out.

I went to my gun safe, grabbing the Smith & Wesson "Dirty Hairy" Model 29 revolver. The Magnum was blued with black Pachmayr grips, a six-inch ribbed barrel, a soft black leather carrying case, a shoulder harness with four speed loaders, already filled with 240-grain wadcutters, the copper-jacketed soft nose hollow point cartridges, twenty-four rounds of maximum heavy loads plus my Winchester

Model 12 pump shotgun with the eighteen-inch nickel barrel with the pistol-style sawed-off grip, along with a full box of twenty-five double aught buckshot. Putting both firearms with the ammunition in the toolbox of the welding rig, I then cleaned the windshield before taking off.

I had a bag loaded with power bars, a thermos of hot black coffee, some cold bottled water, plus my night vision binoculars. Apollo was sitting in the front seat but I made him get out, needing him to watch the ranch and cabin, as I wasn't quite sure what I was going to do when I got to Eric's shop. Putting the transmission in "granny" low gear I drove slowly down the long private entrance wondering if this was the last time I would ever drive away from my reclusive hideaway. I looked at Apollo walking beside the rig with his head down. He knew something was up and was thinking he should be going with me.

Driving down out of the Martinez hills I checked the time on my wristwatch: almost 5:00 p.m. It would be dark in four more hours but I could not just sit waiting so I drove off down the winding mountain roads in deep thought. Plan A: Drive to Eric's shop, get up all the speed I could then crash through the gates into the building "gangster style," guns blazing. But the closer I got the more I realized how stupid that would be, although it would definitely make me feel better, having just gotten out of jail that morning. Besides the fact that I didn't want to be back in that stinking jail, I wouldn't do Olivia any good if I was behind bars. On the way through Martini town I stopped at the 76 filling station topping off the saddle tank and putting 40 gallons in the drag up. Driving across the Benicia Bridge I looked at the Moth Ball Fleet, wishing I was on my own like I used to be, just sitting at the helm of the *Sturgeon General* with a full charter, an ice chest full of cold beer without a worry in the world. I guess those days were gone. The thing that kept popping up over and over was why I didn't go to the authorities to try and get help, but then again what proof did I have of anything—besides, that would have an effect on the plan I was forming in my head.

When I got to the shop it looked completely deserted with the gates shut and locked. The welding rig was as inconspicuous as it could possibly be in this heavy industrial area. Driving to a place up the hill from the shop where I could pull over, tucking Old Yeller off to the side on a turnout, I sat low in the saddle deciding to wait it out and see what developed.

I watched for about one hour but saw no sign of activity, figuring if I waited until dark, if Eric was inside, possibly with Olivia, then I would have to see some lights on. I nibbled a power bar with a bottle of water and was able to catch a pretty good nap. The sun was setting across the Moth Ball Fleet with the refinery lights starting to flicker across the water. Seeing no movement or any sign of people coming or going, if there was anybody inside it was hard to tell. I recognized the truck that tried to run me off the bridge. Everything was adding fuel to the fire burning inside me. Coming up with a plan to wait until it got good and late, maybe 2:00 a.m., then I'd coast down the hill with my lights off. I would have the "Master Key," my oxygen and acetylene torch at the ready. Using the welding rig to block the view from the roadway I'd cut my way in through the gates, an old trick I learned from one of the most "Red Ass" pipeline rig welders on the planet.

"Howard the Horrible" would show up for work two hours early while it was still dark, string out his cutting torch leads then cut his way through the gates, loading up his two and half ton welding rig with anything not nailed down: 50 pound cans of rod, grinding discs, etc, including filling his one hundred gallon drag up tank.

Cutting my way in would only take seconds, making a minimum of noise. Biding my time, a good soldier knows when to rest so I decided to get some much-needed sleep.

After some quick shut eye, feeling a lot better, everything went well as planned with the engine and headlights off, rolling the welding rig silently down the hill, blocking the view from anybody driving by, the torch making quick work cutting off the lock in seconds, careful when I fired up the cutting torch by adjusting the oxygen and acetylene to just the perfect mixture before igniting, so when I fired up the torch there was no excessive flaring, just a quarter-inch blue flame. I made a precision cut on the shank next to the hasp of the big Master lock so I could false-lock the gate behind me. Unless somebody looked really close they would never know the lock wasn't intact without actually trying to open it themselves.

I drove in then shut the gate behind me, hiding my rig behind the big truck with the reefer box on the back. I backed my truck up where I could string out my oxygen and acetylene cutting leads then made my way in the warehouse. The 12-gauge was at the ready in the top of the toolbox, one in the chamber then four more in the magazine tube. The heavy forty-four felt comforting, the weight of the big revolver, loaded in the shoulder rig strapped on over my black T-shirt but underneath the overalls very reassuring. Filling the big pockets of my overalls with the speed loaders, ten extra rounds of the double ought buck and a folding Spyderco stainless steel knife with serrated blade, a small Maglite, some small hand tools including a pair of heavy wire cutters, a four-way screwdriver, a pair of smaller 420 channel lock pliers, a spool of number ten insulated wire, plus a sixteen-ounce mechanic's ball-peen hammer with the wooden handle cut off short and a hole drilled in the end of the handle with six-inch raw hide loop to go around my wrist. Putting a single-beam adjustable light with a two-inch elastic strap on my forehead, I proceeded to make my way inside.

After running a jumper wire from the door connection to the jamb, so as not to break the connection, setting off the primitive alarm, I crossed my fingers, saying a small prayer as I repeated the procedure with the cutting torch. Sliding open the door with no alarm, rolling up the cutting leads, I made my way inside. After I shut the big sliding door the shop was pitch black, with no light coming in whatsoever. Standing as still as a statue for a long, full minute, my mind racing, I expected the lights to come on with a gun pointed at my head. Taking long, slow, deep breaths to get control of my racing heart I felt like a blind man, it was so dark I couldn't see my hand in front of my face. Out of the silence a compressor kicked on and I almost went through the roof. Holding the 12-gauge pump with my left hand on the pump action and my right-hand white knuckled on the sawed-off grip, if I would have had my finger on the hair trigger instead of safely on the trigger guard I would have burned off a round when the compressor fired up.

I squinted, letting my dilating pupils react. With my vision improving I regained my composure as I was waiting for the compressor to build up pressure before it would automatically shut itself off. With my breathing under control, no more heartbeat ringing in my ears, the dark shop was silent again. I picked up the faint noise of some kind of air-conditioning or a running fan. After a few minutes it would shut off again. Waiting a good ten minutes, which seemed like an eternity, I switched on my headlight, taking a long look around.

The inside was the most meticulously organized shop anybody ever saw. Everything was in order, every tool, every possible square foot of space utilized, with remotely controlled overhead trolley cranes, plasma arc cutting machines, every style of welding equipment from standard, shield arc stick welding to high frequency heliarc gear, orbital computer-operated welding devices as well as underwater welding gear, rolling positioners for fabrication of the fuel tankers from Eric's father's business, motorcycle stands with tool boxes in straight rows, large red rollaway, upright Snap-on toolboxes, without one speck of dirt or grease on any surface. There were several motorcycles on elevated stands, mounted upright in various stages of custom construction. Seeing the one Eric had been riding when he tried to make the hit on the freeway, the handle grip had been replaced so I pulled out the folding Spyderco knife, cutting off the end of the grip to see the end of the shot gun barrel. Even though Eric had attempted to murder me and Olivia both, I still couldn't help admire the genius behind the madness.

Remembering Olivia telling me about Eric's private part of the warehouse, still gazing in awe, checking myself from marveling at the meticulously organized shop, I went about my business, finding another set of doors that wasn't locked. After a while I was able to trace some electrical conduit to a series of switches. Using just my head light I studied the box, finding it was locked, the key missing from the switch. Disassembling the box with the screwdriver, after several attempts at hot-wiring I was able to open the door, which opened like a false wall. Opening it just enough to walk through, I stopped and waited. Checking the time on my Seiko wrist watch I couldn't believe it was already past 3:00 a.m. Not knowing what to expect next I started cautiously looking around. There was everything from drafting tables to cars and trucks under car covers, all of them plugged in to battery monitors. There was every type of priceless '60s Muscle collector car stacked on custom racks, three high, wall to wall in the giant warehouse. There were vintage Harley-Davidsons of every style, from the newer Evolution, then Shovelheads, Pans, Knuckleheads and Flathead models dating back to the 1920's era, a few OG Indian bikes and a British model I didn't recognize. It was hard to keep my mind on the business at hand, which was looking for Olivia, not knowing if she was dead or alive. All I had to go on was hope.

Walking along the expansive shop I wondered how a person who had everything in the world at his fingertips could be more interested in the life of a career criminal. Spotting a refrigerator I opened the door looking for something to drink. Inside were stacked boxes of anabolic steroids: testosterone ampules and Primobolan tablets, daily doses of HGH and hypodermic syringes. Shutting the door I went back to work. In one corner was the most ingenious, custom-fabricated gymnasium with a stainless steel universal structure, cables and plates. The machine was equipped with every style and every exercise setup I had ever seen. There were curl bars on racks, from 25 up to 75 pounds, complete racks of dumbbells from 5 pounds to 120 pounds, bench presses fixed in three different positions, guillotine, incline and decline, all organized on wall mounted racks,

Olympic bars, pull-down bars of every sort, all in order from lightest to heaviest, gymnastic parallel bars as well as a pommel horse, tread mill, elliptical and rowing machines and stationary bike—all of this in a corner where the walls were mirrored from floor to ceiling. I just stood there for a minute nodding my head up and down in recognition of the way the gym was laid out.

Walking along in complete amazement I stopped dead in my tracks. In the far corner of the shop was a car under a cover. Thinking my eyes were playing tricks on me, recognizing the long low body style, I walked over barely able to breathe lifting off the car cover. I stared as the cover slid off the Pimpala. My memory started working, going back in time to the day Eric drove by with Olivia on the back of his bike. While I was getting hauled into Concord Police Station Eric had gone back and stolen my car. Standing there for a while in shock, I couldn't help but notice it was still cherry, having been well maintained. Shaking my head in disbelief at the thought of him pulling off the caper, throwing another log on the fire that was burning inside me I looked at the walls, finding drawings and designs of what appeared to be a mini submarine. There were elaborate drawings with details indicating wall thickness of the fuselage, ".500 wall" equaling half an inch, with the sketches of 55-gallon drums and details like parts of ammonia nitrate mixed with certain amounts of diesel. Walking around in a daze with everything I was seeing in plain sight, I noticed drawings of the Benicia Railroad Bridge, with a schedule of a liquefied petroleum gas shipping company on the wall.

BLACK GOLD

When I heard voices outside the building they were talking in broken English. Turning off my headlight I stood still trying to listen. The voices I heard were mixed Russian, from the sound of it they had been drinking pretty heavy. The first voice was slurred, asking the second if he was positive Eric would be gone all morning, the second one answered hell yes, he was positive, screw that arrogant bastard anyway, saying if Eric hadn't been so greedy trying to raise the price of the caviar they wouldn't have to steal it. All this was too much for me to comprehend; the two Russians were ripping off Eric at the same time that I had broken into the shop. The first voice exclaiming how Eric thought he was so smart all the time, not even locking his gates, stupid-ass American, serves him right, we have been making him a rich man long enough, etc. I figured the drunken condition of these two was to my advantage, where it would be easier to get the drop on them.

Staying low I walked from the back of the shop, watching from behind a row of toolboxes as the drunks backed a van in through the sliding door. They slid the big door shut behind them not even noticing the thin jumper wire on the floor. They knew right where they were going, as they walked up to what looked like a walk-in freezer. I knew right away that the faint humming sounds I had heard earlier were the compressors that operated the freezers. Without wasting any time they started loading the van with boxes while smack talking Americans, cussing Eric, talking about with this last load being free, they could go back home to their own country and retire as rich men. I thought I heard the word caviar again but couldn't be sure, hearing them say they had at least a quarter million in product plus the quarter million in cash. Sitting on the back of the van with the doors open, taking a break, they produced a handle of cheap vodka, which they passed between themselves drinking straight from the bottle, the smaller of the two saying this cheap American vodka was not good enough to clean a toilet. I noticed they were sitting awfully close to each other with their legs swinging together off the back of the van, like two school kids in love. These two were clearly partners. I'm far from homophobic but I couldn't help but think, "Cum Sucking Communist Bastards."

I didn't know how or why Eric had such large amounts of the expensive delicacy in a walk-in refrigerator but I knew it was highly illegal. The boxes were loaded with four 1-quart jars each of refrigerated raw caviar, otherwise known as black gold. The full-length van was loaded to the top with one gallon per box. Staying in the shadows trying to come up with a plan on how to subdue the two Russians then turn over the evidence to California Fish & Game, if somehow I got the jump on these guys and was able to hold them until I could get word to the authorities, Eric's shop would be crawling with cops. Eric would probably go to jail for a little while, but I figured he would just slither his way out like a snake, interrupting my plan.

Still not knowing if Olivia was dead or alive, my main focus was her safety but in the back of my mind, looking far into the future I was coming up with a plan that was almost as deceptive as some of Eric's scams. Never having been criminally minded I surprised myself at the simplicity of how it could turn out. This was no gentleman's game but I justified my plan by defending Olivia and myself. It was going to be "double or nothing," but first I had to take out the rich and famous E.Z. Money. Looking too far ahead, getting the cart before the horse, I decided to deal with the matters at hand. Listening to the Russians, who were discussing how Eric had managed to come up with all the caviar, and how they had been purchasing it from him at the end of every spawn for the last three seasons, one Russian tells the other that Eric was using an old poaching system known as a trot line, catching every sturgeon that came up the river on its way to shallow waters where the ripe females would lay their eggs. Every male sturgeon from the surrounding area would follow on their migratory run every year. The Russians went on that the other freezer was full of whole-bodied sturgeon that Eric was selling through the black market to some Asians.

I couldn't believe my ears but it was all becoming crystal clear that Eric had somehow had something to do with the dwindling sturgeon population, possibly forcing the species into near extinction. This was all I could stand. Twenty years ago, this guy steals my girl and my car all in the same day. Second, he repeatedly tries to kill me and Olivia, resulting in me burning up the engine and totaling my El Camino, me spending the night in that stinking jail and, to top things off, he had been messing with my livelihood, getting rich while destroying the sturgeon population, strike three.

There was a fire burning inside me. Realizing I was clenching my teeth so hard my jaw was starting to hurt I calmed myself with deep breathing until I was no longer seeing red. It was hard to hold back from killing both of the Russians on the spot, visualizing mowing them both down with the 12-gauge. Time was running out. I knew I had to keep a cool head and not let my anger overrun my thought process. The Russians were finishing loading the van when I saw what I had to do. They were still working with the light from their handheld Maglites and had completed their task of loading up the bootleg caviar. I heard one tell the other all they had to do now was take the raw cavvy to their rented house, then cure it before it got warm. When they got ready to drive out, as one was going to open the sliding door, I waited behind a large red toolbox. Before he reached the door handle I was stepping out from behind the toolbox and cracked him a good one, right dead in the middle of his forehead with the butt of the 12-gauge, thinking I must have killed him the way he dropped like a sack of potatoes. The second man yelled at his partner to hurry up, they had to leave immediately.

By now the sun was coming up. Not wasting any more time I quickly dragged the knocked out Russian out of sight by the ankles then waited for the second man. When he came around the front of the van looking for his partner I pistol-whipped him hard with the heavy barrel of the .44, coming down with a full swing like a golfer swinging his driver. With their hands and feet bound with electrical zip ties from the toolbox, somehow, running on pure adrenaline alone, I was able to lift the deadweight bodies of the two men into the back of the van.

Placing them in the rear of the van I bound them together around their chests and heads with duct tape, also gagging them with numerous wraps of the tape wound tightly around their mouths, the back of their heads against each other. Just as I was completing this task they started to come around, their eyes ablaze with anger and fear. I was completely out of time and thought about driving the welding rig off the property, parking it on the side of the road then coming back for the van. But I decided it didn't matter, having to forfeit the rig, and drove out in the van with the two Russians tied in the back with the load of caviar. I'd had the welding rig for a long time but it had no real cash value. I just wrote it off as a sacrifice, grabbing my bag of hand tools, throwing them in the van as I checked the vehicle for up-to-date registration, the rear license plate having current tags. The thought crossed my mind to use the gas from my drag up tank to burn down Eric's entire shop—spread the forty gallons from the auxiliary tank, then burn it all to the ground—but I had good reasons why I couldn't do it. One, time was short, two, Olivia could be hidden somewhere on the property and three, this would interfere with my overall plan.

NICE GUYS FINISH LAST

Leaving the van outside, then parking the welding rig right in front of the gates, I started the welding machine, strung out the leads then welded his gates shut, sending Eric a message. It was not only time for me to get inside Eric's head, but this was step one of my plans. I drove the van to an older deserted part of the industrial park where I knew no one would be around, parking behind an abandoned warehouse where I opened the back doors. After checking the ropes, duct tape and zip ties to make sure there were going to be no surprises, I studied my two prisoners, letting fear and intimidation work for a while. Eating a power bar while drinking the rest of my coffee, I inspected the big mouse on the forehead of the first Russian, then the big crease in the top of the head of number two, deciding they would survive.

Checking the obvious hiding places in the van for the $250,000 cash I came up empty handed, but found the plastic handle of cheap vodka from Long's Drugs, $4.98 for a half gallon. I took a long well-deserved pull of the disgusting vodka. I studied to see who was the weaker of the two Russians. They were both between 30 and 40 years old, one wore an overly large wristwatch. I didn't recognize the make but I knew it was an expensive European chronometer. The small one looked hardened and mean, a little man with a big small man complex, who had to fight for everything he ever had, where somebody bigger probably took it away from him. He needed a shave but his complexion was smooth and tanned, his eyes a piercing silver blue, full of hatred and fire. The other guy was outfitted with blue and white camouflage pants with ankle-high, cheap Kmart, waffle-bottom, lace-up, hiking style boots. He was a big man, probably used his size to intimidate people his whole life. He tried to look at me hard but it was plain to see he was scared. I figured the larger of the two to be the cow and the smaller the bull, thinking this information may come into effect.

I checked the load of the .44 in front of them both, dramatically swinging the cylinder out the side of the double action Magnum, revealing six full chambers. Taking out four of the rounds I then rotated the cylinder into the position where when I pulled back the hammer the next round would rotate to discharge. Pulling the duct tape from the mouth of the cow, I held the big revolver next to his ear then busted a cap. The .44 rocked the van like a cannon, the sun shining through the half inch hole in the roof of the van like a laser, the dust in the air illuminated by the bright sunlight. The rear of the van smelled like cordite from the Winchester

Smokeless Super X Gunpowder. Telling the big one, I'm only asking you this one time; where is the cash? He spat at me trying to look tough but he looked like he was close to tears. I told him as ironic as it sounded we were going to play a little game of Russian roulette, pulling back the hammer in the halfcocked position as I was spinning the cylinder, the loud distinct clicks of the Smith & Wesson magnified in the van. Putting the end of the fat warm barrel in his ear, I pulled back the hammer then waited, silently praying as hard as I could that the firing pin would land on an empty chamber, telling him his odds of survival were five to one. I squeezed the hair trigger and let the hammer fall. Thank God it came up on an empty chamber.

Without hesitation I pulled back the hammer and said, "Four to one," pushing the barrel harder into the hole of his ear. When I pulled the hammer back his bowels jellied, filling the air with the smell of human waste, next his bladder released as the warm yellow liquid formed a shadow on his camouflage pants as the tears rolled down his face. Telling the cow I didn't care about the sturgeon roe and that I just wanted the cash, when the big man started to cry harder, without hesitation I turned the muzzle of the .44 to the face of the little bull, the hammer cocked with my finger white knuckled on the hair trigger, knowing the larger of the two would never talk for fear of his partner. He didn't care about himself, but he couldn't stand to let his lover get hurt. His irregular breathing was uncontrolled. Between sobs he started to spill his guts. The little bull tried to stop big boy from talking by swinging his head back trying to bang their heads, so I stuck the muzzle against his face to keep him still.

The big man told me to look behind the door panel on

the driver's side door. Using my four-way screwdriver to remove the panel, the cash was stacked in bundles of crisp one-hundred-dollar bills, ten thousand per bundle. Slitting open one bundle I pulled one of the stacks then replaced the door skin, putting the remaining bundles in my bag then cutting big boy loose. Holding the Magnum on him while I had him untie his boyfriend I told to him to leave his partner's hands tied. I told them both to sit on the pavement. Knowing I was making a big mistake I counted out fifty one-hundred-dollar bills and handed the big man the stack, leaving myself $45,000 in cold, hard cash. I told them that should be enough money to get them safely out of town. If Eric found them it couldn't be helped; live by the sword, die by the sword. I knew I was making a big mistake letting these guys go free, but I gambled, taking the risk anyhow.

Getting behind the wheel and checking the gas gauge the van had a full tank. At first I had planned to turn the two over to Fish & Game with the sturgeon roe, but I knew they would rat out Eric and I wanted him for myself. I left the two smugglers as I drove away feeling pains of hunger plus anxiety as the adrenaline was wearing off. Recapping the situation, the bizarre events that were unfolding, the new information about the sturgeon eggs, I knew I was in too deep and there was no turning back. I felt exhausted from the events that had taken place the night before, but I had no time to rest and pushed on.

NEW WHEELS

I drove the van to a supermarket and purchased all the 20-pound bags of ice that were available along with some bottled water and some power bars. There was a Denny's in the parking lot. Grabbing my thermos, I went inside to re-lieve myself, using the men's room, splashing plenty of fresh cold water on my face, using the palm comb to slick back my hair, noting that I needed a haircut, wondering if I would be alive long enough for it to matter. Inside the restaurant a beautiful young lady helped me recharge the thermos with hot black coffee. The waitress naturally flirt-ing, fishing for a tip, the name pinned on her uniform said Loretta. She was short but hell for stout with an hourglass waistline, extremely top heavy with overly large "breeder hips," but a looker with the nice curves. She had those mag-nificent Celtic, twinkly-blue, sparkly-green eyes that matched her spectacular smile. I thought to myself, here I am trying to save the "damsel in distress" but girls are falling out of the sky all around me, go figure.

I asked her if she was Irish. Loretta swelled up as she proudly told me her name was Loretta Wallace, 100% Scot-tish descending from the "Buchannon clan." I knew right away that I was completely fascinated with this young lady. She had been in the U.S. for almost ten years. When she talked it was the voice of an angel. Her heavy Scottish accent made it hard to understand what she was saying, her mouth was moving but it sounded like music was coming out. Giv-ing her an appraising look, Loretta was covered in tats with long blonde hair in dreadlocks, where I couldn't resist to asking if she came from the "hood" in Scotland. She ex-plained it was part of her heritage, dating back to William Wallace, the famous warrior who led his people in the thir-teenth century, and that the Scottish women fought side by side with their husbands where she was well versed in train-ing: hand to hand combat, the staff, short and long sword. I nodded in acknowledgment and said "Get back Loretta."

Thinking to myself, *truly amazing,* I made a mental note never to piss her off explaining that I was from Welsh-German descent and recognized her heritage.

She asked me if I had ever been to the Scottish Games and Celtic celebration. Loretta said everybody dressed for the occasion, saying with a grin that she thought I would look good in a skirt. Laughing out loud I felt just a second of peace, realizing we would get along "like gin and tonic." Promising to take her up on her offer, explaining that I really wished I had time to flirt back with her but time was short. I promised to come back and see her when the smoke cleared, giving her my business card saying goodbye for now. Loretta said she could see I was on a mission, telling me to be careful.

Outside in the parking lot, I packed the ice around the jars of sturgeon roe in the back of the van then got on the highway. It was the same stretch where I had chased Eric with Olivia. Thoughts of her flooded my mind as paranoia crept into my head, wondering if she was still alive. If she was, what kind of evil was Eric putting her through? E.Z. had kidnapped Olivia almost twenty-four hours ago. Thoughts filled my head that maybe she had gone with Eric willingly, but I tried to block this from my mind having to keep my brain going in a forward direction and not let fear or feelings interfere with moving ahead.

Gulping bottles of water and wolfing down several of the power bars the nutrition revitalized my thought process. I sipped the coffee as the caffeine kicked in, catching a second wind where I felt more aggressive. Driving up to Sacramento the day was warming up. I pulled into a gas station getting directions to California Fish & Game and a used car dealership.

At the car lot I removed the remaining tools from the small bag, stuffing it full of the "blood money" where it was a tight fit, not believing the weight of the cold hard cash. Parking the van in the shade with the motor running and the air conditioning on the maximum setting, I took a walk around the lot carrying my bag. The car lot was small but it had several used trucks sitting around. I had my eye on a good-looking white Ford F-150, a short fleetside Super Cab that was only a couple of years old, outfitted with a rack on the bed, stock wheels with low miles. There was no other vehicle that would blend in and be as incognito as a typical white construction worker's truck.

The owner of the car lot came walking up explaining that they were not open yet, but upon seeing the bag and the look in my eyes he sensed I was in some kind of trouble, and smelling a quick sale he asked with a smile how he could help me out. Looking right at him saying I would give him asking price for the F-150 plus an additional five hundred if he was ready to cooperate with a few details.

The old slick only said three words, "Got the money?"

I patted the bag as we walked inside and explained that he had to hold the paperwork for 72 hours. He would also have to follow me to Fish & Game.

After counting out the cash and signing the paperwork I pulled the truck over to the van then removing the sawed-off shotgun and the .44 Mag. from the van, hid them in the truck under the back seat. I took the $200,000 out of the door, stuffing it under the rear seat of my new truck. The sly used car salesman looked away whistling a little tune.

I asked if he knew the way to Fish & Game, explaining it was a major national emergency. Following him in the van, parking in front of the entrance doors, I left the van running with the A/C on max. I drove the car salesman back to his lot then back to the gas station, topping off the truck and using a pay phone to call Fish & Game, explaining that there was a van full of fresh, raw sturgeon eggs in front of the Fish and Game Department. The man on the other end of the line asked me where I had acquired the eggs. I told him he wouldn't believe me if I told him but the important thing was they had very little time to get the eggs and take them to a hatchery where the sturgeon were being farmed.

GAME OF CHESS

Driving the F-150 back to Martinez, when I got close to the cabin I put the loaded Magnum on the front seat with me. My remote for the gate was in the El-Co so I had to pull up to the keypad and press in the code as Apollo came out of the manzanita bushes without making a sound, his hackles raised on his back. I couldn't remember ever being so glad to see him. He didn't know who I was yet but he was doing his job being on point as usual. Puckering up my lips and making a double kiss sound that I knew he would recognize, as soon as he heard this he was wagging his stubby little tail so hard his back legs were coming off the ground. Opening the driver's door and patting the seat on my right, before I was finished with the second pat he was in the cab looking for Olivia. Apollo jumped over the armrest into the backseat sniffing for signs of her then without hesitation he was riding shotgun on point. I knew he sensed something was wrong, Apollo had the look of let's go fix it, that dog always knows what time it is.

Seeing no sign of anything wrong at the cabin, where it had been 48 hours since I had been home, I fed Apollo then myself, taking a long hot shower then a little cat nap. When I woke up my eyes slammed open, wide awake. Apollo on guard at the foot of the bed was letting me get some much-needed rest. He looked at me like what are you waiting for, let's go! Apollo was leading the way looking over his shoulder at me wanting me to hurry it up. I went to the gun safe then ran the combination. I couldn't believe what I was actually doing; grabbing my M-1 Garand and making sure it was empty by operating the slide. In the bottom of the safe there was a cigar box full of .30-06 ammunition. Having found these rounds at a garage sale years ago, half of the rounds were military tracer ammunition left over from Vietnam, the maximum load hollow points filled with pyrotechnic flare material. The magnesium in the hollow point ignites from the friction. These rounds were primarily used at night for anti-aircraft, to help follow the track of the projectiles through the dark night sky. The other half were armor piercing rounds that have tungsten hardener combined with lead wrapped in a full metal jacket. I thought to myself that if this submarine in Eric's drawings existed, the armor piercing rounds would come in handy.

Gathering up and counting the loot, I had spent $26,000 on the F-150 and $5000 to the Russians. I had $19,000 left, excluding the $200,000 under the seat of the F-150, not a bad chunk of change for one night's work. I didn't like the dirty money, for I knew bad karma would be right behind it, but it made me feel good for once to take something from Eric, guessing there is a first time for everything. If Olivia was still alive and I could keep her that way, once I got her back, if things went as planned the cash was a drop in a bucket. Stuffing a fold of the money in both shirt pockets then putting the rest in a black plastic garbage bag and tying it in a knot, I took a spade from the barn and walked up the hill from the cabin, making sure nobody was bird dogging me from a distance, digging a hole then burying the rest of the loot. After refilling the hole and putting a large rock over the fresh dirt, I kicked leaves over the area in an effort to hide my work.

Apollo was watching from close by, on point as usual. I wasn't hungry but forced down some food, wondering if this would be my last meal, saying a short prayer asking God for guidance, strength and forgiveness for what I had planned. Apollo knew he was going with me and jumped into the truck as I opened the driver's door. I went back in the house to grab my firearms, the .44, Model 13 - 12-gauge breakdown and the ought-six, putting them all in an army duffel bag, and all the extra ammo plus bottles of water with the remaining power bars in a green, military ammunition bag. On my way out I was taking a good look around the grounds. Even though the property didn't belong to me I thought I better get a long look in case it was my last.

I parked at the marina then slung the strap of the duffle bag over my shoulder, carrying the ammo bag in my hand. As my feet hit the floating dock I realized how good it felt to be on the water, my sea legs came instantly back to life. Every time I see the water a feeling of euphoria comes over me, I didn't know until just that exact point in time thinking about how long it had been since I was on the water and how much I missed it. Walking down the dock with Apollo heeling at my side with no leash, just getting to my two boats when Jason came walking up, seeing the duffle and the ammo bag.

He said, "Those are some funny looking fishing rods you got there, Stoner." Apollo walked over and sniffed him, recognizing him at once then without hesitation the big black dog started to do a perimeter check of both the *Aquaholic* and the *Sturgeon General*.

Jason must have seen that something was wrong from the look on my face, because he got real serious when he asked if I was in some kind of trouble, asking if he could help me out. I was removing the mooring cover from the *Aquaholic* when I answered Jason thanks but no.

He said, "Be careful, Mike," and went about his way.

The 23-foot power launch looked better than I remembered, with the sleek lines and all the teak. The big block fired up on the second try, I couldn't remember ever hearing anything as sweet as the open exhaust coming directly from the transom, reverbing from being backed into her slip. Letting her run on high idle while I stored the firearms, I loaded the M-1 with eight armor-piercing rounds in the top loader slide clip, the pump with one in the chamber, four more in the magazine tube. Taking a quick look at my gauges I saw everything was in order, both fuel tanks were topped off. Casting off the final mooring line then slapping the passenger bucket seat with my open palm, Apollo was in the boat fast as graceful as a gazelle.

Getting up on plane in seconds, trimming out as I backed off on the throttle then started to set my electronics. The water was a little choppy with the tide on its way out, with signs of a fog bank over toward the west. It was common for coastal fog to blanket the San Francisco Bay Area at night, the SF locals refer to this as free A/C when the "cool whip chills the city."

I knew right away without looking that the old standby Hummingbird combination fish finder and depth sounder was functioning. The newer Sidefinder had the latest capabilities:

it could not only view the bottom directly under the boat but could scan to the right or left off the starboard and port sides as far as the banks of both sides of the channel. After fine-tuning the Sidefinder and setting the fish indicator so it would only show larger fish, I plotted my course running directly up the middle of the channel. The Sidefinder would only mark anything three feet or bigger, the old Humming-bird would indicate black square blocks one eighth per foot, one inch equaling eight feet. The electronics were doing their job, showing an occasional sturgeon here and there on the bottom with some sign of stripers halfway between the surface of the water and the bottom of the channel.

I was cruising at about ten knots—fast enough to cover some water but slow enough not to create cavitation from my props, so the electronics could get a solid view of the bottom plus port and starboard readings. The Shell Oil Re-finery came up on the starboard side of the channel. I saw the steam from the cooling tower, indicating the normal southeast prevailing wind was starting to shift, reversing its normal direction. This wasn't unusual for this time of year but it would result in the fog from the San Francisco Bay coming in toward the afternoon. Heading upriver I passed a large oceangoing ship, a car carrier full of brand new Toy-otas that had come all the way across the pond from Japan. Being on the water was like therapy for me. Even though I was armed to the teeth and hell bent on a crazy insane mis-sion, the naturally euphoric feeling of being on the water overpowered the anxiety that was eating away at the back of my mind.

Heading downriver passing Eric's shop off the portside, I took a quick look at the docks behind his shop, seeing no activity. I split a power bar with Apollo then drank a bottle of water as I headed under the Benicia Bridge, coming directly in line with the *Glomar Explorer*—just looking like an average everyday common fisherman, out scoping the channel trying to find a sturgeon on the bottom.

As the fog was blowing in all the other fishermen in the area hightailed it in. Even with GPS when the fog sets in it is still dangerous due to the traffic in the main shipping channel. Not being able to keep my mind on track wondering on how crazy this whole thing seemed, even to me, after a couple of hours I took a break I beached the *Aquaholic* on Ryer Island. Apollo never took his eyes off mine waiting for permission to leave the boat then to relieve himself. Giving the dog the signal with a snap of my fingers pointing toward the island, he silently left the boat to go explore and take care of business.

Sticking the heavy .44 in the back of my belt I went for a quick walk. The low grassy piece of land called Ryer Island is rectangular, fairly long but narrow and maybe five acres at the most, with dilapidated docks, what was left of the ancient pilings that had long ago rotted away. We went for a long walk where I got to stretch my legs and clear my head. When we got back in the boat I put on my foul weather gear. Checking my tide table book, the outgoing tide would bottom out about 4:00 p.m. I did some quick calculating, figuring just as it was going to be full dark it would be slack tide. The channel would be completely deserted with the exception of an occasional large ship and naval patrols from the fleet, knowing for a fact the naval patrols made their rounds at exactly 0900, then again at 2100 hours. I crossed the channel above the big sand bar that separated the fleet from the Shell Oil Refinery then came down river running parallel with the long rows of ships. The sun was all but gone with the wind completely stopped, leaving the surface of the water smooth as glass.

The fog was becoming denser as the wind dissipated, catching glimpses of the refineries but not for long as the fog increased. I heard what sounded like twin big blocks with open exhaust coming up the river. Just as I was getting the direction of the loud open pipes and the growl of the engines, I heard the boat change course then take off. I figured it had to be a work boat of some kind or a tug, but the noise sounded like something high performance. Letting it go, figuring I was just getting paranoid out in the fog in pitch blackness, pea soup so thick you could cut it with a knife.

Deciding to make a run at Eric's shop then scope the area between there and the *Glomar*, Apollo was letting out a low growl from deep in his chest where I went on full alert. I did one complete circle around the *Glomar* then was heading across toward Benicia and Eric's dock when I heard the roar of the big blocks coming right at my bow. The noise was definitely high performance. The 42-foot Fountain offshore cigarette boat came out clearing the fog, gaining speed, with the hull painted in three-dimensional ghost flames with skulls forming out of the feathering flames. Eric passed me head-on doing 80 mph, leaving only two to three feet between our boats.

Making a U-turn for another pass, Eric's face looked like a death mask of horror; his creepy long blonde hair blowing in the wind with his dilated eyes looking like two black dimes, circles of lifeless obsidian. E.Z. $ had gained a lot of size since I had seen him last, his arms looked bigger than I remembered. He was wearing a black sweatshirt with the sleeves cut off, a yellow upside-down smiley face with the words "Have a Nice Day Asshole," biceps the size of dinner plates, triceps like horseshoes.

As Eric roosted my boat, Apollo lunged toward the other boat with white fangs bared, hackles higher than I had ever seen them, his big black head with his short ears pinned back on his skull emerging through the water, teeth snapping at the waves. Grabbing the 12-gauge, setting the short shotgun barrel first in the gunwale next to the captain's seat, I heard my engine miss and then die. He had succeeded in swamping my motor compartment.

Taking a good look around for Eric, I couldn't see or hear him, wondering if he had radar on the boat. Lifting the doghouse motor cover off, I dried the inside of the distributor cap, reassembled the distributor then turned the key. She didn't fire right away. I crossed my fingers and said a prayer. I heard the growl of big blocks coming from behind when Eric veered off at the last second, killing his engines.

We both knew I was dead in the water. I held off turning the key because I didn't want him to hear the starter turning, in case he didn't already know he had swamped my motor compartment, killing my only engine. Holding my breath, getting low in case Eric opened up with a firearm, I listened for the sound of the offshore boat's ignition turning over. Drifting along in the slack tide, I could feel the gentle surge from the incoming as the tide was beginning to turn, knowing there was nothing to fear right away but if I kept drifting I would end up at the fleet.

Hearing him fire up the fountain, he made a few runs at me again but turned away before he was in sight. My battery was already getting low so I changed the Perko switch to the "ALL" position, to combine the remaining power of both batteries in a final effort when I heard him coming. I held the key in the start position as she caught fire at the last instant, the 409 roaring back to life. Knowing I was on the edge of the channel, I could hear the twin big blocks from Eric's cigar boat as he shifted the transmissions into gear, letting her idle to hold position with the tide. I knew he was trying to listen to make my position while maintaining his own. It was as though we were playing a game of chess with our boats. The bilge pump was all but stopped, only discharging an occasional spout of water as the gentle waves rocked the hull side to side. The heat from the 409 rapidly dried out the motor compartment, the batteries still too low to risk shutting off my engine.

I convinced myself that I had come out here looking for Eric. As it turned out, he had turned the table where he had found me, the hunter becoming the prey. The *Aquaholic* was outmatched by his boat where my only advantage was my knowledge of the river plus the fire that was burning inside of me with Olivia's life at stake. Floating toward the tip of the fleet, Apollo stood on the passenger seat with his front legs on the dash where he heard it before I did: a low idling engine of a boat, the naval patrol, right on time as always, making their routine patrols.

E.Z., hearing the navy patrol shut off both his engines. He couldn't risk possibly being seen. I knew he had every intention to deep six me but he couldn't afford any witnesses. Knowing Eric, he most likely had stolen the offshore cigarette-style boat. He planned on ramming my boat, capsizing me then running me down with his boat, taking me out with his props. I knew I had better come up with a defensive plan.

The naval boat lit me up with its spotlight, announcing that I was way too close to the off-limits zone. I yelled back telling them that I'd just got my motor running and that I

would get out right away. I came up with a strategy. With
the incoming tide increasing the fog was starting to dissi-
pate, it was still so thick that precipitation was dripping off
my hair, every surface on the boat covered in moisture,
Apollo picked up a scent.

I knew right away where Eric was, sitting waiting for me
to get too close to the fleet. As soon as he heard me engage
my gear shifter the onslaught would start, and he wouldn't
give up until one of us was dead. I put on a life jacket just
for good luck. Pulling out my old standby wooden oar I
silently positioned my boat by paddling where my bow was
headed, in the same direction Apollo was pointing.

The first noise I heard was the deep rumble of a tugboat's
twin 16-cylinder diesel engine coming from upriver. The
second noise was the gently rocking ships where they are
kept separated with large wood crates. The timbers are 12-
inch by 12-inch and 10 feet long, the heavy creosol-treated
lumber serving as bumpers between the ships. I heard the
eerie sound of the ancient wood with the sound of the increasing tide as it bottlenecked between the ships creating
turbulence, indicating I was close to the fleet.

I whispered to Apollo ever so low, "You ready, boy?"
Apollo just wagged his little tail.

Making sure the 12-gauge was at the ready, I fire-walled
the fuel feeder all the way to its stop. In the same instant I
heard the thunderous high-performance exhaust come to
life from the fountain boat. There was no way Eric would
try to ram me with both of us being so close to the ships, it
was just too risky. Holding the steering wheel with my
knees, the shotty at my right side, right hand wrapped
around the sawed-off pistol style grip, finger on the trigger
guard, the first big roller wave from the wake of the tug

came across the water and I heard Eric's hull slap the waves. Both his twin screws were momentarily spinning in thin air, the twin 502s redlining the tachometers, the rollers creating instant havoc.

The *Aquaholic* took the first wave, getting air. I tried to stuff the barrel of the shotgun in the gunwale but had to grab the steering wheel with both hands as the antique Model 12 disappeared into the drink, gone forever. Getting control of the boat as I hit the second set of rollers, I saw that Eric was close enough to where I could feel his exhaust blasting in my face. His wake was smoothing out the rollers from the tug. I was closing the gap between our boats with my big claw anchor above his stern. Eric's twin big blocks were digging in, with the Mercury Bravo outdrives doing their jobs, pushing massive water.

My plan was to ram my bow into the back of his boat, when Eric produced a 9 mm fully-automatic mini machine gun pistol as gracefully as a symphonic orchestra leader waving his wand. His right arm arced from his waist to his shoulder as he raised the short barrel squeezing the trigger, burning off a thirty-round clip in less than three seconds, the muzzle producing a five-foot flame illuminating Eric's demonic face grinning ear to ear, the 120-grain copper-jacketed bullets ripping holes in the side of the *Aquaholic*, leaving a trail of perfectly symmetrical holes. I knew Eric could have taken me out then and there but he wasn't through toying with me. E.Z. wanted the game of cat and mouse to last longer.

The 9-mil' did its job on my engine, the 409 was through, dropping power immediately as my bow was already on its way down, losing all my momentum. I hit the toggle switch for the automatic anchor hoist, letting the anchor line freewheel, dropping the big galvanized claw-style anchor in the back of his boat, taking the risk of the anchor rope becoming entangled in his propellers.

The Fountain boat took off like a raped ape, the big blocks filling the air with the loudest roar, exhaust filling my lungs, the taste of gasoline in my mouth. Eric looked over his shoulder, when I saw the insanity in his face. He was actually enjoying this game of life or death. The slack was getting tight as Eric's boat was finding its own on the water, demonstrating its superior power and technology. My engine being dead, I could still read my speed on my depth sounder. We were already doing 50 miles per hour. The anchor slipped once, losing its bite. It started to grab on the rear bench seat of the Fountain but ripped free like a hot knife through soft butter, shredding the upholstery. Chunks of seats with cushions flew out of the boat before the claw dug in, taking hold.

Somehow, I managed to get my hands on my rifle. Eric was heading upriver away from the industrialized part of the channel, towing me to a more isolated area, when I let one fly. The M-1 felt better than anything I had ever remembered, the butt of the heavy gun recoiled into my shoulder. When Eric heard the firearm discharge he cut the wheel hard to the right then the left, running a zigzag pattern. Missing twice more, I found pay dirt on the fourth round, placing a tracer round next to Eric, the 180-grain projectile splintering the beautiful dash of the fountain, wreaking havoc on his gauges. The magnesium round exploded like the Fourth of July, showing Eric's wicked face in multiple colors. He whipped the steering right then left, causing my anchor hoist to strip its gears, slowly but surely giving up more feet of anchor line with each passing second.

We were traveling at speeds between 80 and 90 mph. I used my rudder to steer back and forth over his wake as he dragged my boat like an inner tube. Hefting the Garand, I burned off rounds, aiming for the motor house and fuel tanks. As we traveled upriver the channel was becoming narrow with more turns. I burned off the remaining four shots without a hit, not knowing I had nicked a high-pressure fuel line on his port side. Because it was one of the armor-piercing projectiles it went right through. If it had been a magnesium tracer round the Fountain would have exploded, blowing this demon to Hell, where he belonged. The ruptured fuel line, not causing an explosion but draining one of his twin gas tanks, the O2 sensors on the port side of the cigar boat did their job, shutting both motors down. The gasoline, pouring out of both sides with the bilge pumps activated, spread across the surface of the water. Eric, thinking fast, hit the switch to operate the hydraulic motor cover. When it was raised to its max 60-degree angle E.Z. kicked the cover off to let out the gasoline fumes then grabbed the fire extinguisher, emptying its contents on and around both of the 502s. Taking a chance firing up his only remaining motor, he drove off with the fountain listing to one side from operating on only one screw, gasoline pouring from both of the bilge pumps.

Reloading the carbine while operating the boat, I managed to feed eight more rounds from the top using the slide clip, six armor-piercing with tracers being the last two rounds. The tide spread the gasoline toward the stranded *Aquaholic* with the acrid fumes burning my throat and eyes. Eric started a wide sweeping turn. Figuring he was heading back for open water, my anchor line came to its end, leaving 150 feet of line between our boats. E.Z. was going to try to drag my boat across the sand bar. The big boat looked as graceful as a figure skater as it turned effortlessly across the water, the single big block screaming with its roaring exhaust. I burned off the first six rounds, the trusty M-1 Garand barking loud. Taking full aim with the last two rounds I set my sights on the water surface next to his bilge pump, trying to ignite the fuel on the surface of the water. The tracer indicated the first round went wide. Just as I let my last round fly, Eric must have had a seventh sense because in the nick of time he spun 180 degrees, causing the magnesium round to miss.

The fog was clearing fast as the big cigarette boat got closer. The 42-foot Fountain had "Frenched-in" navigation lights to go along with its custom paint job, with multiple skulls blending in with the ghost flames, the portside light shining red from deep in the eye socket of a skull, looking as menacing as all evil on the black water. Eric now had enough slack that he could have doubled back and cut my anchor loose from his stern, then driven by taking shots at me, being a sitting duck. But apparently he had other plans. He continued to tow my boat to the sand bar, to then strand the *Aquaholic* high and dry, where he could toy with me, making the game last longer. Knowing Eric was down to one motor, even this small detail lifted my hopes of survival. I considered using my VHF ship to shore radio, channel 16 to contact the coast guard, but turning on the power switch it was deader than a doornail. Looking underneath the fire wall I noticed the wires had been tampered with. I felt my bow rise up as my speed dropped from fifty to zero.

I held the steering wheel for support as Apollo slid across the wet deck. It was still pitch dark but the wind was picking up with the incoming tide reaching full force. I heard Eric reverse his boat then disengage my anchor from his stern. Hand signaling to Apollo, we got on the opposite side of the boat, using the hull as cover in case Eric attempted a drive-by attack. By 2:00 a.m. the tide would come in and my boat would be carried off the sandbar. Getting back in the boat, I was able to pull in my anchor line with the electric hoist, retrieving the big claw anchor. I could hear Eric's boat staying at a safe distance. Dreading what I was about to see, I lifted the doghouse motor cover off to inspect for damage. The motor compartment was filled with oil from where the bullets had ripped through the valve covers, damaging the valves on my beautiful 409. There were a few holes in the hull below what would have been the water line. Taking advantage of the boat being exposed, I corked the holes with empty brass from the M-1, necessity being the mother of invention. Time marched on as the tide came in. Apollo followed me out of the stranded boat, both of us hiding behind it for protection. Eric must have given up, knowing he would have to get close for his gun to be effective. I heard him throttle up then take off, operating the Fountain with only one screw. I thought he would run down river to his shop, but he took off in the opposite direction.

We got back in the boat and waited. The tide peaked, then when it was on its way out I shoved off, able to use my oar to get out into some running current, setting my rudder straight and positioning my bow in the direction of Martinez. I fashioned a "sea anchor" from a sleeping bag, tying the four corners "parachute style" with twenty feet of lead line, a trick the old sailors used to rely on when they had no trade wind. They would lower their sails under the surface to move their mighty ships. I thought I saw Eric a hundred times materializing out of the dark, so I kept the M-1 at the ready, but he never came back. When the marina was in sight I pulled in my sea anchor and was able to row to the entrance of the break water. Exhaustion was taking its toll, so I tied up in the first available slip, not noticing I was next to Jason's sailboat.

DROP MY GUARD

Wet and tired, exhaustion creeping in, I must have dropped my guard. As Apollo and I walked down the dock toward the *Sturgeon General*, I noticed footprints in the moisture on the dock. Apollo picked up a scent and with hair up he headed onto the *General*. One of the Russians was lying in wait. They had broken into my party boat, burglarizing the *General*. Using my sturgeon snare like a dog catcher he had Apollo around the neck. Even though Apollo had the cable tight around his throat he sprang off the deck like a cheetah, the big black dog flying horizontally across the gunwale with ears back, white fangs bared, sinking all four teeth in the upper arm of the smaller man, leaving four holes the size of silver dollars. Screaming in pain, the smaller Russian used the snare to choke out the dog, causing him to lose his bite. The Russian was able to wrestle the dog off the dock into the water.

The same instant the big man grabbed me from behind, big boy had my rifle. Coming from behind, using the M-1 like a night stick, holding his hands wide, he pulled the stock under my chin as he yanked me off my feet. As I was watching the little bull trying to drown my dog, Apollo thrashing underneath the surface of the water, I lashed out with a straight defensive kick as the big man jerked me away. My right boot heel caught the little bull, opening a gash in the end of his chin. The heel kick was solid enough to ring his bell but not enough to knock him out. He had to catch himself, and lost his grip on the sturgeon snare and control of my dog, who was fighting for his life.

Giving Apollo hand signals to swim to the bank, without hesitation the big black dog swam away with the snare around his neck. The small man was temporarily TKO'd from the kick so I went to work on big boy. While struggling with the big man I was able to set a hook with the toe of my boot inside the man's leg, twisting hard at the same time. He had lost his choke hold but was doing a good job trying to break my neck with the rifle. My right arm was free so I started swinging blindly with my right fist, landing blows on his thick skull when I heard the distinct click of the hammer of my own .44 Magnum.

The little bull had moved fast, standing there with blood running down his neck from the gash on his chin. Apollo was trying to climb up the rocks, thrashing the water, the snare hanging from his neck. I was hoping Jason was sleeping in his boat and would be woken up from the noise, but no such luck. This side of the marina was deserted, quiet as a graveyard.

The little bull pointed the fat barrel in my face, saying, "Lucky for you, it's a good thing we need you alive." He let the hammer down slowly then whacked me across the head with the heavy barrel of my own gun.

REFUSE TO LOSE

When I came to, my hands were tied behind my back in an ocean-going cargo van, the sea van with the big, hinged doors on both ends. My first thoughts were of Olivia and

Apollo, were they alive? What condition could Olivia be in after this much time around Eric? The sea van was an older model that had been converted to some type of construction storage where Unistrut-style shelves had been used to store tools and materials but were now completely bare. Not being able to see what my hands were tied with I was able to spin around and find a sharp surface. I started to grind up and down in an effort to cut whatever it was holding my hands tied behind my back.

Not knowing how much time before the Russians came and started to torture the information out of me, I stayed busy with the slow grind of trying to get my hands free. My wrists were blistered from the friction against my denim shirt; my shoulders felt like somebody had driven a sixteen-penny nail through both sides. Feeling something give on my wrist binds, it wasn't much but at least one thin layer of something gave way. I went on with a renewed energy, counting the movement, 25 times up and down then I took a short break to avoid complete exhaustion, 25 more as the bindings cut deeper into my wrists.

The pain was overtaking my efforts when the second wind kicked in, irritated inflamed flesh burning with salty sweat, the pain fueling the fire of determination. Picking up speed I started to cut through layers of what turned out to be insulated copper wire.

Getting my hands free felt better than anything I had ever experienced. I untied my ankles then searched the van for weapons, finding a heavy, steel-toed lace-up logger's boot. I hefted the heavy boot giving it a few practice swings, removed the woven lace and put it in the back pocket of my Wranglers. I crawled onto the top level of the storage shelves. It wasn't much of a plan, and just a little bit crazy but right now crazy was better than nothing.

KILL OR BE KILLED

Waiting for the two Russians I actually fell asleep, but was instantly awake when I heard the key rattle. The little bull was smarter than the big man and waited outside. Big boy stepped in the van as I rolled off the shelf like a wild man, wielding the boot like Sampson swinging the jawbone of an ass, holding it by the toe, using the heel for a weapon I connected pretty good on the top of his big ugly head. I landed on my feet ready to pounce when from behind I heard the hammer come back on the .44 Magnum. I knew they still needed me alive to get back what I had taken from them, so knowing in my heart he wouldn't pull the trigger just yet, no time to waste, spinning and getting low at the same time, I dove for the little bull going for the gun. In a panic he accidently squeezed off a round. When the Magnum discharged it rocked the sea van like a bomb going off. The shot went between my arm and chest, the heat from the passing projectile, the muzzle energy, burning my shirt, blistering the skin between my bicep and the right side of my chest.

The bullet passed by me, but the big man wasn't so lucky. The 240-grain copper-jacketed hollow point entered his face below his left eye. I was already closing the distance between me and the little bull, but he was faster than I thought, with no remorse whatsoever for killing his friend. He took a step back, pulling the hammer back on the Smith & Wesson. I was close enough to swing the boot, but he started to talk. Less than one second after killing his buddy he was trying to negotiate a deal. The first thing he says is now that his partner is out of the way we could talk business. Trying to buy time I told him I was listening. He asked me what I had done with the caviar and I lied, telling him it was in a safe place, stored at forty degrees, nobody but me knew where it was safely hidden. Then he wanted to know how much money was left from the quarter million; I answered with the truth. He told me to drop the boot and back up into the sea van.

THE FISTS OF STONE

Faster than a feline I lunged for the gun again, positioning my body sideways to present a narrower target. Hearing the hammer release I drove my hand downward, wedging the skin between my thumb and my trigger finger under the firing pin, where it landed with a dull thump but kept the pin from indenting and igniting the primer, saving my life. People have always told me that I was just like a cat and that I had to have nine lives, but I was starting to wonder how many I had left. Still standing sideways, my left hand still held low, locking my thumb over my trigger and my "courting" finger, rolling my two knuckles forward like ball peen hammers, I came around with a big right cross, twisting my hips, pushing off my planted right foot. My knuckles connected with his temple. When the punch landed and drove the little bull's head from left to right it should have knocked him into next week, but the little bull was fierce. I hit him so hard I felt the thin carpal bones of my wrist actually bow from the impact and thought I'd broken my wrist for sure.

The bull wasted no time, I'd rung his bell hard but he had already come in at my feet. He was a grappler, where I was able to latch on to him making him lose his grip on the

Magnum, pulling him with me as the heavy gun clanked on the floor of the sea van, out of our reach. The little man obviously had a lot of ground experience, quick as a cat and strong as an ox he quickly took full control of the fight. In less than a second he had me in a choke hold. Not being able to break free I knew I had less than a minute before I lost consciousness, after only fifteen seconds the lights were going out, the ringing in my ears was getting louder with every beat of my heart. Everything went into slow motion as the lights got dim, thoughts of Olivia and Apollo flooded my mind, giving me a surge of determination. Feeling around with my free hand my fingers probed in desperation, my hand going under the belt line of his loose fitting sweats. I didn't realize it at the time, but I had dug my fingers into his genitals. When I came up with a handful of his scrotum I squeezed hard in a last futile attempt at making the little bull lose his grip. Crushing one of his testicles in my right hand, he let out a scream like a banshee. It was just enough for me to roll out, turning the table on the little bull.

We toppled over the big man's still warm body, the smell of his last bodily function filling my nose with human stench. The little bull slipped in the black puddle of the still warm blood from his dead partner and when our combined weight landed on top of the dead man the stale air was forced from his lungs, coming out in a whoosh. The smell of the bad air burned in my nostrils, I knew it was the smell of death. I could not believe the fierceness of the little man as he went straight back to work on me with no hesitation whatsoever. He should have been tiring and slowing down, but instead he was gaining momentum as the fight went on. His blows were fast and sharp, every time we moved or changed position he would sneak in a punch here and there,

the blows not big enough to do any real damage but definitely taking a toll on me in my already exhausted condition.

I got him in a good position, with me on the bottom, having his back against my chest. With one arm I was applying
an old-fashioned choke hold. Finally managing to reach the
bootlace and wrap it in one of my hands then around his
throat, I used it for a garrote. Releasing my grip with my
other hand, I crossed my clenched hands behind his neck
when the little bull let go and went for the reversal. I pulled
the boot string tight, digging into the flesh of his throat, the
bootlace stopping the critical flow of blood from the jugular
vein to his brain. Pulling with everything I had until the
string was actually cutting into my own hands, the bootlace
sliced into his throat like a piano wire. Hearing him gurgle
as the string severed his throat, he tossed then pitched trying
to get his fingers under the bloody garrote, but it was use-
less. I heard the death rattle in his lungs, lying there breathing deep until my senses cleared. No longer feeling him
breathe, I was positive he was dead.

Pushing the sweaty, dead bull off me, I stood up and
looked around the room. Not remembering how long it had
been since I had actually cried, warm tears streamed down
my dirty face. Every bone in my body felt like it was frac-
tured or broken, my muscles were quivering and cramping.
This was the first time I had ever had to kill another man,
but could justify it to myself knowing it was in self-defense,
kill or be killed. I prayed to God for forgiveness for having
to spill another man's blood. Grabbing the gun, I stuck it in
my waist band and covered it with my shirttails. When I
went outside the fresh air felt incredible. If anybody had
seen me I would have been caught red-handed with the still
warm, wet blood on my hands.

Standing in a shipping yard in Port of Oakland trying to remember what day it was, knowing I had been knocked out for only a few hours, made it Sunday morning. I saw my white Ford F-150 parked outside the fence with the keys in the ignition. When I got control of my emotions, I realized there was a slug from my .44 in the skull of the big man. Could the slug from the unregistered gun be connected to me? It was either toss the gun out the window of the truck going over the Benicia Bridge, or go back inside to find the spent slug. Thinking this through, I still needed my trusty .44, so I knew I had to go back in the sea van and face the grizzly scene.

Taking a deep breath of clean, fresh morning air, I went back inside. The smell was overpowering as I walked into the chamber of death, fly's buzzing around the already congealing blood. Looking for tools I found a welding rod on the ground, using it for a probe, searching for the projectile in the back of his emptied-out brain cavity. Finding nothing there I followed the trajectory, where I found the slug embedded in the insulation of the rear wall. Digging it out with the welding rod I dropped the slug in my shirt pocket as I looked around the van, picking up the boot and the lace, locking the doors behind me. The van was being shipped overseas, where the Russian Mafia was waiting for their cured shipment of bootleg American caviar. Boy, were they in for a surprise.

Back to thinking things through, I put the truck in gear and left the two dead Russians, heading to a gas station to clean up. When I asked for the key which was attached to a piece of grease-stained wood, the man asked me, "Looks you've been working hard all night my friend?"

Trying to smile I answered, "Yessir, they had me tied up all night."

THE WHARF INN

I didn't dare to go anywhere near the cabin for I knew Eric had my location dialed in, after scrubbing the filth from my hands and cleaning up as well as possible, tossing the bloody boot with the lace in the dumpster behind the filling station I then threw the slug from the Magnum as far as I could into a field of tall grass. I got on Highway 24 heading east back to Martinez. Pulling into the Marina, I drove to the boat launch ramp where I could see the *General* sitting peacefully at its berth. Rolling down the window I whistled for Apollo, and watched his big black head look over the gunwale of the boat. First thing I noticed the sturgeon snare was missing from around his neck. He came down the dock at a full run, and when he got to the security gate of the dock he didn't even hesitate, jumping into the water at full speed. Apollo's ninety pounds hit the water like an explosion, his paws turning whitewater like the blades of paddle wheel river boat, as his webbed toes spread and he made quick work of swimming the fifty something feet to the top of the ramp. He ran toward the truck, shaking the water from his thick black coat. Apollo was as glad to see me as I was him. Letting the wet dog into the cab of the F-150, Apollo looked at me like *what are waiting for, we got work to do.*

A vehicle pulled in and I recognized Jason's van as it pulled up. He got out walking to the passenger side of the truck. He stuck his hand out to Apollo, who nuzzled it.

Jason looked at me dead in the eye, the first thing he says is, "Mike, I don't want to know what's going on but if you need help you know you can count on me in any way."

Jason said he'd covered up the *Aquaholic* with the mooring

cover to hide the bullet holes and had found Apollo sitting in the *General* with a sturgeon snare around his neck, which Apollo let him take off. Jason tried to get him to go to his sailboat, but he wouldn't budge. I told Jason thanks but no, and that if I ever needed him I would be sure to let him know.

Thanking God that Apollo was safely in the cab of the truck, I drove to a restaurant in Martini town, ordering two double orders of steak and eggs to go, one order for me, one for my faithful companion. We pulled into the seediest motel in Martini town, called the Wharf Inn, where no identification is required to check in and you could rent a room for only thirty minutes, half or full day, nothing but class. Parking the F-150 in the back parking lot, out of sight from the street, I went inside, paying with cash for the room, a week in advance, no ID required. As I walked in, Apollo heeling with no leash, another tenant was hanging out in his doorway, peddling cheap dope to the locals. The gutter rat asked me if I was the guy who ran the *Sturgeon General*. I answered, "No, but people have asked me that before," playing it off saying that happens a lot.

The smalltime dope dealer asked if I wanted to buy any "gangster," stating he had quarter T's, an old school term from back before they had scales readily available—the dopers would use a teaspoon for a measuring device, quarter T being a quarter teaspoon—for $15, but he would accept $10 because he was broke and hungry. I answered no, that I was straight, and then I gave him a fiver so he could get something to eat. Carrying the bag with the tools and the .44 I entered the room, where it smelled like mold, liquor and stale tobacco smoke.

We wolfed down the grub like starved animals. Feeling

better after a clean shave, I put the .44 in the plastic bag from the trash can liner to bring it in the shower, just in case. After a long hot shower I took the big revolver, putting it in my right hand and wrapping duct tape around my fist with the grip of the revolver inside, leaving my thumb and trigger finger free. No matter what happened I was armed to the teeth. Lying down we both gave in to exhaustion, sleeping motionless for six straight hours. With the dog at my feet between me and the door, if anybody came through it Apollo would be on the job. Knowing where the Magnum was no matter what, I was able to catch some much needed rest.

When I came to lying in the bed, looking up at the peeling paint on the moldy ceiling, I turned on the only light in the room, round white glass covering a single bulb in the middle of the ceiling. There were bugs running around in circles inside the globe, cockroaches over two inches long absorbing the heat from the dull 75-watt bulb. Looking down, there was my faithful companion, as quiet as a church mouse, gently wagging his stubbed tail, obediently waiting for me to take him for a walk outdoors so he could take care of business.

Everything that had happened in the past 72 hours came back like a nightmare of grisly, reoccurring flashbacks. I couldn't believe my own train of thought, going over the whole scenario again and again in my mind to make sure I had covered my tracks, that no evidence could be traced to me. If I got locked down the chances of finding Olivia would be eliminated. The slug from the .44 was long gone, the boot with the lace as well. The next detail was to get rid of my filthy clothes, so after taking care of Apollo with a short walk we drove to a Goodwill to stock up on some used, ordinary clothes as part of the plan forming in my head.

THE AQUADESIAC

We headed east on Highway 4 to a marina upriver in Pittsburg. There's a broker there named Tocci, with used boats for sale year-round. I came across a 23-foot late model Crownline. She had a 9-foot beam with hose-down decks, white upholstery, a single swivel captain's high back bucket seat, with wrap-around sectional seating. The body of the boat was ivory white with burgundy wine panels and gold pin striping, the two-tone colors showing off her lines. With less than a hundred hours on the engine hour meter she was equipped with a head, a denatured alcohol stove topped with a stainless steel sink, green and gold laced marble countertops, surround sound music system and romantic mood rope lights that supplied soft lighting in the luxurious quarters. Looking around the pimped out cabin of the boat I thought to myself that this was much more than I was used to but could see where I could appreciate the upgrades, knowing the romantic setting of the "stabbin' cabin" would come in handy someday, the sooner the better.

Lifting up the rear bench seat that rolled back on hinges and was incorporated into a motor cover / doghouse, I saw the cleanest engine and bilge area I had ever seen on a used boat. The Volvo Penta M-300, a fuel-injected 305-cubic-inch 300 hp small block, looked like it was brand new out of a crate. Checking the fluids and belts I found everything was in good repair, the oil on the end of the dipstick looked brand new. The hull was designed with a semi-modified deep V that would eat waves effortlessly. She was capable of well over 50 miles an hour with the new style of hull and updated Volvo Penta 280 dual, state of the art, counter-rotating props.

Talking with the salesman, an older man with the obvious permanent tan of a river rat, Tocci said he recognized me, that he had been on the *Sturgeon General* before and had success, catching a keeper sturj'.

Now was the best time to negotiate. He was asking $33,000 for the beautiful power launch, but I knew the asking price was inflated. After negotiations we worked out a deal at $29,000, and after hours of paperwork I gave him $4,000 cash as a down payment then worked out a payment plan. The fuel tank was full at maximum capacity of seventy gallons. I couldn't believe she had a "side finder 3000 depth sounder/fish finder." I turned the key where she caught fire on the first bump. The high output, small block purred like a kitten, she ran so quiet you could barely hear her at all. Asking the old river rat if I could keep the trailer and my truck there for a week or two, he said it would be all right but if it went longer than the end of the month I would have to pay a storage fee. He gave me the combination to the lock on the gate, where I left the F-150 parked next to the boat trailer, grabbing the bag with the .44 and the soft zipper case with the M-1 inside. Tocci saw the gun case and said that duck season ended over a month ago. Thinking fast I told him I'd been to the target range and didn't want to leave it behind.

Walking back down to the slip, seeing my new boat moored in its slip, I got that same old feeling of excitement that any mariner gets when he is ready to untie the mooring lines and shove off. No matter what is on your mind or how bad a day you're having, it seems like as soon as you untie your last rope you are leaving it all behind. Apollo jumped right in like it was his boat, taking his position on point in the passenger side. The salesman offered to help me shove off.

As I was standing there Tocci asked me what I was going to name her. Right then and there, looking right at him, I told him my old boat was named the *Aquaholic* and that the way this boat makes me feel when I look at her I think the *"Aquadesiac"* has a nice ring to it. Never having had the luxury of being able to afford anything like this boat or the F-150, I have to admit, it felt good spending Eric's money.

CHAPTER 11

GATHERING INTEL

Two hours of daylight left there was light cloud cover with prevailing Delta winds blowing ten to fifteen knots, heading directly upriver. With an incoming tide the water would lay flat all 20 miles, from the "City of Pitty" to Martini town. Leaving the entrance of the marina, I tapped the horn twice as I throttled up then pointed the bow of my new boat upriver to a restaurant named Humphrey's, after a wayward whale that had come up river years ago. I was getting to know my new toy. The synthetic wood grain steering wheel was gorgeous, smaller than I was used to as the boat came equipped with power steering. Because of the newer design of the outdrive she didn't need additional trim tabs to get on plane, and the throttle was more responsive than I had expected with the semi-modified deep V. The waves would normally fly up past the boat at forty-five-degree angles as the bow powered through the water, but with the newest technology of the hull, the waves seemed to spray like flat sheets of water, horizontally, away from the bottom of the hull across the surface of the river. She rode so smooth you could drink from a champagne glass without spilling a drop.

Being able to motor at top speeds we were making excellent time, enjoying the gracefulness of the sweet little boat. The gauges were all reading perfectly with amperage, water temperature and oil pressure right on the money. The fuel gauge didn't seem to move at all even though I was running hard upriver against the incoming tide. I stopped at Humphrey's, with access by land or water, then took the dog for a quick walk. Pointing at the boat, snapping my fingers, Apollo walked down the dock and jumped back in the boat without so much as looking back. He could smell the food and knew exactly what I was doing. Going inside, ordering from the bar, I ordered a draft beer to drink while waiting for the food. I found the men's room, taking care of business, splashing cold clean water on my face then slicking my hair back in the mirror. Wearing my used clothes as a sort of disguise I looked like any other typical river rat that might wander through the door. I didn't care for the appearance, but I could play it off and get away with it if I had to. Shoving off, motoring slowly, getting back on course, I set one order for the big black dog on the floor. I took a minute to enjoy the grub; Apollo was done in seconds, the four quarters of his club sandwich with fries seemed to disappear. Apollo looked at me then pushed his big head against my leg, giving thanks for the food. He went down into the cabin where he made himself at home, taking over the ample-sized V berth bed with the overstuffed pillows. A good soldier knows when to rest, and he was asleep in seconds.

Having finished the food, I felt instantly revitalized from the nutrition and the bounce from the draft beer. The carbohydrates with the protein made for good brain food. I cleared my mind of everything going on. It was like wiping down a large chalkboard where I could think more clearly with a clean slate. I was motoring down river past Pitsburg with the sun on it's way down. The reflection of the sun sinking in the west looked like an endless highway of gold bricks on the surface of the water. The long line of commute vehicles coming downhill on highway 4 with the sun making the chain of endless headlights look like a woman's diamond tennis brace. Heading all the way downriver past the Fleet, I motored into the Benicia Marina, where "waspy" Yacht Club Members were hanging out. Motoring in I got a lot of hard looks from the regulars, not that I was doing anything wrong but I was an outsider. The gas dock and visitors' slips were incorporated into the harbormaster's quarters. As I idled up, Ron, the harbormaster recognized me. He came out to help tie me off.

Ron said, "How you been, Mike? ...haven't seen you in a coon's age." He let out a long, low whistle, saying the Crownline was the prettiest boat he had ever seen, asking if she was brand new.

I said, "Glad to see you, Ron," answering the boat was new to me, but she was a few years old. Asking Ron if I could moor her in the guest slip in the back row for a few days, I explained that I needed to make arrangements to have the *Aquaholic* towed from the Martinez Marina then stored in dry dock. Paying in advance, I collected the keys to the guest dock.

After taking care of business with Ron, Apollo and I launched, feathering the fuel feeder as we motored past the yacht club, trying not to disturb the peaceful, serene setting. We headed further downriver to a dock at the end of 9th Street. The sleepy little town of Benicia was the original site of the state capitol before it was moved to Sacramento. Benicia is one of the oldest towns on the river, famous for being a historical fishing village, populated with Italian and Portuguese ancestry. I gave a hand signal to Apollo with my flat palm to stay behind and guard the boat. As I walked into town it felt great to stretch my legs, and I stocked up on supplies.

Once in the deepwater channel, stabbing the fuel feeder to its stops, I was on plane in seconds. The beautiful boat handled like a Ferrari. The surface of the channel was covered in a light chop, my bow cutting through the waves effortlessly. The breeze in my face carried the scents and smells of the refineries that operate seven days and nights all year round. The smell made me think back to my first day on the job in an oil refinery where I was complaining about the rank odor. An old slick told me that was the smell of money, and that over a period of time I would get used to it. I motored up the Carquinez Straits, past Martinez, under the Benicia Bridge, steering between the columns with the *Glomar Explorer* coming up off the port side bow. There would be no naval patrol until later, at 9:00. Taking a chance I killed my navigation lights and stealthily approached the west side of the channel, coming up above Eric's shop on the deserted bank of the river. There is a frontage road that follows the channel, but the traffic was sparse at this time of evening on a Sunday night.

Killing the engine I let the outgoing tide carry the boat silently with the fast-running current. Apollo was working his keen nose, trying to catch a scent of anything in the air. The boat was drifting maybe ten feet off the bank. When I got within 150 feet of Eric's dock I hit the toggle switch dropping the claw anchor, letting it freefall. The anchor dug in as the boat positioned itself. After making sure the anchor had a good bite holding solid, I released the toggle letting out maybe 50 feet more anchor line, then locked the hoist again and checked my position. There was not a soul in sight from the back of the shop and nothing stirring on the dock. The lights were all off. Deciding to get a little more daring I let out more anchor line, getting close enough where I could see more of the front of the shop, but still nothing worth seeing. Sitting there for another hour, I was now close enough that I could safely step off the swim deck on the back of my boat and walk across Eric's dock toward his property.

Apollo looked at me for an order where I gave him a hand signal, snapping my fingers to sit then an open flat palm to stay. He sat and stayed without hesitation. With the .44 in my hand, I crept up toward the shop. Walking past the covered berth, the first thing I saw was the HydroHoist. I had seen a lot of this style of hoist in my day but never one that sat this deep, submerged in the water.

Olivia had told me there was an apartment on the second story of the shop. Walking around until I was directly below what had to be the living quarters, I stopped and listened but heard nothing but traffic on the nearby bridge and the gentle breeze blowing through the grass surrounding the shop. Shutting my eyes I listened, hearing the sounds of nature, crickets then small nocturnal animals scrambling looking for food or fleeing from predators for survival. I opened my eyes, hearing the wind off the wings of an owl flying overhead, then a small feral cat working its way through the tall grass like a tiger in the jungle. I could hear my heartbeat pounding in my ears. Standing there listening for all of fifteen minutes, I convinced myself that if anybody was inside, they were in a deep sleep.

I climbed a utility stairway, then using a four-inch rainwater downspout I managed to climb onto the roof, certain there was nobody there. Putting my ear to a two-inch vent riser penetrating the roof, any sound at all from inside the small apartment-style living area would be amplified. Any noise whatsoever would be easily detected in the quiet stillness of the night. I found the door and entered the lavishly furnished apartment, walls lined with historical nautical and naval hangings, complete with every type of submarine in history, including illustrations of the U-80, the first sub used in U.S. military operations. After a complete search I came up empty-handed, no sign of Olivia whatsoever. Now armed with the knowledge that she was not in the shop or the apartment, my brain was in gear. Walking outside I breathed the fresh air deep into my lungs, then headed back to the boat. Hearing a metal-on-metal sound, I stopped and got low, squinting to let my eyes adjust to the darkness. Not hearing anything more, I waited for five minutes, knowing better than to underestimate my enemy. After I sensed everything was safe I made my way back to the boat, stepping on the swim deck, where Apollo was waiting on point as usual. Operating the toggle on the dash, I reeled in about half of my anchor line, putting a safe distance between me and Eric's shop. The water was the color of dark gray steel, the current streaming past the boat with the stern moving gently back and forth, everything so peaceful. Looking around and listening for a full five minutes I then reeled in my remaining line, weighing anchor, slowly cruising the boat out past the *Glomar Explorer*. I turned on the depth sounder / fish finder to make it look like I was an everyday fisherman, scoping the bottom for a sturgeon.

Out of the peace and quiet, the Sidefinder indicated a signal from 60 feet off the starboard. The tide was now on its way in. I swung the nose of the boat so I would stay in the same position. By using my lower unit as a rudder, with the southeast prevailing wind and leaving the boat in gear at the lowest possible throttle setting allowed the boat to hold position. The signal came again, this time marking at 40 feet. I held my position in the current and waited. Apollo stirred awake and came out to his favorite spot, right across from me on the passenger side. He kept his eyes glued to the *Glomar Explorer* while constantly working the wind with his nose. That big black dog knew something was up with the *Glomar*. Apollo was trying to tell me something, but I couldn't figure out what. The big black dog rarely barks. When he is on alert he never makes a sound so he can surprise intruders. Apollo, looking at the *Glomar* barked so loud it scared the daylights out of me, so powerful I could feel the bark in my chest.

Another signal at 20 feet off the starboard and then another one directly under my boat; seeing bubbles appear on the surface and smelling a distinct scent I remembered from the night I hooked the big sturgeon and lost him under the *Glomar*, I knew I was getting warmer, closer to figuring something out.

As suddenly as the indications on the Sidefinder appeared, they were gone. I searched the area for several more hours, running in a grid like mowing a lawn, then starting where I saw the last signal, motoring in circles with each rotation getting larger, the electronics showing no sign. I gave up the search, motoring back to Benicia to stash the new boat in the visitor slip. I put the dog on a leash and walked him for a while before leaving him locked him in the cabin to guard the *Aquadesiac*.

PEEPHOLE

I got in the F-150 then drove back toward Martinez,

stopping at a store to buy a shaving kit with all the needed toiletries. After a long hot shower at the hotel, I checked the cylinders in the Magnum, duct-taping the Pachmayr grip in my right hand, lying down on the bed for just long enough to clear my head, as the exhaustion crept in on me.

I must have dosed off, waking slowly, hearing pipes from some kind of hot rod, deep throaty exhaust from some radical high-performance engine just idling in the street in front of my room. The dope dealer in the hallway must have been in contact with Eric and ratted me out.

Slowly unwinding the duct tape off the .44, my face against the door peering through the peephole I saw a Chop Top 1970 Chevrolet Caprice Classic, black with a lot of blue pearl paint, all the windows down. As I sat there admiring the car through the peephole there was a reflection from the sun glaring back at me from inside the car. Instantly I pulled my head away from the peephole, realizing I was looking at the optical glass of the scope of a rifle, just as I was pulling my head away the first shot came through the peephole. If I hadn't moved when I did the 120-grain soft-nosed jacketed hollow point from the silenced, semi-automatic Ruger Mini-14 would have gone straight through my eye and out the back of my skull.

Without hesitation I dove for the floor as the bullets stitched the door from the peephole down. Hearing the tires burn when he stepped on the gas, there was no way I could burn off a round without attracting heat, so I held my fire. I couldn't go out the front door so I grabbed everything I could fit in my bag then went out the back window to where I had the F-150 stashed. I drove away slowly as the Martinez Police were pulling in. Looking like an average, everyday construction worker driving an everyday white work truck and wearing the used Goodwill clothing, nobody gave me a second glance as I drove out of Martinez, hoping I hadn't left anything behind that could possibly tie me to the room. I drove back to Benicia to catch some more shut eye in the Aquadesiac.

CHAPTER 12

SUPER BOWL STURGEON DERBY

When I woke up my eyes slammed open, wide awake—understanding Apollo's reaction to the *Glomar* I knew I had no time to waste. Leaving Benicia, the first thing I noticed were all the boats on trailers heading toward the marina. The General was not booked, but the biggest fishing tournament of its kind was going to start the following morning. The Super Bowl Sturgeon Derby takes place every year, first week of February, Super Bowl weekend. From Thursday night until Sunday at noon, there are trucks with boats on trailers backed up for miles waiting to launch. The Derby is the biggest tournament of its type in the world. Under normal circumstances I would have the *Sturgeon General* chartered both days, two shifts: the first all day, the second all night.

The tournament starts at 7:00 a.m. on Saturday morning. Anglers from everywhere fish from every kind of boat until noon on Sunday, the hearty fisherman trying their luck and angler skills for 36 hours straight, rain or shine. Back in the day I used to rent a slip for the weekend, where the party started on Friday night, featuring a live bluegrass band, numerous tapped kegs of cold beer, half a side of barbeque beef turning on a spit, plus a pig in the ground—all you can eat and drink for ten bucks a head. In the morning, after they spin the roulette-style wheel to determine the target length of the sturj', the anglers all motor out of the two inlets running parallel away from both marinas, McAvoy's and Harris Yacht Harbor. Watching the hundreds of boats pulling out in the morning it looks like some kind of naval force of fishing boats coming out in formation. It always reminded me of the scene from the movie Jaws where they had offered a reward for the shark, with all the boats full of drunken fisherman, chumming as they left the marina. The only chumming going on here would be from hung-over anglers paying the price for partying all night.

The boundaries of the Derby are the Antioch Bridge on the east and then thirty miles downriver to the San Rafael Bridge at the mouth of San Pablo Bay on the west. There are as many as ten thousand boats entered so it is quite a party. Sturgeon anglers talk about and prepare for the derby for months. They tie up next to each other, camp, party and fish with friends and relatives. To compete officially, every boat has to fly a banner off the bow in plain sight and every sturgeon entered must be alive and fresh, since every kind of trick has been attempted from every kind of cheater. Back in the day there were two marinas side by side in Pittsburg: McAvoy's and Harris Harbor. Back then the rules were you had to launch out of either harbor on Saturday morning. After spinning the roulette style wheel to pick the target length between 46-inch minimum and 72-inch maximum. The slots being called out to one-sixteenth of an inch. First prize was usually $17,000 to $20,000, depending on how many contestants enter the derby.

I thought back about all the Derbies I had fished in over the years, the first one when I was ten years old. My father had told everybody that worked for him at Southern Pacific Pipeline, SPPL. Dad had explained to his crew from the PL outfit that anybody who had a boat was entering the Derb'.

This wasn't a direct order but when the old man talked, people listened. My father rigged it where SP had to pay the entry fees, the grub, the gasoline for the boats and all the beer they could drink, writing off the whole trip as a company picnic. One thing you can say about my dad, he was "slicker than spit on a gold tooth."

Going back in time, I remembered fishing out of smaller, older boats, a lot of alcohol-related, cloudy, cold nights exposed to all kinds of weather. As I got older, to where I could afford bigger and better boats, I would always have a fishing partner onboard for the Derby so I could put out four rods with a two-rod sturgeon stamp. Whoever I brought usually crashed out in the small but comfortable cabin of the boat, which was okay with me because it enabled me to fish with five rods: my two-rod stamp, his two plus an extra. I'd bait up then cast out wide to the starboard side, letting the current bring the bait directly behind the stern—cast one out, reel one in, so four rods were in the water at once, increasing my odds of setting the hook. I'd use four identical rods, Ugly Stik Medium Lights, with various different baits: fresh live grass shrimp, ghost and mud shrimp, lamprey eel, salmon roe, night crawlers, blood worms, just to name a few. As we got older the Derby was an annual event where we were able to afford lobster tails to go along with elk back straps or wild boar sausage, eating like kings, consuming large amounts of alcohol and fishing like madmen. Out of maybe fifteen derbies in my life, I've only entered one fish where I was "on the board," for about an hour. There have been a lot of heated arguments plus a few good fist fights at the Derby headquarters over the actual length of an entered sturj'.

Focusing in, I couldn't believe that my boat, the *Sturgeon*

General was sitting at its berth collecting dust, covered in seagull droppings, but I had to get Olivia back if she was still alive. Eric had attempted to kill me on four separate occasions. I knew time was running out. Driving back to Benicia where I had the *Aquaholic* towed and stored in dry dock, I loaded up my truck with fishing equipment, a small inflatable raft with a 12-volt electric trolling motor, foul weather gear and a few odds that I might need including the VHF ship to shore radio and antennae. I drove to the bait shop in Benicia, where local fishermen were hanging out drinking beer while waiting for their precious, fresh bait they had reserved in advance for the Derby, telling long tales of past tournaments and getting up to speed on the latest hotspots.

When I got to the marina and let the dog out of the cabin of the boat, where he'd been locked down for over eight hours, the first thing I did was take him for a long walk. Apollo hadn't touched his food or water, not knowing when I would return. Coming back to the boat he made quick work of the food then drank the water bowl dry. I took him for another run then waited for darkness to execute the next part of my plan. Looking around the luxurious cabin of the boat, I said a small prayer thanking God for my blessings and keeping me alive up to this point. I broke out the Stoli, filling a red Solo plastic cup with ice, topping it off with voddy and raising the glass in salute to the dog, telling Apollo he was the best partner a man ever had, human or canine. Apollo nuzzled my hand in recognition, and then was instantly asleep. The Stoli calmed my nerves where I was starting to relax. I knew I had better get some shut eye myself, slipping off into a short but deep slumber.

KISS - KEEP IT SIMPLE, STUPID

When I woke up everything was crystal clear, I knew what Apollo had been trying to tell me and where to find Olivia. Man's best friend had saved the day. Knowing a man has to do what a man has to do, it was time to get started. My plan was to keep it simple, transporting the raft to the slip, borrowing the fully charged 12-volt battery from the F-150, connecting the terminals then testing the electric trolling motor, tying off the raft to the back of the boat and rig the VHF radio in the 23-footer. Setting the fishing rods in the holders I motored out as slow as possible with the small gray rubber dingy in tow. Even though it was 1:00 a.m. it did not surprise me to see a few fishermen milling around the marina. After all, this was Super Bowl Sturgeon Derby weekend.

Cruising the Crownline downriver past Benicia and then positioning my boat between the bridge and the *Glomar Explorer*, I dropped anchor, setting my tines three times, releasing twenty feet of line in between each pull to ensure the anchor would stick. Even though I wasn't flying the banner from the derby, I cast a rod out the back with no bait just to make it look like I was just a fisherman pulling an all-nighter. I switched on the anchor light, tuned in the electronics and waited. Seeing no sign of light or any kind of activity, I put on my insulated overalls and a black night watchman's cap, filling my pockets with three sets of speed loaders for the .44, plus six in the cylinders. I strapped on a headlight and pulled on some black gloves made of wet suit type material, waterproof and thick enough for what I had planned.

Loading the rubber raft with gear then releasing the mooring line, I spun her around and ran with the current toward the *Glomar,* where she made good time running with the tide. The 12-volt motor ran almost completely silent, only making a slight whine. Sitting in the back of the dingy with my 200 pounds on the back bench, my right hand operated the small tiller, twisting the throttle grip as I navigated to the west side of the *Glomar* on the opposite side of the main deepwater shipping channel. The four mooring chains of the *Glomar,* two off each side of the bow and two more off each side of the stern, were secured to large concrete mooring anchors on the bottom of the channel. I tied off to the rope handles of the gray rubber raft using a bowline knot, the other end of the rope through the large link of the mooing chain.

As I stepped from the raft, placing my heavy black neoprene gloves in the 12-inch links of the chain, the toe of my boots barely fit in the large oval links. I let out line as the little gray rubber dingy floated lazily away with the current until the slack in the 100-foot rope was drawn tight with the resistance from the current, with the little gray boat tucked in along the waterline of the behemoth flat gray sides of the *Glomar Explorer.* The gray dingy was camouflaged against the primer gray *Glomar* where it seemed to disappear from sight.

Climbing up the anchor chain was quite a chore, having to stop and rest several times. Finally getting to the top, I secured the .44 in my belt, taking a break sitting on the deck behind a bulkhead, knowing I had gotten onboard without being detected. Exploring the ship, the gangways were lit up just enough from the reflection of the primer gray and red oxidized paint that covered every surface of the exposed deck. I stopped and pulled the binoculars from inside the overalls, studying the surrounding waters. With the Crownline holding steady, everything seemed to be in order, so I started to explore the massive decks, imagining what the ship must have looked like with a fully manned crew, steaming off the coast of Hawaii in crystal clear blue water and tropical sunshine. After walking the entire perimeter I followed a set of fresh footprints, finding a small micro-cassette video recorder mounted on a rail where it was pointed in the direction of the draw section of the railroad trestle. The camera was set on ultra-slow speed, which would record up to eight hours. I looked through the lens and saw that it was focused in on the "H" section of the drawbridge, where the bridge was raised for the passing of large ships. The camera was connected to a coaxial cable that ran down an air shaft, Eric's crude but effective security.

My senses all automatically switched to high alert. Closing my eyes to small slits to let my pupils dilate and adjust to the dark, every nerve in my body was tighter than a bow string magnifying every noise. Layers of bird droppings were crunching under my feet, sounding like broken glass under my boots. The footprints led me down a series of stairs. Having to clear thick cobwebs, I came to a door that I couldn't budge. I found a deck scraper with a heavy, five-foot handle, using it to pry open the door. The hinges squeaked in protest, but the door came free. The first thing I noticed was the smell of fresh air. I pulled the Magnum and opened the cylinders, double checking that the six chambers were loaded. Working my way down the stairwell I entered a cavernous area maybe five stories tall, where I saw a dim light. Getting low, I killed my strap on headlight. As my eyes adjusted I got out the binoculars and studied.

The longer I looked the less I believed what I was seeing. It looked like a giant swimming pool in the bottom of the cavern. The water seemed to be alive. Overhead numerous trolley cranes with remote controls hung down within arm's reach. I was close enough to hear the water running underneath the bowels of the ship. All the rumors I had been hearing for many years were true, about the *Glomar Explorer* being designed for covert operations, with the hollow cavity designed to recover the Russian sub under the cover of stealth.

There was a dock running down one side of the water, leading to a living area where Eric had set up camp; a small machine shop that had been converted to a sleeping area with a door that was locked with a heavy padlock. Hanging on the wall I saw my sturgeon rod with leader, complete with my padlock that I had lost the night I thought I had hooked the big sturgeon. I couldn't suppress my grin when I realized that I had snagged his submarine.

Next to Eric's quarters there was what looked like parts from a water propulsion system out of a jet ski. I realized Eric's sub had sucked my leader into its water intake, the 100-pound monofilament leader wrapping itself around the impellor. This had slowed him down but the padlock had done the trick, causing irreversible damage to the blades. Thinking this over, I remembered he had lost half his power when I sent the padlock down my fishing line. Sensing a weakness in the design of the sub, I knew I had discovered his Achilles heel. This confirmed all my suspicions of the miniature sub, making me feel better knowing I wasn't completely insane. Eric had been hiding in the bowels of the ship. Everybody knew Eric was highly intelligent, but this was truly amazing.

Studying the area, Eric had rigged a paddle wheel, with

the current from the continuous tide rotating the shaft supplying energy from a miniature hydroelectric plant, charg-
ing the ship's large deep cycle batteries, a never-ending
supply of free electricity. Eric kept his modern day "pirate's
lair" fully illuminated with the existing large overhead low-
sodium lighting. Exploring the surrounding structure, I
found a large padlock on a heavy metal door, but also a
handy oxygen & acetylene rig. I turned on the gauges then
strung out the leads. Using the striker I lit the torch, the
feathers of the flame casting an eerie light in the dark part
of the cavern. I cut off the lock and opened the door. I was
in shock at what I saw.

Olivia still wore the cocoa brown dress. She was tied to
a steel beam with her bare dirty feet barely touching the
ground, her arms stretched wide like she was nailed to a
crucifix. Sitting on a stand in front of her was a monitor
showing a bird's eye view of the railroad bridge. She was
unconscious, her filthy matted hair hanging down covering
her face, dress ripped to shreds barely covering her body,
covered in dirt and grime. Pulling her hair out of her face I
could see where tears had cut runnels through the dirt on
her cheeks. Holding my hand over her mouth, I shook her
gently to wake her up. It took a while but she slowly regained consciousness. Olivia had obviously been drugged.
That's when I started to feel the black rage burning inside.

When Olivia finally came to she didn't even know who I
was at first. When she recognized me the first thing she said,
"They call you Stone because you ROCK!"

I cut her loose and looked in the small fridge, finding a
cold bottle of water. She tried to gulp the water at first,
because she was obviously heavily dehydrated. As I made
sure Olivia sipped the water slowly, she started to cry,

trying to tell me that Eric had confessed to her that he had killed his father when he was eighteen, making it look like an accident at the shop.

"Eric told me the whole story..." Olivia was fading in and out, but she made sure I understood what she was trying to tell me. E.Z. had actually been born with the name Elias. Eric was his younger brother, who was only three at the time but big for his age, where people would mistake him for Elias, the older but smaller brother. When E.Z. was just six years old, his mother along with his younger brother Eric got in a bad automobile accident, killing both of them. His father knew that Elias was to replace him someday, to run his empire, and although young Elias showed signs of high intelligence his dad thought that his smaller size would challenge his confidence, handicapping him. When Eric got killed the father told the authorities that the boy's badly damaged dead body found after the accident was the older boy, switching the birth certificates where Elias was really Eric and vice versa. The highly intellectual "Eric" now had full advantage over every kid in his age group—imagine thirteen-year-olds competing against ten-year-olds.

Eric's father had told him all of this on his eighteenth birthday. It was too much for him to comprehend, going into a blind rage. In his own mind he thought he was super-human, being physically as well as mentally superior to everyone—in his school studies, sports, fistfights—in everything. This was when E.Z. $ turned his talents toward becoming a career criminal. Eric's father was found dead the next day.

His father still loved to weld where he often worked by himself, running beads over Eric's welds. E.Z. was the fastest welder that ever struck an arc, but maybe with a few repairs here and there. His father would not even tell Eric, he would just add metal in low spots, maybe tie in an edge or repair small pinholes. Eric's dad had bad lungs from decades of burning rod. When he welded he had a custom hood that supplied medical grade oxygen into the helmet while sucking the smoke out with a built-in ventilator. Eric had switched the labeling on the cylinders where his dad was breathing odorless and tasteless argon, which was too much for the seventy-year-old lungs to handle, resulting in his father's death.

Confidence shattered from being misled since the age of six, Eric had killed his own father to get his hands on the family business. E.Z. had told Olivia his plan to kill the both of us. I held her for a minute then told her she had to get it together because we had a long way to go, and that time was short. Olivia stopped in her tracks. She told me to look straight into her eyes and listen carefully to every word she was going to say. She explained that Eric had never beaten me at anything, he'd cheated—his entire life was a lie. Olivia told me it was black and white, goodness over evil, light over darkness.

"You're the good guy Mike Stone. Just remember, Mike; Eric is too smart for his own good. You're going to have to outthink him to win." Looking into Olivia's green eyes, digesting this new information, everything became clear why I could never compete with the rich and famous Eric Zachary... excuse me, make that Elias Zachary.

We started to walk down the dock, my body running on pure adrenaline. When I got to the top deck the fresh air hit me like a gift from heaven. As the narcotics were wearing off, Olivia faded in and out, trying to focus through glazed eyes but nodding on and off. Checking the time, it was 6:15 a.m.

Twenty minutes of darkness left before sunup. I checked on my boat and to my good luck the tide was still coming in, the current heading toward the *Glomar*. I had to figure a way of getting Olivia down to the raft, she had to wake up and wake up quick. After shaking her over and over I slapped her hard across the face. She thought I was Eric and spit in my face. Pulling her hair away from her eyes, I slapped her again. Olivia blinked as she tried to focus, asking me what I wanted her to do. Stripping off my clothes, I tied my overalls around the boots in a bundle, knowing I couldn't swim with the heavy overalls. I found a length of rope and tied my right hand to Olivia's left, with ten feet of rope between us. The loose end of the rope I attached to the bundle of overalls with the boots.

Olivia started to come to, looking around in bewilderment. Kissing her dry, swollen lips I told her she had to do exactly what I said, explaining my plan quickly where she didn't argue. On the count of three we jumped together off the bow of the *Explorer*. The 60 feet down to the surface of the cold water took an eternity, the frigid water felt like hitting concrete. The salty brine burned our eyes as the current drew us toward the raft. We were pushing off the *Glomar Explorer*, the barnacles and growth on the side of the ship cut like a thousand small razor blades drawing blood, the salt working its way into the cuts. As we came up on the raft I held one side as Olivia climbed in, barely able to hold the small boat steady as I pulled myself up. Once onboard I showed her where to sit to balance our weight. We started to lose ground against the current. I showed Olivia how to operate the throttle and steer the tiller and shaking the water out of the heavy revolver, I tossed the Magnum on the floor of the raft. With Olivia operating the handgrip throttle as I was pulling on the rope, the current was still coming in hard, making it a real chore to get back to the safety of the anchored *Aquadesiac*.

While the raft was floating beside the *Glomar Explorer* the rough surface of the bow had worn through the thin quarter-inch rope. Half way back the rope broke and we were quickly drifting the wrong way. Having no choice I jumped back in the water, grabbed onto the stern and started kicking my legs to help move us along. We were maybe fifty feet away when, after three or four minutes I felt the beginning stages of hypothermia setting in, feeling my heartbeat throbbing in my head like somebody beating on a drum, every breath like molten lava burning my throat. The salty, ice-cold water kept getting in my mouth. As my body temperature dropped, my muscles were beginning to seize. I was on the edge of giving in when I heard Apollo hit the water.

Having left him tied in the boat he had slipped his collar then jumped into the icy water. Apollo came swimming to me, and then circled around, heading back to Crownline. Grabbing a handful of his thick black mane he towed us back to safety.

We climbed onto the swim deck as Olivia grabbed the bundle of clothes and the .44 then let the raft drift free in the current. Climbing into the cabin cruiser, I started the engine and let it warm up. Apollo acted like all this was normal, nuzzling Olivia's tear-covered face welcoming her back. I found a sleeping bag and wrapped it around Olivia who was shivering uncontrollably, her straight white teeth chattering. She was also shaking uncontrollably pulling out of her drugged stupor. I lit the white gas stove for heat, saying a silent prayer thanking God I had rescued the damsel in distress.

STURGEON FEVER

CALL OF DUTY

Daylight was just beginning to break, the Super Bowl Sturgeon Derby fishermen on their way to the most famous sturgeon fishing hole on the planet, The Naval Reserve Moth Ball Fleet. What I saw next, if I had not seen with my own eyes I wouldn't have believed. But there it was; the railroad drawbridge was being lifted. It was still halfway dark, coming up the channel past Benicia I saw a large ship painted red and white, fully loaded carrying Liquefied Petroleum Gas coming around the point from Benicia. Flashing back to the drawings in Eric's shop, thinking of the camera aimed at the railroad drawbridge, I knew what was going to happen. Somehow Eric was going to blow up the ship as it passed under the bridge. I picked up the microphone on the VHS marine radio, turning the selector to the coast guard emergency channel number16. The operator came back instantly, with strict instructions that channel 16 was exclusively for coast guard only. Trying to explain that this was a matter of a national emergency, they instructed me to go to channel 22. So I switched channels, where I was instantly stepped on by numerous fishermen who were conversing on every channel.

I told Olivia what Eric had planned, knowing I couldn't afford to waste time. Realizing what I had to do, I put the cabin cruiser in gear and idled up toward the anchor, holding the toggle on the automatic hoist. Anchor retrieved, I told Olivia what she had to get done, explaining about the transfer boat coming our way. She was coming out of her stupor telling me she would do her best. I told her that after I bailed off the boat to head straight for Martinez and put the cabin cruiser in my slip. She asked how I knew the ship's security officers wouldn't shoot me on sight. Explaining to her that in the interest of safety, the cargo of the LPG ship was refrigerated to lower the octane level of the gas. If anybody fired a weapon it would risk blowing up the ship, so they only were allowed rubber bullets in their rifles

The LPG tanker was still a mile and a half away from the bridge, running at twelve knots. When a ship comes "across the pond" there is the ocean captain who navigates from whatever country the ship hails. When the ship reaches the San Francisco Bay, without slowing down the transfer vessel pulls alongside, lowering a gang plank for the captains to walk between ship and transfer vessel. The ocean captain will step off onto the bow of the transfer boat with its oversized whale point and high safety rails and the river captain, who knows the California Delta, can safely navigate the large ocean-going vessel through the tight turns.

Having only one chance, I had to make it count. I'd pull alongside the transfer boat then, with Olivia at the helm of the Crownline, I would simply step across from my boat without stopping and climb aboard the ship. I would calmly explain the situation to the crew of the LPG tanker then play it by ear.

Things didn't quite go as planned. When we pulled alongside I was able to walk from my boat across to the transfer vessel, getting safely onboard the LPG tanker. The crew of the tanker was at the ready, intercepting me with five-armed security officers, the lasers of their fully-automatic rifles, five red dots, trained on my face and chest. Thank God they were only armed with rubber bullets otherwise they might detonate their own boat. I started out by telling everybody this will sound crazy but they had to stop the ship from going under the bridge. I showed the captain the re-fineries on both sides of the channel, telling him that every man onboard, every fishing boat, and everybody that lives next to the refineries plus the impact on the environment was in his hands. He looked at me deep in my eyes search-ing for some kind of an answer. The captain asked me why I didn't call the coast guard.

I told him, "I tried but they kicked me off channel 16, the VHF ship to shore radio was jammed with thousands of fishermen from the Super Bowl Sturgeon Derby." Telling him there was a madman on the loose who was planning a terrorist attack on the three oil refineries, I finished, "I wouldn't have jumped from my boat unless every word I was telling you was the absolute God's honest truth."

The river pilot looked at me, saying I'd better not be mak-ing a fool out of him. We ran together toward the control house, the captain gave the order to throttle down then place both transmissions in neutral. After a pause he placed the transmissions in reverse and pulled the throttles to ten per-cent power. He calmly dropped the ship's anchor on the front starboard side. I was sure all was lost, as I was silently praying; the old river pilot never took his eyes off the bridge, waiting for what seemed like an eternity for the tines of the massive anchor to dig in, then engaged the lock on the chain, we didn't feel anything at first, then slowly but surely the anchor did its job as the massive three-ton anchor with its ten-foot tines slowly but surely dug into the soft clay bottom of the channel, the wise captain let off the throttles then let the ship settle in.

After the LPG tanker slowly rotated 180 degrees, when the stern came to a stop it was less than fifty feet away from the drawbridge. What happened next anybody onboard, all the fishermen in the area, and anybody driving across the bridge will never forget. Eric was watching the entire time from the monitor screen in the *Glomar Explorer*. Having plan B for a backup he detonated the explosives in a last ditch, futile attempt at blowing up the ship.

The waters of the channel opened up like Moses parting the Red Sea, the water erupting straight up into the air. The draw bridge couldn't be seen and the massive giant columns of the bridge were exposed for seconds. The force from the explosion affected the giant tanker like a tsunami, tossing it like a rowboat built from balsa wood. The LPG tanker was rocked from the impact, but suffered no damage. Fishing boats were capsized, pandemonium was everywhere; fishermen in the water, boats capsized, upside down, with many injured but no fatalities.

The crew of the LPG tanker all let out a thunderous yell together in celebration. The old river pilot looked at me and said, "Well kiss my ass, I always wanted to try that." He smiled as he patted me on the back. The fishermen were all helping each other out of the water where it was quite a scene, but everybody knew it could have been a heck of a lot worse.

THE BIG PAYBACK

Remembering the Achilles' heel of the sub, I asked the captain if I could use the ship's VHF radio. I told him I was going to show him an old Indian trick, putting the selector on channel 69, the fishermen's channel.

I listened for a minute, and when there was a break on the air waves I announced over the air, "The sturgeon are practically jumping in the boat all around the *Glomar Explorer*."

After several minutes we watched as dozens of boats came from every direction. Nobody knew why there where boats capsized, the boats virtually surrounded the *Glomar*, dropping anchor, creating a drag net with anchors and fishing lines. Emergency crews as well as coast guard boats were swarming the area, with sheriff helicopters circling overhead. Watching the entire scene from the stern rail of the tanker I saw the first fisherman scream he had a monster sturgeon on his line. I knew what was going to happen next.

The submarine tried to power its way out and make its escape, when another fisherman in a different boat screamed that he was hooked up. The sub started towing both boats, entangling them with dozens of other fishermen. The sub was soon tied up with numerous boats but didn't have the power to get away. The water intakes for the propulsion systems sucked up fishing hooks, leaders and lead fishing weights, rupturing the stainless steel impellors and distorting the housing that pushed the massive supply of water that propelled the underwater vessel. As the sub self-destructed from the inside out, Eric's ingenious invention was now his coffin. The submarine surfaced for a few seconds, with its large rudder and periscope it looked like a giant sturgeon. Nobody said a word, just staring in bewilderment as the sub sank from sight. Only air bubbles and tangled fishing lines were left, the fishermen would swear forever that they had hooked the biggest sturgeon of all time.

The captain and the river pilot looked at me and said I had some explaining to do and the captain offered me some dry clothing. After changing into dry gear we went to the ship's galley to eat. The food tasted better than anything I ever remembered. After we ate the plates of bacon, lettuce and tomato sandwiches served with hot black coffee, the captain told me a coast guard helicopter would land topside on the helipad in a few minutes, asking me if I was all right to talk to authorities. I answered that I really couldn't afford to stick around. The captain then told me that every man onboard, every fishing boat in the area, not to mention the countless lives that I saved in the refineries and surrounding residential neighborhoods, the impact on the environment, the cost of rebuilding both the railroad and automotive bridges, the price of the three major crude oil refineries, the cost alone not counting the human lives was astronomical, somewhere in the hundreds of billions of dollars, and let it be known from this day forward that you shall be hailed as a national hero.

I told the captain, "Thanks for the acknowledgement but I was just doing my red-blooded American duty, that's all." We traded business cards and the captain told me to call him if I needed help with the authorities.

The wise old captain asked if I knew who was responsible for all this, and I told him somebody had to go look inside the *Glomar*, saying that by the looks of things some of those fishermen still had their lines attached to whatever was on the bottom. I couldn't explain it all to him then but the answers were on the bottom of the river. The captain told the river pilot that the ship would not be leaving its present location and that he had called for transportation to pick him up right away.

Bumming a ride with the river pilot we motored over to the Martinez Marina where I jumped off at the guest dock, thanking him for the lift. As I walked down the dock toward my two slips I saw Apollo on point waiting in the Crownline. Olivia opened the door. She had cleaned herself up some, still wrapped in a sleeping bag. I gave her a long hug, asking her if she needed to go to a hospital. She answered firmly, thanks but no, and asked if Eric was still alive. I told her truthfully I didn't have an answer until his body was found.

BLUE COLLAR TO CAPITALIST

I started up the cabin cruiser, letting it run while I untied the mooring lines. Pulling the bottle of Stoli out of the refrigerator I took a long pull straight from the bottle, passing the jug to Olivia who followed suit. She didn't ask where we were going. I slowly made my way on the short trip to Benicia, then home. My own bed felt like a million dollars when my head hit the pillow and I was out like a light. When I awoke the next day to Apollo licking my hand and the sound of a car in the driveway, I really didn't know what to expect, but I knew it wasn't the landscapers because I would have recognized the sound of their truck. I figured my luck had run out, and the authorities were here to haul me in.

Peeping out the window I saw the old gentleman who owned the property. He hadn't been around in over a year but there he was, bigger than life and he wasn't alone. The chauffer got out opening the rear door as Mr. Ellington was helping an older woman get out. I tried to remember if I had ever seen Mr. Ellington smile, because he was definitely smiling now. They walked off hand in hand like two teenagers in love—she was obviously in love with him as much as he was with her. The love birds strolled off together, Ms. O'Malley appraising the ranch with a big smile on her face. Grabbing my robe and slippers, I met him at the driveway. First Mr. Ellington tended to Ms. O'Malley, then after some brief catching up, he gave me instructions that dinner would be served at 7:00 sharp. He said to bring some fresh sturgeon if I had any, but if not fresh then frozen would do. He didn't wait for an answer and went about his business. Mr. Ellington instructed Leon the chauffer/assistant to open up the house to let in some fresh air, then remove the coverings from all the furniture while he walked his new lady around the premises, showing her the sights.

At 7:00 sharp we all sat at the long dining table. Mr. Ellington introduced Ms. Charlotte O'Malley. They had found each other on a cruise in the Mediterranean, where they fell in love at first sight.

After introducing Olivia, Mr. Ellington said with a twinkle in his eye, "Oh yes, the old high school flame, took you long enough to get her back, Mike."

Mr. Ellington called everyone in close, then we toasted to new beginnings. We were all seated at the table with candles lit and lights down low. The wine had been allowed to breathe in an ancient antique crystal decanter. The finest 1961 Napa merlot was poured into oversize goblets where it complemented the savory leg of lamb, blackened then simmered in a red wine sauce. The sturj' was prepared the old fashioned way: cut into fish sticks, soaked in egg, rolled in flour, salt and pepper, dipped in a simple but savory tartar sauce consisting of mayo, red wine vinegar and garlic salt, a little parsley for color. There were dark green patties of sautéed spinach, with several other gourmet sides, plenty of bread along with the wine.

While we waited for dessert the eccentric old gentleman asked what had happened to Olivia and me. Mr. E. said "Nothing personal, but you two look like you've been through a war."

I explained to him that we had been in a wreck in the El Camino and that he probably wouldn't believe the rest of what had happened, adding that I really didn't believe it myself. The old gentleman said when I was ready to tell him the story he couldn't wait to hear it. Then he asked who had been in the tack room, saddle soaping all the leather and straightening things out. He said whoever it was knew what they were doing. Olivia's eyes came back to life like somebody turned on a light switch. Mr. E. asked Olivia about her folks and background where it turned out he had done business with her family years ago and that her parents were famous, reputable thoroughbred breeders. As soon as she mentioned the horse ranch in Montana the conversation went to horse flesh and breeding, where the two of them shared the same opinions about the mare being the most critical part of producing a stud of superior quality. As the old man's eyes clouded, I could see he was going back in time to when he and his former wife were younger, with every stall full of top-end horses. Olivia told the story about when we in high school, sitting on the bale of hay and her black stallion wouldn't let me near her.

Mr. E. laughed long and loud saying, "*That's* why Mike never showed interest in the horses."

After dinner, dessert was served—blackberry cobbler fresh out of the oven served with homemade hand-churned cherry vanilla ice cream. After some serious grubbing, thanking Leon for the screaming dinner and dessert, we all went to the formal living room. The two women acted as though they had known each other all their lives where they were instantly best friends. This gave me a chance to talk to Mr. Ellington. The landlord broke out a bottle of Remy Martin Louis XIII Cognac with two large crystal snifters. Out of his blazer breast pocket he produced two Cuban cigars. Standing on the back deck, lighting up then dipping the Cuban in the cognac, we relaxed for several minutes, letting the food settle, enjoying the peace and tranquility of the cool night air.

This is when Mr. Ellington said, "Mike, I want you to pay close attention to what I am going to tell you. My late wife passed on over fifteen years ago. You know that I sold off all the horse stock because it reminded me of her. I have been traveling the world ever since hoping that by looking at something new every day it would somehow soften the pain of losing the only thing that ever truly meant anything to me." The old timer looked up at the sky, then looking all around as if seeing the ranch for the first time he said, "Mike, I never had children. You're the closest thing to a son I have ever had. Ms. O'Malley is a blue blood—her family has old money that you wouldn't even begin to imagine. If you want it I wish to sign over the deed to the property to you. I have no more use for it and I want it to make somebody as happy as it did me and my late Missus." Mr. Ellington went on, saying he knew I never cared anything about horses and that my only thoughts were for those boats, the skirts and the sturgeon. He said, "Mike, if it works out with the girl, I want you to stock the ranch with thoroughbreds, play a little house with that gal. I don't know much but I know you two make a nice couple. It doesn't matter what has happened in the past, just don't look back—think about how bright your future could be together."

I told Mr. Ellington I would be honored to accept his generous proposal, but I had to sleep on it before answering. The old gent gave me a hug, saying we could talk tomorrow.

He said, "Mike, you look like you could use some rest."

After gathering up Olivia, then saying goodnight to the two love birds, Olivia and I walked out together. As soon as the front door was shut, Olivia asked me why the funny look on my face. Telling her I would answer that question in the morning, after she got ready for bed I kissed her goodnight then tucked her in, me back on the couch, Olivia with Apollo in the bed. I stretched out and tried to absorb some of things Mr. Ellington had told me.

In the morning Olivia was awake sitting at the table drinking a cup of tea, looking worlds better after some good sleep. After telling her of the conversation I'd had the night before with Mr. Ellington, I asked her if she was interested in breeding horses again right here on the ranch. Olivia couldn't talk; she just started bawling her eyes out, the dam breaking as runnels of heavy tears flooded her face. She tried to gather her composure as the recent events caught up with her. The thought of ranching took her to a better place. She kissed me hard on the mouth where I could taste the sweet, salty tears running down her face. I told her she could take her time before she answered, when she jumped up with a renewed freshness, hurrying to take off her robe and putting on her jeans. I asked her what she was doing. Olivia told me she had so much to do. She said she was angry at me because I should have woken her up earlier. Running a ranch like this is a lot of hard work and we were burning daylight. Then she stormed off toward the barn with Apollo on her heels. I said to myself, "I'll take that for a yes."

After breakfast Mr. Ellington said that he already knew the answer to his question, telling me to enjoy the property as much as he had. He'd already been to the barn, bird-dogging Olivia. The old gent asked me if it was all right if he stuck around a month or so, to help Olivia pick out some breeding stock and hire some help. Of course, I couldn't say no. We were standing on the front porch when the sheriff arrived at the front gate. After opening the gates then inviting the sheriff into the cabin for coffee, they explained to Olivia and me that Eric's submarine had been recovered. They wanted Olivia to identify Eric's remains. Although Olivia and E.Z. were never married she had been living with him long enough to be considered his legal wife, where she was legally next of kin. She had run his business while he was doing time and she had power of attorney, her name was on everything he owned, to where my plan was in effect. Five acres of waterfront property, the vast shops, warehouses and everything in them belonged to Olivia, not that she wanted any of it.

TOE TAG

Downtown at the morgue they pulled the sheet off Eric's corpse. We both stared in disbelief at the rich and famous Eric Zachary, E.Z., the famous Eazy Money, no more expensive jewelry, just a toe tag, laid down to rest for eternity. We gave statements about the events that took place. California Fish & Game verified the part of the story about the sturgeon eggs. They claimed that by artificially fertilizing the eggs they would produce a hundred times more fish than in their natural habitat, boosting the sturgeon population for decades to come. The oil companies had come forward with the information about Eric's terrorist demands, the remains of the two Russians were discovered in the sea van, where I claimed self-defense, and that I didn't have time to report it at the time because I had to save Olivia and prevent the attempted terrorist attack on the L.P.G. tanker. All charges were dropped, including the felony speeding ticket for driving 150 miles an hour—80 miles an hour over the posted speed limit—eluding the law, endangering other people on the highway, etc.

After Olivia looked at Eric's face she went into a trance, she couldn't or wouldn't talk. I took her home and put her in the bed to rest. The next day she was up before dawn. She and Mr. Ellington were out near the stalls instructing hired hands, receiving shipments of fresh straw, feed and other supplies. The ranch was alive with activity like I had never seen. The next day horses started showing up from all parts of the country. As happy as I was to see the ranch active, with Olivia as well as Mr. Ellington happy, I knew my ten years of peace and quiet were gone.

As the days went by I started spending time at Eric's old shop, making sure everything was locked and secure. Olivia refused to go anywhere near the compound with the horrific memories. I moved the *Sturgeon General* to the service dock where I had to admit it looked pretty good, the big cigarette boat in the HydroHoist and the Crownline in the covered berth. When I went home that night, I tried to talk to Olivia about the property. She told me she wanted nothing to do with it and asked me if I wanted it. Olivia said if I didn't want it, to sell it, keep the money or donate the whole thing to charity; she didn't care which. She didn't want to talk about it or hear about it ever again. Remembering the buried loot, I dug up the ammo can with the two hundred thousand, putting most of it in the bank, less a little pocket money, because I had a few bills to pay.

THE EL CORVETTO

Olivia and I were driving a brand new white Ford F-350, Super Duty Club Cab King Ranch Truck, a present to Olivia from Mr. Ellington. It came equipped with every option except a snowplow. My car trailer in tow to bring home the remains of the El-Co, we pulled into the impound yard where the El Camino had been in storage. The biker working the counter smiled at me and told me to walk around back, explaining that the boss was on his way here. Then here came Russell on his bike, a radical new Road Glide, custom paint, with 20-inch ape hanger handlebars thrown forward. Russell was so big he made the big Road Glide look like a Schwinn Stingray. The dual thunder headers created noise you could feel in your teeth. Russell parks the bike, raised his big arms wide, smiling ear to ear. I told him I didn't want trouble, just my El Camino.

The overgrown biker walks up saying, "Mike Stone, Stone to the Bone, rock hard, hard bone, Mike stone."

Looking at Russell, nodding toward Olivia, I said, "That's what she said."

I asked Russell how tall he was and he said he was only six-four, but with his boots on and a good hair day, if he stood up straight he was all of six-seven. I then asked him his age. Grinning the whole time he said he was born on February 29th, leap year, so he was really only twelve years old and just big for his age. Finally, I couldn't resist so I asked him what size his obviously-too-small T-shirt was, boy's medium? I said the sleeves were so tight it looked like he shopped at BabyGap.

Russell, still roaring with laughter shaking his big head

back and forth, smiled even harder when he said, "Well, about the El-Co...We heard that you took out E.Z. Money." Russell went on to explain that Eric had enough information on the club to put them all in the pokey, and that by me eliminating Eric I had done the club a very big favor. Russell fished around in the pocket of his black leather cut out— PRES stenciled on the front, flying his colors with the rocker on the back in black and gold, SATAN'S SOLDIERS—producing a remote control. Pointing the fob at a roll-up door as he depressed the button, the heavy steel door rolled up revealing the El Camino.

I was in shock. Expecting to see the remains of my totaled pick up, the body work had been repaired, the paint completely redone, a perfect match, new tonic cover, with brand new chrome bumpers. The first thing I noticed was that the El Camino had a completely different stance, including two Corvette turbo mufflers spaced close together tucked up tight behind the rear bumper. The wheel wells were full showing off 22-inch Corvette rally wheels tubbed into the rear end, staggered with 20-inch wheels in the front, the brand new Michelin Z-rated tires freshly juiced with Armor All.

Russell just stood there smiling then said, "Let me explain. Your truck was toast—frame bent, big block completely destroyed, Jaguar independent rear end twisted up like a pretzel. We had a new Corvette in impound that had somehow disappeared after the owner was away doing time. That was E.Z.'s Corvette, and we thought it was only right that we rebuilt your El-Co with Eric's car parts. After a frame off rebuild-slash-conversion, we welded on the front clip, including rack and pinion steering, computerized suspension, McPherson struts with five different settings eliminating your existing Air Ride equipment. You now have a state of the art, twin caliper, quad piston braking system, onboard computer, etc. Your truck is now equipped with a brand new fuel-injected 475 hp small block, a six-speed automatic transmission, with high and low gears, five different suspension modes from SS to luxury ride, including the Corvette independent rear end. You won't be needing the nitrous anymore—E.Z. had ordered the Corvette new with dual turbochargers. At six thousand rpm the small block will produce up to 650 horsepower. We call it the El Corvetto. This restoration as well as your bill is a present from the club to you. That evil bastard E.Z. Money has been ripping us off for years. We couldn't retaliate because he had enough information to put us all in the "slammer."

Russell said, "Just throwing this out there, Mike. The club has your back from now on. If you ever have to 'save the world' again Satan's Soldiers are ready." Russell took off his pimp shades, the biker glasses with the rose colored glass. Looking at me like the cat that ate the canary, his ear-to-ear grin exposing big white teeth, so big they looked like white Chiclets, he turned one eye at me saying, "How does it look?"

Knowing without asking he was talking about the dental impressions I left in his eyebrow, I told him it didn't look that bad, over time it would probably not be visible at all. He said he liked the way it looked and hoped it would stay there forever, for it was a badge of honor. Russell said pain is temporary, scars are forever. Adding with a loud laugh if he caught anybody in the club biting each other in the face he would pull their patch. Tilting his big bucket head back opening his large mouth, his jaw hinged like a Pez dispenser letting out a thunderous laughter. I could see the sincerity in Russell's eyes as I felt the bond growing between us.

Firing up the El-Co listening to the crisp exhaust, tapping

the floor feeder listening to the responsive small block, leaving the impound yard I hit the freeway on ramp hard, using the Steptronic transmission selector. I dropped her into SS, Super Sport mode, the computerized Steptronic six-speed transmission shifting through the gears, the lowered front end of the 1970 El Camino feeling its way through the corners with ease, sweeping across four lanes as I hit a sweet power band, doing 55 miles per hour when I dropped the hammer. The suspension adjusting itself, I could feel the chassis drop, as the G-forces were calculated by the computer, the steering becoming stiffer, the back tires trying to break traction almost power sliding through the on ramp across to the number four lane, the Michelin Z tires sticking like glue with the independent rear end propelling the pickup forward with ease, pushing 160 miles an hour in seconds, the El Corvetto riding as smooth as a "rocket sled on rails." I couldn't believe my El Camino was faster and with better handling than ever, thinking to myself how ironic my pickup had been brought back to life using E.Z.'s car. Justice and karma served in one dish.

That night while eating dinner at the big house, Mr. Ellington announced that he and Ms. O'Malley would be departing in the morning. He and Olivia had set up everything we needed to breed horses. I told him there were no words to express how grateful I was for his generosity and kindness. He told me to thank him by being happy and living a clean life.

CLOSURE

EASY LIKE SUNDAY MORNING

After the smoke cleared Olivia insisted that the Benicia property be transferred to my name where my plan had panned out. After going through Eric's personal effects, I set up the loft apartment then spent most of my nights there. Eric had a very large weapons collection, everything from full standing medieval knights in sheet metal armor or chain mail suits with spears and swords, to muzzle loaders, every kind of weapon ever used by American armed forces, a handgun collection that covered the walls of one room, state of the art fully-auto grease guns, all in order. Eric must have been fascinated with Rolex wrist watches for he had at least one of every style and model ever sold. I picked out a newer Submariner chronometer stainless with a black face for myself. I must admit it looked good and felt even better on my wrist. The boat collection was just as extensive with several different styles, including a 16-foot 1961 Uniflite Sportabout. The little two-tone red and white boat had been upgraded in '81 with a 70-horse Johnson. I remembered many days on the lake with my fishing mentor, Uncle Jimmy, back east in South Carolina. This little boat became my favorite automatically, so easy to untie from my dock, turn the little key and you were free, plus I could fill her up for less than five bucks.

Now that I had unlimited spare time on my hands, I joined the U.S. Volunteer Auxiliary Coast Guard, where I

soon patrolled the Delta from as high up on the San Joaquin
River as Stockton to the beginning of the San Francisco Bay.
This gave me the opportunity to stay on the water, helping
people out and giving something back to the community.

Olivia had moved into the main house. On the rare
nights I slept there I stayed in the cabin. Olivia slept with
Apollo in the master bedroom of the big house. I couldn't
hold that against him for I would be doing the same thing if
I had a choice. I think it made her feel more secure. We had
lost whatever connection we'd had. I wasn't that worried
about it for now; the way things had worked out we had
kind of traded each other the ranch for the Benicia property,
but legally everything was in my name. Olivia set up pro-
grams through 4H to entertain a youth group at the ranch
every Sunday, where she insisted her share of the massive
profits could be donated to the battered women's society.

I made arrangements with a union pipe fabrication contractor to lease out some of the industrial sections of the
shop, using the rent money to cover the payments Eric left
behind. I auctioned off the frozen sturgeon, donating the
profits to charity. The *Aquaholic* was almost done and my
FLH was complete. Looking at my pager the call back numbers were stacked like firewood, numerous calls from fishermen wanting to book a charter, and four calls from Eileen,
Cassy, Andrea and the only one that I was thinking about,
Loretta Wallace.

I had a hundred problems to deal with but a skirt was
not one of them. Returning calls to the anglers I explained
that I was no longer in the charter business, at least for the
time being. Everyone told me the sturgeon bite was back in
full force. With an ear-to-ear grin on my face, looking up at
the sky I laughed out loud, saying a quick prayer to God,

giving thanks for guidance, strength against my weakness, asking for forgiveness for my sins and giving thanks to him for hearing all my prayers.

Olivia was friendly, but still no sign of improvement in our relationship, so feeling no guilt when I wrote down the numbers of the four women, making it a point to follow up. Reaching into the cooler, twisting the cap off a brew, knocking back an ice-cold bottle of Coors, the old notion crossed my mind. I could feel the fever coming on strong, the urgin' to catch a sturgeon. It was time to rip some lips.

We walked over to my dock, fired up *Little Red* and shoved off in no hurry. I was easy like Sunday mornin'. The sun was setting on the steel-colored flat water as I looked back at my wake, seeing my shop with the El-Co parked in front, my boats and the car collection in the back, the California sky with the sun setting a lava-like orange, gold and purple pastel colors reflecting off the water, smiling with Apollo at my side, on the water where we belonged. I couldn't help but think without feeling the least bit guilty, the winner takes it all.

THE END

Robert Owen's Next Novel
Coming Soon

R.I.P.

Death of the Delta

California is suffering from a seven year drought. The Sierra Nevada Forests are burning out of control. The San Joaquin Valley, the world's biggest supplier of agriculture, is only producing at fifty percent, causing a global crisis. A catastrophic flood, making Hurricane Katrina look like a mud puddle, enables a madman to put a stranglehold on California's precious supply of drinking water. Is the man of stone in too deep? Find out in Mike Stone's next adventure.

A Mike Stone Adventure

ABOOKS

ALIVE Book Publishing and ALIVE Publishing Group
are imprints of Advanced Publishing LLC,
3200 A Danville Blvd., Suite 204, Alamo, California 94507

Telephone: 925.837.7303
alivebookpublishing.com